THE
PUTTERMESSER
PAPERS

THE
PUTTERMESSER
PAPERS

CYNTHIA OZICK

ALFRED A. KNOPF   NEW YORK   1997

THIS IS A BORZOI BOOK
PUBLISHED BY ALFRED A. KNOPF, INC.

http://www.randomhouse.com/

"Puttermesser in Paradise" first appeared
in slightly different form in *The Atlantic Monthly*.
Three of the sections herein—"Puttermesser: Her
Work History, Her Ancestry, Her Afterlife,"
"Puttermesser Paired," and "Puttermesser and the
Muscovite Cousin"—have appeared in *The New
Yorker*. "Puttermesser and Xanthippe" first
appeared in *Salmagundi*.

"Puttermesser: Her Work History, Her Ancestry, Her
Afterlife" and "Puttermesser and Xanthippe" were
published in *Levitation: Five Fictions* (Knopf, 1982).

Library of Congress Cataloging-in-Publication Data
Ozick, Cynthia.
The Puttermesser papers / by Cynthia Ozick. — 1st ed.
p.   cm.
ISBN 0-679-45476-4 (alk. paper)
1. Jewish women—New York (State)—New York—
Fiction. 2. Women mayors—New York (State)—New
York—Fiction. I. Title.
PS3565.Z5P8 1997
813'.54—dc21   96-39155   CIP

Manufactured in the United States of America
Published June 12, 1997
Reprinted Once
Third Printing, August 1997

FOR

Elaine, Esther,

Francine, Gloria, Helen,

Johanna, Lore,

Merrill, Norma, Sarah,

Susan, Susanne

Flaubert does not build up his characters, as did Balzac, by objective, external description; in fact, so careless is he of their outward appearance that on one occasion he gives Emma brown eyes; on another deep black eyes; and on another blue eyes.

—A comment by Dr. Enid Starkie, quoted (disapprovingly) in *Flaubert's Parrot*, by Julian Barnes

THE
PUTTERMESSER
PAPERS

Puttermesser: Her Work
History, Her Ancestry, Her Afterlife

Puttermesser and Xanthippe

Puttermesser Paired

Puttermesser and the Muscovite Cousin

Puttermesser in Paradise

PUTTERMESSER:
HER WORK HISTORY,
HER ANCESTRY, HER
AFTERLIFE

uttermesser was thirty-four, a lawyer. She was also something of a feminist, not crazy, but she resented having "Miss" put in front of her name; she thought it pointedly discriminatory; she wanted to be a lawyer among lawyers. Though she was no virgin she lived alone, but idiosyncratically—in the Bronx, on the Grand Concourse, among other people's decaying old parents. Her own had moved to Miami Beach; in furry slippers left over from high school she roamed the same endlessly mazy apartment she had grown up in, her aging piano sheets still on top of the upright with the teacher's X marks on them showing where she should practice up to. Puttermesser always pushed a little ahead of the actual assignment; in school too. Her teachers told her mother she was "highly motivated," "achievement oriented." Also she had "scholastic drive." Her mother wrote all these things down in a notebook, kept it always, and took it with her to Florida in case she should die there. Puttermesser had a younger sister who was also highly motivated, but she had married an Indian, a Parsee chemist, and gone to live in Calcutta. Already the sister had four children and seven saris of various fabrics.

Puttermesser went on studying. In law school they called her a grind, a competitive-compulsive, an egomaniac out for aggrandizement. But ego was no part of it; she was looking to solve something, she did not know what. At the back of the linen closet she found a stack of her father's old shirt cardboards (her mother was provident, stingy: in kitchen drawers Puttermesser still discovered folded squares of used ancient waxed paper, million-creased into whiteness, cheese-smelling, nesting small unidentifiable wormlets); so behind the riser pipe in the bathroom Puttermesser kept weeks' worth of Sunday *Times* crossword puzzles stapled to these laundry boards and worked on them indiscriminately. She played chess against herself, and was always victor over the color she had decided to identify with. She organized tort cases on index cards. It was not that she intended to remember everything: situations—it was her tendency to call intellectual problems "situations"—slipped into her mind like butter into a bottle.

A letter came from her mother in Florida:

> Dear Ruth,
>   I know you won't believe this but I swear it's true the other day Papa was walking on the Avenue and who should he run into but Mrs. Zaretsky, the thin one from Burnside not the stout one from Davidson, you remember her Joel? Well he's divorced now no children thank God so he's free as a bird as they say his ex the poor thing couldn't conceive. *He* had tests he's O.K. He's only an accountant not good enough for you because God knows I never forget the day you made Law Review but you should come down just to see what a tender type he grew into. Every tragedy has its good side Mrs. Zaretsky says he comes down now practically whenever she calls him long distance. Papa said to Mrs. Zaretsky well, an accountant, you didn't over-educate your son anyhow, with daughters it's different. But don't take this to heart honey Papa is as proud as I am of your achievements. Why don't you write we didn't hear from you too long busy is busy but parents are parents.

Puttermesser had a Jewish face and a modicum of American distrust of it. She resembled no poster she had ever seen: she hated the Breck shampoo girl, so blond and bland and pale-mouthed; she boycotted Breck because of the golden-haired posters, all crudely idealized, an American wet dream, in the subway. Puttermesser's hair came in bouncing scallops—layered waves from scalp to tip, like imbricated roofing tile. It was nearly black and had a way of sometimes sticking straight out. Her nose had thick, well-haired, uneven nostrils, the right one noticeably wider than the other. Her eyes were small, the lashes short, invisible. She had the median Mongol lid—one of those Jewish faces with a vaguely Oriental cast. With all this, it was a fact she was not bad-looking. She had a good skin with, so far, few lines or pits or signs of looseness-to-come. Her jaw was pleasing—a baby jowl appeared only when she put her head deep in a book.

In bed she studied Hebrew grammar. The permutations of the triple-lettered root elated her: how was it possible that a whole language, hence a whole literature, a civilization even, should rest on the pure presence of three letters of the alphabet? The Hebrew verb, a stunning mechanism: three letters, whichever fated three, could command all possibility simply by a change in their pronunciation, or the addition of a wing-letter fore and aft. Every conceivable utterance blossomed from this trinity. It seemed to her not so much a language for expression as a code for the world's design, indissoluble, predetermined, translucent. The idea of the grammar of Hebrew turned Puttermesser's brain into a palace, a sort of Vatican; inside its corridors she walked from one resplendent triptych to another.

She wrote her mother a letter refusing to come to Florida to look over the divorced accountant's tenderness. She explained her life again; she explained it by indirection. She wrote:

> I have a cynical apperception of power, due no doubt to my current job. You probably haven't heard of the Office for Visas and Registration, OVIR for short. It's located on Ogaryova Street, in Moscow, USSR. I could enumerate for you a few of the innumerable bureaucratic atrocities of OVIR, not that anyone knows them all. But I could give you a list of the names of all those criminals, down to the women clerks, Yefimova, Korolova, Akulova, Ar-

khipova, Izrailova, all of them on Kolpachni Street in an office headed by Zolotukhin, the assistant to Colonel Smyrnov, who's under Ovchinikov, who is second in command to General Viryein, only Viryein and Ovchinikov aren't on Kolpachni Street, they're the ones in the head office—the M.D.V., Internal Affairs Ministry—on Ogaryova Street. Some day all the Soviet Jews will come out of the spider's clutches of these people and be free. Please explain to Papa that this is one of the highest priorities of my life at this time in my personal history. Do you think a Joel Zaretsky can share such a vision?

Immediately after law school, Puttermesser entered the firm of Midland, Reid & Cockleberry. It was a blueblood Wall Street firm, and Puttermesser, hired for her brains and ingratiating (read: immigrant-like) industry, was put into a back office to hunt up all-fours cases for the men up front. Though a Jew and a woman, she felt little discrimination: the back office was chiefly the repository of unmitigated drudgery and therefore of usable youth. Often enough it kept its lights burning till three in the morning. It was right that the Top Rung of law school should earn you the Bottom of the Ladder in the actual world of all-fours. The wonderful thing was the fact of the Ladder itself. And though she was the only woman, Puttermesser was not the only Jew. Three Jews a year joined the back precincts of Midland, Reid (four the year Puttermesser came, which meant they thought "woman" more than "Jew" at the sight of her). Three Jews a year left—not the same three. Lunchtime was difficult. Most of the young men went to one or two athletic clubs nearby to work out; Puttermesser ate from a paper bag at her desk, along with the other Jews, and this was strange: the young male Jews appeared to be as committed to the squash courts as the others. Alas, the athletic clubs would not have them, and this too was preternatural—the young Jews were indistinguishable from the others. They bought the same suits from the same tailors, wore precisely the same shirts and shoes, were careful to avoid tie clips and to be barbered a good deal shorter than the wild men of the streets, though a bit longer than the prigs in the banks.

Puttermesser remembered what Anatole France said of Dreyfus: that he was the same type as the officers who condemned him. "In their shoes he would have condemned himself."

Only their accents fell short of being identical: the "a" a shade too far into the nose, the "i" with its telltale elongation, had long ago spread from Brooklyn to Great Neck, from Puttermesser's Bronx to Scarsdale. These two influential vowels had the uncanny faculty of disqualifying them for promotion. The squash players, meanwhile, moved out of the back offices into the front offices. One or two of them were groomed—curried, fed sugar, led out by the muzzle—for partnership: were called out to lunch with thin and easeful clients, spent an afternoon in the dining room of one of the big sleek banks, and, in short, developed the creamy cheeks and bland habits of the always-comfortable.

The Jews, by contrast, grew more anxious, hissed together meanly among the urinals (Puttermesser, in the ladies' room next door, could hear malcontent rumblings in the connecting plumbing), became perfectionist and uncasual, quibbled bitterly, with stabbing forefingers, over principles, and all in all began to look and act less like superannuated college athletes and more like Jews. Then they left. They left of their own choice; no one shut them out.

Puttermesser left too, weary of so much chivalry—the partners in particular were excessively gracious to her, and treated her like a fellow-aristocrat. Puttermesser supposed this was because *she* did not say "a" in her nose or elongate her "i," and above all she did not dentalize her "t," "d," or "l," keeping them all back against the upper palate. Long ago her speech had been standardized by the drilling of fanatical teachers, elocutionary missionaries hired out of the Midwest by Puttermesser's prize high school, until almost all the regionalism was drained out;

except for the pace of her syllables, which had a New York deliberateness, Puttermesser could have come from anywhere. She was every bit as American as her grandfather in his captain's hat. From Castle Garden to blue New England mists, her father's father, hat-and-neckwear peddler to Yankees! In Puttermesser's veins Providence, Rhode Island, beat richly. It seemed to her the partners felt this.

Then she remembered that Dreyfus spoke perfect French, and was the perfect Frenchman.

For farewell she was taken out to a public restaurant—the clubs the partners belonged to (they explained) did not allow women—and apologized to.

"We're sorry to lose you," one said, and the other said, "No one for you in this outfit for under the canvas, hah?"

"The canvas?" Puttermesser said.

"Wedding canopy," said the partner, with a wink. "Or do they make them out of sheepskin—I forget."

"An interesting custom. I hear you people break the dishes at a wedding too," said the second partner.

An anthropological meal. They explored the rites of her tribe. She had not known she was strange to them. Their beautiful manners were the cautiousness you adopt when you visit the interior: Dr. Livingstone, I presume? They shook hands and wished her luck, and at that moment, so close to their faces with those moist smile-ruts flowing from the sides of their waferlike noses punctured by narrow, even nostrils, Puttermesser was astonished into noticing how strange *they* were—so many luncheon martinis inside their bellies, and such beautiful manners even while drunk, and, important though they were, insignificant though she was, the fine ceremonial fact of their having brought her to this carpeted place. Their eyes were blue. Their necks were clean. How closely they were shaven!—like men who grew no hair at all. Yet hairs curled inside their ears. They let her take away all her memo pads with her name printed on them. She was impressed by their courtesy, their benevolence, through which they always got their way. She had given them three years of meticulous anonymous research, deep, deep nights going after precedents, dates, lost issues, faded faint politics; for their sakes she had yielded up those howling morning headaches and half a diopter's worth of sight in both eyes. Brilliant students make good aides. They were pleased though not regretful. She was replaceable: a clever black had been hired only that morning. The palace they led her to at the end of it all was theirs by divine right: in which they believed, on which they acted. They were benevolent because benevolence was theirs to dispense.

She went to work for the Department of Receipts and Disbursements. Her title was Assistant Corporation Counsel—it had no meaning, it was part of the subspeech on which bureaucracy relies. Of the many who held this title most were Italians and Jews, and again Puttermesser was the only woman. In this great City office there were no ceremonies and no manners: gross shouts, ignorant clerks, slovenliness, litter on the floors, grit stuck all over antiquated books. The ladies' room reeked: the women urinated standing up, and hot urine splashed on the toilet seats and onto the muddy tiles.

The successive heads of this department were called Commissioners. They were all political appointees—scavengers after spoils. Puttermesser herself was not quite a civil servant and not quite *not* a civil servant—one of those amphibious creatures hanging between base contempt and bare decency; but she soon felt the ignominy of belonging to that mean swarm of City employees rooted bleakly in cells inside the honeycomb of the Municipal Building. It was a monstrous place, gray everywhere, abundantly tunneled, with multitudes of corridors and stairs and shafts, a kind of swollen doom through which the bickering of small-voiced officials whinnied. At the same time there were always curious farm sounds—in the summer the steady cricket of the air-conditioning, in the winter the gnash and croak of old radiators. Nevertheless the windows were broad and high and stupendously filled with light; they looked out on the whole lower island of Manhattan, revealed *as* an island, down to the Battery, all crusted over with the dried lava of shape and shape: rectangle over square, and square over spire. At noon the dark gongs of St. Andrew's boomed their wild and stately strokes.

To Puttermesser all this meant she had come down in the world. Here she was not even a curiosity. No one noticed a Jew. Unlike the partners at Midland, Reid, the Commissioners did not travel out among their subjects and were rarely seen. Instead they were like shut-up kings in a tower, and suffered from rumors.

But Puttermesser discovered that in City life all rumors are true. Putative turncoats are genuine turncoats. All whispered knifings have happened: officials reputed to be about to topple, topple. So far Puttermesser had lasted through two elections, seeing the powerful become powerless and the formerly power-less inflate themselves overnight, like gigantic winds, to suck out the victory of the short run. When one Administration was razed, for the moment custom seemed leveled with it, every-thing that smelled of "before," of "the old way"—but only at first. The early fits of innovation subsided, and gradually the old way of doing things crept back, covering everything over, like grass, as if the building and its workers were together some inex-orable vegetable organism with its own laws of subsistence. The civil servants were grass. Nothing destroyed them, they were stronger than the pavement, they were stronger than time. The Administration might turn on its hinge, throwing out one lot of patronage eaters and gathering in the new lot: the work went on. They might put in fresh carpeting in the new Deputy's office, or a private toilet in the new Commissioner's, and change the clerks' light bulbs to a lower wattage, and design an extrava-gant new colophon for a useless old document—they might do anything they liked: the work went on as before. The organism breathed, it comprehended itself.

So there was nothing for the Commissioner to do, and he

knew it, and the organism knew it. For a very great salary the Commissioner shut his door and cleaned his nails behind it with one of the shining tools of a fancy Swiss knife, and had a secretary who was rude to everyone, and made dozens of telephone calls every day.

The current one was a rich and foolish playboy who had given the Mayor money for his campaign. All the high officials of every department were either men who had given the Mayor money or else courtiers who had humiliated themselves for him in the political clubhouse—mainly by flattering the clubhouse boss, who before any election was already a secret mayor and dictated the patronage lists. But the current Commissioner owed nothing to the boss because he had given the Mayor money and was the Mayor's own appointee; and anyhow he would have little to do with the boss because he had little to do with any Italian. The boss was a gentlemanly Neapolitan named Fiore, the chairman of the board of a bank; still, he was only an Italian, and the Commissioner cared chiefly for blue-eyed bankers. He used his telephone to make luncheon appointments with them, and sometimes tennis. He himself was a blue-eyed Guggenheim, a German Jew, but not one of the grand philanthropic Guggenheims. The name was a cunning coincidence (cut down from Guggenheimer), and he was rich enough to be taken for one of the real Guggenheims, who thought him an upstart and disowned him. Grandeur demands discreetness; he was so discreetly disowned that no one knew it, not even the Rockefeller he had met at Choate.

This Commissioner was a handsome, timid man, still young, and good at boating; on weekends he wore sneakers and cultivated the friendship of the dynasties—Sulzbergers and Warburgs, who let him eat with them but warned their daughters against him. He had dropped out of two colleges and finally graduated from the third by getting a term-paper factory to plagiarize his reports. He was harmless and simpleminded, still devoted to his brainy late father, and frightened to death of news conferences. He understood nothing: art appreciation had been his best subject (he was attracted to Renaissance nudes), economics his worst. If someone asked, "How much does the City invest every day?" or "Is there any Constitutional bar against revenue from commuters?" or "What is your opinion about taxing exempt properties?" his pulse would catch in his throat, making his nose run, and he had to say he was pressed for time and would let them have the answers from his Deputy in charge of the Treasury. Sometimes he would even call on Puttermesser for an answer.

Now if this were an optimistic portrait, exactly here is where Puttermesser's emotional life would begin to grind itself into evidence. Her biography would proceed romantically, the rich young Commissioner of the Department of Receipts and Disbursements would fall in love with her. She would convert him to intelligence and to the cause of Soviet Jewry. He would abandon boating and the pursuit of bluebloods. Puttermesser would end her work history abruptly and move on to a bower in a fine suburb.

This is not to be. Puttermesser will always be an employee in the Municipal Building. She will always behold Brooklyn Bridge through its windows; also sunsets of high glory, bringing her religious pangs. She will not marry. Perhaps she will undertake a long-term affair with Vogel, the Deputy in charge of the Treasury; perhaps not.

The difficulty with Puttermesser is that she is loyal to certain environments.

Puttermesser, while working in the Municipal Building, had a luxuriant dream, a dream of *gan eydn*—a term and notion handed on from her great-uncle Zindel, a former shammes in a shul that had been torn down. In this reconstituted Garden of Eden, which is to say in the World to Come, Puttermesser, who was not afflicted with quotidian uncertainty in the Present

World, had even more certainty of her aims. With her weakness for fudge (others of her age, class, and character had advanced to martinis, at least to ginger ale; Puttermesser still drank ice cream with cola, despised mints as too tingly, eschewed salty liver canapés, hunted down chocolate babies, Kraft caramels, Mary Janes, Milky Ways, peanut brittle, and immediately afterward furiously brushed her teeth, scrubbing off guilt)—with all this nasty self-indulgence, she was nevertheless very thin and unironic. Or: to postulate an afterlife was her single irony—a game in the head not unlike a melting fudge cube held against the upper palate.

There, at any rate, Puttermesser would sit, in Eden, under a middle-sized tree, in the solid blaze of an infinite heart-of-summer July, green, green, green everywhere, green above and green below, herself gleaming and made glorious by sweat, every itch annihilated, fecundity dismissed. And there Puttermesser would, as she imagined it, *take in*. Ready to her left hand, the box of fudge (rather like the fudge sold to the lower school by the eighth-grade cooking class in P.S. 74, The Bronx, circa 1942); ready to her right hand, a borrowed steeple of library books: for into Eden the Crotona Park Branch has ascended intact, sans librarians and fines, but with its delectable terrestrial binding-glue fragrances unevaporated.

Here Puttermesser sits. Day after celestial day, perfection of desire upon perfection of contemplation, into the exaltations of an uninterrupted forever, she eats fudge in human shape (once known—no use covering this up—as nigger babies), or fudge in square shapes (and in Eden there is no tooth decay); and she reads. Puttermesser reads and reads. Her eyes in Paradise are unfatigued. And if she still does not know what it is she wants to solve, she has only to read on. The Crotona Park Branch is as paradisal here as it was on earth. She reads anthropology, zoology, physical chemistry, philosophy (in the green air of heaven, Kant and Nietzsche together fall into crystal splinters). The New Books section is peerless: she will learn about the linkages of genes, about quarks, about primate sign language, theories of the origins of the races, religions of ancient civilizations, what Stonehenge meant. Puttermesser will read Non-Fiction into eternity; and there is still time for Fiction! Eden is equipped above all with timelessness, so Puttermesser will read at last all of Balzac, all of Dickens, all of Turgenev and Dostoevsky (her mortal self has already read all of Tolstoy and George Eliot); at last Puttermesser will read *Kristin Lavransdatter* and the stupendous trilogy of Dmitri Merezhkovsky, she will read *The Magic Mountain* and the whole *Faerie Queene* and every line of *The Ring and the Book*, she will read a biography of Beatrix Potter and one of Walter Scott in many entrancing volumes and one of Lytton Strachey, at last, at last! In Eden insatiable Puttermesser will be nourished, if not glutted. She will study Roman law, the more arcane varieties of higher mathematics, the nuclear composition of the stars, what happened to the Monophysites, Chinese history, Russian, and Icelandic.

But meanwhile, still alive, not yet translated upward, her days given over to the shadow reign of a playboy Commissioner, Puttermesser was learning only Hebrew.

Twice a week, at night (it seemed), she went to Uncle Zindel for a lesson. Where the bus ran through peeling neighborhoods the trolley tracks sometimes shone up through a broken smother of asphalt, like weeds wanting renewal. From childhood Puttermesser remembered how trolley days were better days: in summer the cars banged along, self-contained little carnivals, with open wire-mesh sides sucking in hot winds, the passengers serenely jogging on the seats. Not so this bus, closed like a capsule against the slum.

The old man, Zindel the Stingy, hung on to life among the cooking smells of Spanish-speaking blacks. Puttermesser walked up three flights of steps and leaned against the crooked door, waiting for the former shammes with his little sack. Each evening Zindel brought up a single egg from the Cuban grocery. He boiled it while Puttermesser sat with her primer.

"You should go downtown," the shammes said, "where they got regular language factories. Berlitz. NYU. They even got an *ulpan*, like in Israel."

"You're good enough," Puttermesser said. "You know everything they know."

"And something more also. Why you don't live downtown, on the East Side, fancy?"

"The rent is too much, I inherited your stinginess."

"And such a name. A nice young fellow meets such a name, he laughs. You should change it to something different, lovely, nice. Shapiro, Levine. Cohen, Goldweiss, Blumenthal. I don't say make it *different*, who needs Adams, who needs McKee, I say make it a name not a joke. Your father gave you a bad present with it. For a young girl, Butterknife!"

"I'll change it to Margarine-messer."

"Never mind the ha-ha. My father, what was your great-great-grandfather, didn't allow a knife to the table Friday night. When it came to kiddush—knifes off! All knifes! On Sabbath an instrument, a blade? On Sabbath a weapon? A point? An edge? What makes bleeding among mankind? What makes war? Knifes! No knifes! Off! A clean table! And something else you'll notice. By us we got only *messer*, you follow? By them they got sword, they got lance, they got halberd. Go to the dictionary, I went once. So help me, what don't one of them knights carry? Look up in the book, you'll see halberd, you'll see cutlass, pike, rapier, foil, ten dozen more. By us a pike is a fish. Not to mention what nowadays they got—bayonet stuck on the gun, who knows what else the poor soldier got to carry in the pocket. Maybe a dagger same as a pirate. But by us—what we got? A *messer*! Puttermesser, you slice off a piece butter, you cut to live, not to kill. A name of honor, you follow? Still, for a young girl—"

"Uncle Zindel, I'm past thirty."

Uncle Zindel blinked lids like insect's wings, translucent. He saw her voyaging, voyaging. The wings of his eyes shadowed the Galilee. They moved over the Tomb of the Patriarchs. A tear for the tears of Mother Rachel rode on his nose. "Your mother knows you're going? Alone on an airplane, such a young girl? You wrote her?"

"I wrote her, Uncle Zindel. I'm not flying anywhere."

"By sea is also danger. What Mama figures, in Miami who is there? The dead and dying. In Israel you'll meet someone. You'll marry, you'll settle there. What's the difference, these days, modern times, quick travel—"

Uncle Zindel's egg was ready, hard-boiled. The shammes tapped it and the shell came off raggedly. Puttermesser consulted the alphabet: *aleph, beys, gimel*; she was not going to Israel, she had business in the Municipal Building. Uncle Zindel, chewing, began finally to teach: "First see how a *gimel* and which way a *zayen*. Twins, but one kicks a leg left, one right. You got to practice the difference. If legs don't work, think pregnant bellies. Mrs. *Zayen* pregnant in one direction, Mrs. *Gimel* in the other. Together they give birth to *gez*, which means what you cut off. A night for knifes! Listen, going home from here you should be extra careful tonight. Martinez, the upstairs not the next door, her daughter they mugged and they took."

The shammes chewed, and under his jaws Puttermesser's head bent, practicing the bellies of the holy letters.

Stop. Stop, stop! Puttermesser's biographer, stop! Disengage, please. Though it is true that biographies are invented, not recorded, here you invent too much. A symbol is allowed, but not a whole scene: do not accommodate too obsequiously to Puttermesser's romance. Having not much imagination, she is literal with what she has. Uncle Zindel lies under the earth of Staten Island. Puttermesser has never had a conversation with him; he died four years before her birth. He is all legend: Zindel the Stingy, who even in *gan eydn* rather than eat will store apples until they rot. Zindel the Unripe. Why must Puttermesser fall into so poignant a fever over the cracked phrases of a shammes of a torn-down shul?

(The shul was not torn down, neither was it abandoned. It disintegrated. Crumb by crumb it vanished. Stones took some of the windows. There were no pews, only wooden folding chairs. Little by little these turned into sticks. The prayer books began to flake: the bindings flaked, the glue came unstuck in small brown flakes, the leaves grew brittle and flaked into confetti. The congregation too began to flake off—the women first, wife after wife after wife, each one a pearl and a consolation, until there they stand, the widowers, frail, gazing, palsy-struck. Alone and in terror. Golden Agers, Senior Citizens! And finally they too flake away, the shammes among them. The shul becomes a wisp, a straw, a feather, a hair.)

But Puttermesser must claim an ancestor. She demands connection—surely a Jew must own a past. Poor Puttermesser has found herself in the world without a past. Her mother was born into the din of Madison Street and was taken up to the hullabaloo of Harlem at an early age. Her father is nearly a Yankee: his father gave up peddling to captain a dry-goods store in Providence, Rhode Island. In summer he sold captain's hats, and wore one in all his photographs. Of the world that was, there is only this single grain of memory: that once an old man, Puttermesser's mother's uncle, kept his pants up with a rope belt, was called Zindel, lived without a wife, ate frugally, knew the holy letters, died with thorny English a wilderness between his gums. To him Puttermesser clings. America is a blank, and Uncle Zindel is all her ancestry. Unironic, unimaginative, her plain but stringent mind strains beyond the parents—what did they have? Only day-by-day in their lives, coffee in the morning, washing underwear, occasionally a trip to the beach. Blank. What did they know? Everything from the movies; something—scraps—from the newspaper. Blank.

Behind the parents, beyond and before them, things teem. In old photographs of the Jewish East Side, Puttermesser sees the teeming. She sees a long coat. She sees a woman pressing onions from a pushcart. She sees a tiny child with a finger in its mouth who will become a judge.

Past the judge, beyond and behind him, something more is teeming. But this Puttermesser cannot see. The towns, the little towns. Zindel born into a flat-roofed house a modest distance from a stream.

What can Puttermesser do? She began life as the child of an anti-Semite. Her father would not eat kosher meat—it was, he said, too tough. He had no superstitions. He wore the mother down, she went to the regular meat market at last.

The scene with Uncle Zindel did not occur. How Puttermesser loved the voice of Zindel in the scene that did not occur!

(He is under the ground. The cemetery is a teeming city of toy skyscrapers shouldering each other. Born into a wooden house, Zindel now has a flat stone roof. Who buried him? Strangers from the *landsmanshaft* society. Who said a word for him? No one. Who remembers him now?)

Puttermesser does not remember Uncle Zindel; Puttermesser's mother does not remember him. A name in the dead grandmother's mouth. Her parents have no ancestry. Therefore Puttermesser rejoices in the cadences of Uncle Zindel's voice above the Cuban grocery. Uncle Zindel, when alive, distrusted the building of Tel Aviv because he was practical, Messiah was not imminent. But now, in the scene that did not occur, how naturally he supposes Puttermesser will journey to a sliver of earth in the Middle East, surrounded by knives, missiles, bazookas!

The scene with Uncle Zindel did not occur. It could not occur because, though Puttermesser dares to posit her ancestry, we may not. Puttermesser is not to be examined as an artifact but as an essence. Who made her? No one cares. Puttermesser is henceforth to be presented as given. Put her back into Receipts and Disbursements, among office Jews and patronage collectors. While winter dusk blackens the Brooklyn Bridge, let us hear her opinion about the taxation of exempt properties. The bridge is not the harp Hart Crane said it was in his poem. Its staves are prison bars. The women clerks, Yefimova, Korolova, Akulova,

Arkhipova, Izrailova, are on Kolpachni Street, but the vainglorious General Viryein is not. He is on Ogaryova Street. Joel Zaretsky's ex-wife is barren. The Commissioner puts on his tennis sneakers. He telephones. Mr. Fiore, the courtly secret mayor behind the Mayor, also telephones. Hey! Puttermesser's biographer! What will you do with her now?

PUTTERMESSER
AND XANTHIPPE

I. PUTTERMESSER'S BRIEF LOVE LIFE, HER TROUBLES, HER TITLES

Puttermesser felt attacked on all sides. The night before, her lover, Morris Rappoport, a married fund-raiser from Toronto, had walked out on her. His mysterious job included settling Soviet Jewish refugees away from the big metropolitan centers; he claimed to have fresh news of the oppressed everywhere, as well as intimate acquaintance with malcontents in numerous cities in both the Eastern and Western hemispheres. Puttermesser, already forty-six, suspected him of instability and overdependency: a future madman. His gripe was that she read in bed too much; last night she had read aloud from Plato's *Theaetetus*:

THEODORUS: What do you mean, Socrates?

SOCRATES: The same thing as the story about the Thracian maidservant who exercised her wit at the expense of Thales, when he was looking up to study the stars and tumbled down a well. She scoffed at him for being so eager to know what was happening in the sky that he could not see what lay at his feet. Anyone who gives his life to philosophy is open to such mockery. It is true that he is unaware what his next-door neighbor is doing, hardly knows, indeed, whether the creature is a man at all; he spends all his pains on the question, what man is, and what powers and properties distinguish such a nature from any other. You see what I mean, Theodorus?

Rappoport did not see. He withdrew his hand from Puttermesser's belly. "What's the big idea, Ruth?" he said.

"That's right," Puttermesser said.

"What?"

"That's just what Socrates is after: the big idea."

"You're too old for this kind of thing," Rappoport said. He had a medium-sized, rather square, reddish mustache over perfect teeth. His teeth were more demanding to Puttermesser's gaze than his eyes, which were so diffidently pigmented that they seemed whited out, like the naked eyes on a Roman bust. His nose, however, was dominant, eloquent, with large deep nostrils that appeared to meditate. "Cut it out, Ruth. You're behaving like an adolescent," Rappoport said.

"*You'll* never fall down a well," Puttermesser said. "You never look up." She felt diminished; those philosophical nostrils had misled her.

"Ruth, Ruth," Rappoport pleaded, "what did I do?"

"It's what you didn't do. You didn't figure out what powers and properties distinguish human nature from any other," Puttermesser said bitterly; as a feminist, she was careful never to speak of "man's" nature. She always said "humankind" instead of "mankind." She always wrote "he or she" instead of just "he."

Rappoport was putting on his pants. "You're too old for sex," he said meanly.

Puttermesser's reply was instantly Socratic: "Then I'm *not* behaving like an adolescent."

"If you know I have a plane to catch, how come you want to read in bed?"

"It's more comfortable than the kitchen table."

"Ruth, I came to make love to you!"

"All I wanted was to finish the *Theaetetus* first."

Now he had his coat on, and was crossing his scarf carefully at his throat, so as not to let in the cold. It was a winter night, but Puttermesser saw in this gesture that Rappoport, at the age of fifty-two, still obeyed his mother's doctrines, no matter that they were five decades old. "You wanted to finish!" he yelled. He grabbed the book from her lap. "It goes from page 847 to 879, that's thirty-three pages—"

"I read fast," Puttermesser said.

In the morning she understood that Rappoport would never come back. His feelings were hurt. In the end he would have deserted her anyway—she had observed that, sooner or later, he told all his feelings to his wife. And not only to his wife. He was the sort of man who babbles.

The loss of Rappoport was not Puttermesser's only trouble. She had developed periodontal disease; her dentist reported—with a touch of pleasure in disaster—a sixty-percent bone loss. Loss of bone, loss of Rappoport, loss of home! "Uncontrollable pockets," the dentist said. He gave her the name of a periodontist to consult. It was an emergency, he warned. Her gums were puffy, her teeth in peril of uprooting. It was as if, in the dread underworld below the visible gums, a volcano lay, watching for its moment of release. She spat blood into the sink.

The sink was a garish fake marble. Little blue fish-tiles swam around the walls. The toilet seat cover had a large blue mermaid painted on it. Puttermesser hated this bathroom. She hated her new "luxury" apartment, with its windowless slot of a kitchen and two tiny cramped rooms, the bathroom without a bathtub, the shower stall the size of a thimble, the toilet's flush handle made of light-blue plastic. Her majestic apartment on the Grand Concourse in the Bronx, with its Alhambra spaciousness, had been ravaged by arsonists. Even before that, the old tenants had been dying off or moving away, one by one; junkies stole in, filling empty corridors with bloodstained newspapers, smashed bottles, dead matches in random rows like beetle tracks. On a summer evening Puttermesser arrived home from her office without possessions: her shoes were ash, her piano was ash, her piano teacher's penciled "Excellent," written in fine large letters at the top of "Humoresque" and right across the opening phrase of "Für Elise," had vanished among the cinders. Puttermesser's childhood, burned away. How prescient her mother had been to take all of Puttermesser's school compositions with her to Florida! Otherwise every evidence of Puttermesser's early mental growth might have gone under in that criminal conflagration.

The new apartment was crowded with plants: Puttermesser, who was once afflicted with what she called a black thumb, and who had hitherto killed every green thing she put her hand to, determined now to be responsible for life. She dragged in great clay urns and sacks of vitamin-rich soil bought at Woolworth's and emptied dark earth into red pots. She seeded and conscientiously watered. Rappoport himself had lugged in, on a plastic-wheeled dolly, a tall stalk like a ladder of green bear's ears: he claimed it was an avocado tree he had grown from a pit in Toronto. It reminded Puttermesser of her mother's towering rubber plants on the Grand Concourse, in their ceiling-sweeping prime. Every window sill of Puttermesser's new apartment was fringed with fronds, foliage, soaring or drooping leaf-tips. The tough petals of blood-veined coleus strained the bedroom sunset. Puttermesser, astonished, discovered that if she remained attentive enough, she had the power to stimulate green bursts. All along the bosky walls vegetation burgeoned.

Yet Puttermesser's days were arid. Her office life was not peaceable; nothing bloomed for her. She had fallen. Out of the blue, the Mayor ousted the old Commissioner—Puttermesser's boss, the chief of the Department of Receipts and Disbursements—and replaced him with a new man, seven years younger than Puttermesser. He looked like a large-eared boy; he wore his tie pulled loose, and his neck stretched forward out of his collar; it gave him the posture of a vertical turtle. His eyes, too, were unblinkingly turtlish. It was possible, Puttermesser conceded to herself, that despite his slowly reaching neck and flattish head, the new man did not really resemble a turtle at all; it was only that his name—Alvin Turtelman—suggested the bare lidless deliberation of that immobile creature of the road. Turtelman did not preen. Puttermesser saw at once, in all that meditated motionlessness, that he was more ambitious than the last Commissioner, who had been satisfied with mere prestige, and had used his office like a silken tent decorated with viziers and hookahs. But Turtelman was patient; his steady ogle took in the whole wide trail ahead. He spoke of "restructuring," of "functioning," of "goals" and "gradations," of "levels of purpose" and "versus equations." He was infinitely abstract. "None of this is personal," he liked to say, but his voice was a surprise; it was more pliable than you would expect from the stillness of his stare. He stretched out his vowels like any New Yorker. He had brought with him a score of underlings for what he called "mapping out." They began the day late and ended early, moving from cubicle to cubicle and collecting résumés. They were all bad spellers, and their memos, alive with solecisms, made Puttermesser grieve, because they were lawyers, and Puttermesser loved the law and its language. She caressed its meticulousness. She thought of law as Apollo's chariot; she had read all the letters of Justice Oliver Wendell Holmes, Jr., to Harold Laski (three volumes) and to Sir Frederick Pollock (two). In her dream once she stood before a ship captain and became the fifth wife of Justice William O. Douglas; they honeymooned on the pampas of Argentina. It was difficult to tell whether Turtelman's bad spellers represented the Mayor himself, or only the new Commissioner; but clearly they were scouts and spies. They reported on lateness and laxness, on backlogs and postponements, on insufficiencies and excesses, on waste and error. They issued warnings and sounded alarms; they brought pressure to bear and threatened and cautioned and gave tips. They were watchful and envious. It soon became plain that they did not understand the work.

They did not understand the work because they were, it turned out, political appointees shipped over from the Department of Hygienic Maintenance; a handful were from the Fire Department. They had already had careers as oligarchs of street-sweeping, sewers and drains, gutters, the perils of sleet, ice, rainslant, gas, vermin, fumigation, disinfection, snow removal, water supply, potholes, steam cleaning, deodorization, ventilation, abstersion, elutriation; those from the Fire Department had formerly wielded the scepter over matters of arson, hydrants, pumps, hose (measured by weight, in kilograms), incendiary bombs, rubber boots, wax polish, red paint, false alarms, sappers, marshals. They had ruled over all these corporealities, but without comprehension; they asked for frequent memos; they were "administrators." This meant they were good at arrest; not only at making arrests (the fire marshals, for instance), but at bringing everything to a standstill, like the spindle-prick in Sleeping Beauty. In their presence the work instantly held its breath and came to a halt, as if it were a horse reined in for examination. They walked round and round the work, ruminating, speculating. They could not judge it; they did not understand it.

But they knew what it was for. It was for the spoils quota. The work, impenetrable though it was to its suzerains, proliferated with jobs; jobs blossomed with salaries; salaries were money; money was spoils. The current Mayor, Malachy ("Matt") Mavett, like all the mayors before him, was a dispenser of spoils, though publicly, of course, he declared himself morally opposed to political payoffs. He had long ago distributed the plums, the high patronage slots. All the commissioners were political friends of the Mayor. Sometimes a mayor would have more friends than there were jobs, and then this or that commissioner would suddenly be called upon to devise a whole new management level: a many-pegged perch just between the heights of direct mayoral appointment and the loftier rungs of the Civil Service. When that happened, Puttermesser would all at once discover a fresh crew of intermediate bosses appointed to loiter between herself and the Commissioner. Week after week, she would have to explain the work to them: the appointed intermediate bosses of the Department of Receipts and Disbursements did not usually know what the Department of Receipts and Disbursements *did*. By the time they found out, they vanished; they were always on the move, like minor bedouin sheikhs, to the next oasis. And when a new commissioner arrived right after an election (or, now and then, after what was officially described as "internal reorganization"—demoralization, upheaval, bloodbath), Puttermesser would once again be standing in the sanctuary of the Commissioner's deep inner office, the one with the mottled carpeting and the private toilet, earnestly explaining his rich domain to its new overlord.

Puttermesser was now an old hand, both at the work and at the landscape of the bureaucracy. She was intimate with every folly and every fall. (Ah, but she did not expect her own fall.) She was a witness to every succession. (Ah, but she did not expect to be succeeded herself.) The bureaucracy was a faded feudal world of territory and authority and hierarchy, mainly dusty, except at those high moments of dagger and toppling. Through it all, Puttermesser was seen to be useful: this accounted for her climb. She had stuck her little finger into every cranny of every permutation of the pertinent law. Precedents sped through her brain. Her titles, movable and fictitious, traveled upward: from Assistant Corporation Counsel she became Administrative Tax Law Associate, and after that Vice Chief of Financial Affairs, and after that First Bursary Officer. All the while she felt like Alice, swallowing the potion and growing compact, nibbling the mushroom and swelling: each title was a swallow or a nibble, and not one of them signified anything but the degree of her convenience to whoever was in command. Her titles were the poetry of the bureaucracy.

The truth was that Puttermesser was now a fathomer; she had come to understand the recondite, dim, and secret journey of the City's money, the tunnels it rolled through, the transmutations, investments, multiplications, squeezings, fattenings and battenings it underwent. She knew where the money landed and where it was headed for. She knew the habits, names, and even the hot-tempered wives of three dozen bank executives on various levels. She had acquired half a dozen underlings of her own—with these she was diffident, polite; though she deemed herself a feminist, no ideology could succeed for her in aggrandizing force. Puttermesser was not aggressive. She disdained assertiveness. Her voice was like Cordelia's. At home, in bed, she went on dreaming and reading. She retained a romantic view of the British Civil Service in its heyday: the Cambridge Apostles carrying the probities of G. E. Moore to the far corners of the world, Leonard Woolf doing justice in Ceylon, the shy young Forster in India. Integrity. Uprightness. And all for the sake of imperialism, colonialism! In New York, Puttermesser retained an immigrant's dream of merit: justice, justice shalt thou pursue. Her heart beat for law, even for tax law: she saw the orderly nurturing of the democratic populace, public murals, subway windows bright as new dishes, parks with flowering borders, the bell-hung painted steeds of dizzying carousels.

Every day, inside the wide bleak corridors of the Municipal Building, Puttermesser dreamed an ideal Civil Service: devotion to polity, the citizen's sweet love of the citizenry, the light rule of reason and common sense, the City as a miniature country crowded with patriots—not fools and jingoists, but patriots true and serene; humorous affection for the idiosyncrasies of one's distinctive little homeland, each borough itself another little homeland, joy in the Bronx, elation in Queens, O happy Richmond! Children on roller skates, and over the Brooklyn Bridge the long patchwork-colored line of joggers, breathing hard above the homeland-hugging green waters.

II. PUTTERMESSER'S FALL, AND THE
HISTORY OF THE GENUS GOLEM

urtelman sent his secretary to fetch Putter-messer. It was a new secretary, a middle-aged bony acolyte, graying and testy, whom he had brought with him from the Department of Hygienic Maintenance: she had coarse eyebrows crawling upward. "This isn't exactly a good time for me to do this," Puttermesser complained. It was as if Turtelman did not trust the telephone for such a purpose. Puttermesser knew his purpose: he wanted teaching. He was puzzled, desperate. Inside his ambitiousness he was a naked boy, fearful. His office was cradled next to the threatening computer chamber, just then being installed; all along the walls the computers' hard flanks glittered with specks and lights. Puttermesser could hear, behind a partition, the velvet din of a thousand microchips, a thin threadlike murmur, as if the software men, long-haired chaps in sneakers, were setting out lyres upon the great stone window sills of the Municipal Building. Walking behind the bony acolyte, Puttermesser pitied Turtelman: the Mayor had called for information—figures, indexes, collections, projections—and poor Turtelman, fresh from his half-education in the land of abstersion and elutriation, his frontal lobes still inclined toward repair of street-sweeping machinery, hung back bewildered. He had no answers for the Mayor, and no idea where the answers might be hidden; alas, the questions them-selves fell on Turtelman's ears as though in a foreign tongue.

The secretary pushed open Turtelman's door, stood aside for Puttermesser, and went furiously away.

Poor Turtelman, Puttermesser thought.

Turtelman spoke: "You're out."

"Out?" Puttermesser said. It was a bitter Tuesday morning in mid-January; at that very moment, considerably south of the Municipal Building, in Washington, D.C., they were getting ready to inaugurate the next President of the United States. High politics emblazoned the day. Bureaucracies all over the world were turning on their hinges, gates were lifting and shutting, desks emptying and filling. The tide rode upon Turtelman's spittle; it glimmered on his teeth.

"As of this afternoon," Turtelman said, "you are relieved of your duties. It's nothing personal, believe me. I don't know you. We're restructuring. It's too bad you're not a bit older. You can't retire at only forty-six." He had read her résumé, then; at least that.

"I'm old enough," Puttermesser said.

"Not for collecting your pension. You people have a valuable retirement system here. I envy you. It drains the rest of us dry." The clack of his teeth showed that he was about to deliver a sting: "We ordinary folk who aren't lucky enough to be in the Civil Service can't afford you."

Puttermesser announced proudly, "I earn my way. I scored highest in the entire city on the First-Level Management Examination. I was editor-in-chief of Law Review at Yale Law School. I graduated from Barnard with honors in history, *summa cum laude*, Phi Beta Kappa—"

Turtelman broke in: "Give me two or three weeks, I'll find a little spot for you somewhere. You'll hear from me."

Thus the manner of Puttermesser's fall. Ignoble. She did not dream there was worse to come. She spilled the papers out of her drawers and carried them to a windowless cubicle down the hall from her old office. For a day or so her ex-staff averted their eyes; then they ceased to notice her; her replacement had arrived. He was Adam Marmel, late of the Bureau of Emergencies, an old classmate of Turtelman's at NYU, where both had majored in film arts. This interested Puttermesser: the Department of Receipts and Disbursements was now in the hands of young men who had been trained to pursue illusion, to fly with a gossamer net after fleeting shadows. They were attracted to the dark, where fraudulent emotions raged. They were, moreover, close friends, often together. The Mayor had appointed Turtelman; Turtelman had appointed Marmel; Marmel had succeeded Puttermesser, who now sat with the *Times*, deprived of light, isolated, stripped, forgotten. An outcast. On the next Friday her salary check came as usual. But no one called her out of her cubicle.

Right in the middle of business hours—she no longer had any business, she was perfectly idle—Puttermesser wrote a letter to the Mayor:

The Honorable Malachy Mavett
Mayor, City of New York
City Hall

Dear Mayor Mavett:
Your new appointee in the Department of Receipts and Disbursements, Commissioner Alvin Turtelman, has forced a fine civil servant of honorable temperament, with experience both wide and impassioned, out of her job. I am that civil servant. Without a hearing, without due process, without a hope of appeal or redress (except, Mr. Mayor, by you!), Commissioner Turtelman has destroyed a career in full flower. Employing an affectless vocabulary by means of which, in a single instant, he abruptly ousted a civil servant of high standing, Commissioner Turtelman has politicized a job long held immune to outside preferment. In a single instant, honor, dignity, and continuity have been snatched away! I have been professionally injured and personally humiliated. I have been rendered useless. As of this writing I am costing the City's taxpayers the price of my entire salary, while I sit here working a crossword puzzle; while I hold this very pen. No one looks at me. They are embarrassed and

ashamed. At first a few ex-colleagues came into this
little abandoned office (where I do nothing) to offer
condolences, but that was only at first. It is like being at my own funeral, Mr. Mayor, only imagine it!

Mr. Mayor, I wish to submit several urgent questions to you; I will be grateful for your prompt
views on these matters of political friendships, connections, and power.

1. Are you aware of this inequitable treatment
of professional staff in the Bureau of Summary
Sessions of the Department of Receipts and Disbursements?

2. If so, is this the nature of the Administration
you are content to be represented by?

3. Is it truly your desire to erode and undermine
the professional Civil Service—one of democratic
government's most just, most equitable, devices?

4. Does Commissioner Alvin Turtelman's per-
emptory action really reflect your own sensibility,
with all its fairness and exuberant humaneness?

In City, State, and World life, Mr. Mayor (I have
observed this over many years), power and connections are never called power and connections. They
are called principle. They are called democracy.
They are called judgment. They are called doing
good. They are called restructuring. They are called
exigency. They are called improvement. They are
called functioning. They are called the common
need. They are called government. They are called
running the Bureau, the Department, the City, the
State, the World, looking out for the interests of the
people.

Mr. Mayor, getting the spoils is called anything
but getting the spoils!

Puttermesser did not know whether Malachy ("Matt") Mavett's sensibility was really fair and exuberantly humane; she had
only put that in to flatter him. She had glimpsed the Mayor in
the flesh only once or twice, at a meeting, from a distance. She
had also seen him on Sunday morning television, at a press conference, but then he was exceptionally cautious and sober;

before the cameras he was neuter, he had no sensibility at all; he was nearly translucent. His white mustache looked tangled; his white hair twirled in strings over his temples.

Puttermesser's letter struck her as gripping, impressive; copying it over on the typewriter at home that night, she felt how the Mayor would be stabbed through by such fevered eloquence. How remorseful he would be, how moved!

Still another salary check arrived. It was not for the usual amount; Puttermesser's pay had been cut. The bony acolyte appeared with a memo from Turtelman: Puttermesser was to leave her barren cubicle and go to an office with a view of the Woolworth Building, and there she was to take up the sad life of her demotion.

Turtelman had shoved her into the lowliest ranks of Taxation. It was an unlikely post for a mind superfetate with Idea; Puttermesser felt the malignancy behind this shift. Her successor had wished her out of sight. "I do not consort with failure," she heard Adam Marmel tell one of the auditors. She lived now surrounded by auditors—literal-minded men. They read bestsellers; their fingers were smudged from the morning papers, which they clutched in their car pools or on the subway from Queens. One of them, Leon Cracow, a bachelor from Forest Hills who wore bow ties and saddle shoes, was engaged in a tedious litigation: he had once read a novel and fancied himself its hero. The protagonist wore bow ties and saddle shoes. Cracow was suing for defamation. "My whole love life's maligned in there," he complained to Puttermesser. He kept the novel on his desk—it was an obscure book no one had ever heard of, published by a shadowy California press. Cracow had bought it remaindered for eighty-nine cents and ruminated over it every day. Turning the pages, he wet two of his fingers repeatedly. The novel was called *Pyke's Pique*; a tax auditor named John McCracken Pyke was its chief character. "McCracken," Cracow said, "that's practically Cracow. It sounds practically identical. Listen, in the book this guy goes to prostitutes. I don't go to prostitutes! The skunk's got me all wrong. He's destroying my good name." Sometimes Cracow asked Puttermesser for her opinion of his lawyer's last move. Puttermesser urged him on. She believed in the uses of fantasy. "A person should see himself or herself everywhere," she said. "All things manifest us."

The secret source of this motto was, in fact, her old building on the Grand Concourse. Incised in a stone arch over the broad front door, and also in Puttermesser's loyal brain, were these Roman-style tracings: LONGWOOD ARMS, No. 26. GREENDALE HALL, No. 28. ALL THINGS MANIFEST US. The builder had thought deep thoughts, and Cracow was satisfied. "Ruth," he said, "you take the cake." As usual, he attempted to date her. "Any concert, any show, you name it," he said; "I'm a film buff." "You fit right in with Turtelman and Marmel," Puttermesser said. "Not me," Cracow retorted, "with me it's nostalgia only. My favorite movie is Deanna Durbin, Leopold Stokowski, and Adolphe Menjou in *One Hundred Men and a Girl*. Wholesome, sweet, not like they make today. Light classical. Come on, Ruth, it's at the Museum of Modern Art, in the cellar." Puttermesser turned him down. She knew she would never marry, but she was not yet reconciled to childlessness. Sometimes the thought that she would never give birth tore her heart.

She imagined daughters. It was self-love: all these daughters were Puttermesser as a child. She imagined a daughter in fourth grade, then in seventh grade, then in second-year high school. Puttermesser herself had gone to Hunter College High School and studied Latin. At Barnard she had not renounced Catullus and Vergil. *O infelix Dido*, chanted the imaginary daughter, doing her Latin homework at Puttermesser's new Danish desk in the dark corner of the little bedroom. It was a teak rectangle; Puttermesser still had not bought a lamp for it. She hated it that all her furniture was new.

No reply came from the Mayor: not even a postcard of acknowledgment from an underling. Malachy ("Matt") Mavett was ignoring Puttermesser.

Rappoport had abandoned the Sunday *Times*, purchased Saturday night at the airport; he had left it, unopened, on the Danish desk. Puttermesser swung barefoot out of bed, stepped over Plato, and reached for Rappoport's *Times*. She brooded over his furry chest hair, yellowing from red. Now the daughter, still in high school, was memorizing Goethe's *Erlkönig*:

> Dem Vater grauset's, er reitet geschwind,
> Er hält in Armen das ächzende Kind,
> Erreicht den Hof mit Mühe und Not;
> In seinen Armen das Kind war tot.

The words made Puttermesser want to sob. The child was dead. In its father's arms the child was dead. She came back to bed, carrying Rappoport's *Times*. It was as heavy as if she carried a dead child. The Magazine Section alone was of a preternatural weight. Advertising. Consumerism. Capitalism. Page after page of cars, delicately imprinted chocolates, necklaces, golden whiskey. Affluence while the poor lurked and mugged, hid in elevators, shot drugs into their veins, stuck guns into old grandmothers' tremulous and brittle spines, in covert pools of blackness released the springs of their bright-flanked switchblades, in shafts, in alleys, behind walls, in ditches.

A naked girl lay in Puttermesser's bed. She looked dead—she was all white, bloodless. It was as if she had just undergone an epileptic fit: her tongue hung out of her mouth. Her eyelids were rigidly ajar; they had no lashes, and the skin was so taut and thin that the eyeballs bulged through. Her palms had fallen open; they were a clear white. Her arms were cold rods. A small white square was visible on the tongue. The girl did not resemble Puttermesser at all; she was certainly not one of the imaginary daughters. Puttermesser moved to one side of the bed, then circled back around the foot to the other side. She put on her slippers; summoning reason, she continued to move around and around the bed. There was no doubt that a real body was in it. Puttermesser reached out and touched the right shoulder—a reddish powder coated her fingers. The body seemed filmed with sand, or earth, or grit; some kind of light clay. Filth. A filthy junkie or prostitute; both. Sickness and filth. Rappoport, stalking away in the middle of the night, had been careless about closing the apartment door. God only knew where the creature had concealed herself, what had been stolen or damaged. When Puttermesser's back was turned, the filthy thing had slid into her bed. Such a civilized bed, the home of Plato and other high-minded readings. The body had a look of perpetuity about it, as if it had always been reclining there, in Puttermesser's own bed; yet it was a child's body, the limbs stretched into laxity and languor. She was a little thing, no more than fifteen: Puttermesser saw how the pubic hair was curiously sparse; but the breasts were nearly not there at all. Puttermesser went on calculating and circling: should she call the super, or else telephone for an ambulance? New York! What was the good of living in a tiny squat box, with low ceilings, on East Seventy-first Street, a grudging landlord, a doorman in an admiral's uniform, if there were infiltrators, addicts, invaders, just the same as on the fallen Grand Concourse?

Puttermesser peered down at the creature's face. Ugly. The nose and mouth were clumsily formed, as if by some coarse hand that had given them a negligent tweak. The vomerine divider was off-center, the nostrils unpleasantly far apart. The mouth was in even worse condition—also off-center, but somehow more carelessly made, with lips that failed to match, the lower one no better than a line, the upper one amazingly fat, swollen, and the narrow tongue protruding with its white patch. Puttermesser reached out a correcting hand, and then withdrew it. Once again the dust left deep red ovals on her fingertips. But it was clear that the nostrils needed pinching to bring them closer together, so Puttermesser tentatively pinched. The improvement was impressive. She blew into the left nostril to get rid of a tuft of dust; it solidified and rolled out like a clay bead. With squeamish deliberation she pushed the nose in line with the middle space where the eyebrows ought to have been. There were no eyebrows, no eyelashes, no fingernails, no toenails. The thing was defective, unfinished. The mouth above all required finishing. Forming and re-forming the savage upper lip, getting into the mood of it now, Puttermesser wished she were an artist or sculptor: she centered the mouth, thickened the lower lip with a quick turn, smoothed out the hunch of the upper one—the tongue was in the way. She peeled off the white square and, pressing hard, shoved the tongue back down into the mouth.

The bit of white lay glimmering in Puttermesser's palm. It seemed to be nothing more than an ordinary slip of paper, but she thought she ought to put it aside to look it over more carefully after a while, so she left the bed and set it down on the corner of the teak desk. Then she came back and glanced up and down the body, to see whether there was anything else that called for correction. A forefinger needed lengthening, so Puttermesser tugged at it. It slid as if boneless, like taffy, cold but not sticky, and thrillingly pliable. Still, without its nail a finger can shock; Puttermesser recoiled. Though the face was now normal enough, there was more to be done. Something had flashed upward from that tongue-paper—the white patch was blank; yet it was not only blank. Puttermesser carried it in her palm to the window, for the sake of the light. But on the sill and under the sill every pot was cracked, every green plant sprawled. The roots, skeletal and hairy, had been torn from their embracing soil—or, rather, the earth had been scooped away. The plain earth, stolen. Puttermesser, holding the white scrap, wandered from window to window. There was no pot that had not been vandalized in the same way—Rappoport's big clay urn was in shards, the avocado tree broken. A few sparse grains of soil powdered the floor. Not a plant anywhere had been left unmolested—all the earth in Puttermesser's apartment was gone; taken away; robbed.

In the bedroom the girl's form continued its lethal sleep. Puttermesser lifted the tiny paper to the bright panes. Out of the whiteness of the white patch another whiteness flickered, as though a second version of absence were struggling to swim up out of the aboriginal absence. For Puttermesser, it was as if the white of her own eye could suddenly see what the purposeful retina had shunned. It was in fact not so much a seeing as the sharpness of a reading, and what Puttermesser read—she whose intellectual passions were pledged to every alphabet—was a single primeval Hebrew word, shimmering with its lightning holiness, the Name of Names, that which one dare not take in vain. Aloud she uttered it:

$$השם.$$

whereupon the inert creature, as if drilled through by electricity, as if struck by some principle of instantaneous vitality, leaped straight from the bed; Puttermesser watched the fingernails grow rapidly into place, and the toenails, and the eyebrows and lashes: complete. A configuration of freckles appeared on the forehead. The hair of the head and of the mons Veneris thickened, curled, glistened dark red, the color of clay; the creature had risen to walk. She did it badly, knocking down the desk-chair and bumping into the dresser. Sick, drugged, drunk; vandal; thief of earth!

"Get your clothes on and get out," Puttermesser said. Where were the thing's clothes? She had none; she seemed less pale moment by moment; she was lurching about in her skin. She was becoming rosy. A lively color was in her cheeks and hands. The mouth, Puttermesser's own handiwork, was vivid. Puttermesser ran to her closet and pulled out a shirt, a skirt, a belt, a cardigan. From her drawers she swept up bra, panty-hose, slip. There was only the question of shoes. "Here," she said, "summer sandals, that's all I can spare. Open toes, open heels, they'll fit. Get dressed. I can give you an old coat—go ahead. Sit down on the bed. Put this stuff on. You're lucky I'm not calling the police."

The creature staggered away from the bed, toward the teak desk.

"Do what I say!"

The creature had seized a notepad and a ballpoint pen, and was scribbling with shocking speed. Her fingers, even the newly lengthened one, were rhythmically coordinated. She clenched the pen, Puttermesser saw, like an experienced writer: as if the pen itself were a lick of the tongue, or an extension of the thinking digits. It surprised Puttermesser to learn that this thief of earth was literate. In what language? And would she then again try to swallow what she wrote, leaving one untouchable word behind?

The thing ripped away the alphabet-speckled page, tottered back with the pad, and laid the free sheet on the pillow.

"What's the matter? Can't you walk?" Puttermesser asked; she thought of afflicted children she had known, struck by melancholy witherings and dodderings.

But the answer was already on the paper. Puttermesser read: "I have not yet been long up upon my fresh-made limbs. Soon my gait will come to me. Consider the newborn colt. I am like unto that. All tongues are mine, especially that of my mother. Only speech is forbidden me."

A lunatic! Cracked! Alone in the house with a maniac; a deaf-mute to boot. "Get dressed," Puttermesser again commanded.

The thing wrote: "I hear and obey the one who made me."

"What the hell *is* this," Puttermesser said flatly.

The thing wrote: "My mother," and rapidly began to jerk herself into Puttermesser's clothes, but with uneven sequences of the body—the more vitality the creature gained, the more thing-like she seemed.

Puttermesser was impatient; she longed to drive the creature out. "Put on those shoes," she ordered.

The thing wrote: "No."

"Shoes!" Puttermesser shouted. She made a signpost fist

and flung it in the direction of the door. "Go out the way you came in!"

The thing wrote: "No shoes. This is a holy place. I did not enter. I was formed. Here you spoke the Name of the Giver of Life. You blew in my nostril and encouraged my soul. You circled my clay seven times. You enveloped me with your spirit. Your pronounced the Name and brought me to myself. Therefore I call you mother."

Puttermesser's lungs began to roil. It was true she had circled the creature on the bed. Was it seven times around? It was true she had blown some foreign matter out of the nose. Had she blown some uncanny energy into an entrance of the dormant body? It was true she had said aloud one of the Names of the Creator.

The thing wrote again: "Mother. Mother."

"Go away!"

The thing wrote: "You made me."

"I didn't give birth to you." She would never give birth. Yet she had formed this mouth—the creature's mute mouth. She looked at the mouth: she saw what she had made.

The thing wrote: "Earth is my flesh. For the sake of my flesh you carried earth to this high place. What will you call me?"

A new turbulence fell over Puttermesser. She had always imagined a daughter named Leah. "Leah," she said.

"No," the creature wrote. "Leah is my name, but I want to be Xanthippe."

Puttermesser said, "Xanthippe was a shrew. Xanthippe was Socrates' wife."

"I want to be Xanthippe," the thing wrote. "I know everything you know. I am made of earth but also I am made out of your mind. Now watch me walk."

The thing walked, firmly, with a solid thump of a step and no stumbling. She wrote on the pad: "I am becoming stronger. You made me. I will be of use to you. Don't send me away. Call me what I prefer, Xanthippe."

"Xanthippe," Puttermesser said.

She succumbed; her throat panted. It came to her that the creature was certainly not lying: Puttermesser's fingernails were crowded with grains of earth. In some unknown hour after Rappoport's departure in the night, Puttermesser had shaped an apparition. She had awakened it to life in the conventional way. Xanthippe was a golem, and what had polymathic Puttermesser *not* read about the genus golem?

Puttermesser ordered: "All right, go look on the bookshelves. Bring me whatever you see on your own kind."

The creature churned into the living room and hurried back with two volumes, one in either hand; she held the pen ready in her mouth. She dumped the books on the bed and wrote: "I am the first female golem."

"No you're not," Puttermesser said. It was plain that the creature required correction. Puttermesser flew through the pages of one of the books. "Ibn Gabirol created a woman. This was in Spain, long ago, the eleventh century. The king gave him a dressing-down for necromancy, so he dismantled her. She was made of wood and had hinges—it was easy to take her apart."

The creature wrote: "That was not a true golem."

"Go sit down in a corner," Puttermesser said. "I want to read."

The creature obeyed. Puttermesser dived into the two volumes. She had read them many times before; she knew certain passages nearly verbatim. One, a strange old text in a curiously awkward English translation (it was printed in Austria in 1925), had the grass-green public binding of a library book; to Puttermesser's citizenly shame, she had never returned it. It had been borrowed from the Crotona Park Branch decades ago, in Puttermesser's adolescence. There were photographs in it, incandescently clear: of graves, of a statue, of the lamp-hung interior of a synagogue in Prague—the Altneuschul—, of its tall peaked contour, of the two great clocks, one below the cupola, the other above it, on the venerable Prague Jewish Community House.

Across the street from the Community House there was a shop, with a sign that said v. PRESSLER in large letters; underneath, his hand in his pocket, a dapper mustached dandy in a black fedora lounged eternally. Familiar, static, piercingly distinct though these illustrations were, Puttermesser all the same felt their weary old ache: phantoms—v. PRESSLER a speck of earth; the houses air; the dandy evaporated. Among these aged streets and deranged structures Puttermesser's marveling heart had often prowled. "You have no feelings," Rappoport once told her: he meant that she had the habit of flushing with ideas as if they were passions.

And this was true. Puttermesser's intelligence, brambly with the confusion of too much history, was a private warted tract, rubbled over with primordial statuary. She was painfully anthropological. Civilizations rolled into her rib cage, stone after graven stone: cuneiform, rune, cipher. She had pruned out allegory, metaphor; Puttermesser was no mystic, enthusiast, pneumaticist, ecstatic, kabbalist. Her mind was clean; she was a rationalist. Despite the imaginary daughters—she included these among her losses—she was not at all attached to any notion of shade or specter, however corporeal it might appear, and least of all to the idea of a golem—hardly that, especially now that she had the actual thing on her hands. What transfixed her was the kind of intellect (immensely sober, pragmatic, unfanciful, rationalist like her own) to which a golem ordinarily occurred—occurred, that is, in the shock of its true flesh and absolute being. The classical case of the golem of Prague, for instance: the Great Rabbi Judah Loew, circa 1520–1609, maker of that renowned local creature, was scarcely one of those misty souls given over to untrammeled figments or romances. He was, instead, a reasonable man of biting understanding, a solid scholar, a pragmatic leader—a learned quasi-mayor. What he understood was that the scurrilous politics of his city, always tinged with religious interests, had gone too far. In short, they were killing the Jews of

Prague. It had become unsafe for a peddler to open his pack, or a merchant his shop; no mother and her little daughter dared turn in to an alley. Real blood ran in the streets, and all on account of a rumor of blood: citizens of every class—not just the gutter-snipes—were muttering that the Jews had kneaded the bodies of Christian infants into their sacral Passover wafers. Scapegoat Jews, exposed, vulnerable, friendless, unarmed! The very Jews forbidden by their dietary code to eat an ordinary farmyard egg tainted with the minutest jot of fetal blood! So the great Rabbi Judah Loew, to defend the Jews of Prague against their depredators, undertook to fashion a golem.

Puttermesser was well acquainted with the Great Rabbi Judah Loew's method of golem-making. It was classical; it was, as such things go, ordinary. To begin with, he entered a dream of Heaven, wherein he asked the angels to advise him. The answer came in alphabetical order: *afar, esh, mayim, ruach*: earth, fire, water, wraith. With his son-in-law, Isaac ben Shimshon, and his pupil, Jacob ben Chayim Sasson, the Great Rabbi Judah Loew sought inner purity and sanctification by means of prayer and ritual immersion; then the three of them went out to a mud-bed on the banks of the River Moldau to create a man of clay. Three went out; four returned. They worked by torchlight, reciting Psalms all the while, molding a human figure. Isaac ben Shimshon, a descendant of the priests of the Temple, walked seven times around the clay heap bulging up from the ground. Jacob ben Chayim Sasson, a Levite, walked seven times around. Then the Great Rabbi Judah Loew himself walked around, once only, and placed a parchment inscribed with the Name into the clay man's mouth. The priest represented fire; the Levite water; the Great Rabbi Judah Loew designated himself spirit and wraith, or air itself. The earth-man lay inert upon earth, like upon like. Fire, water, air, all chanted together: "And he breathed into his nostrils the breath of life; and man became a living soul"—whereupon the golem heated up, turned fiery red, and rose! It rose to become the savior of the Jews of Prague. On its forehead were imprinted the three letters that are the Hebrew word for truth: *aleph, mem, tav*.

This history Puttermesser knew, in its several versions, inside out. "Three went out; four returned"—following which, how the golem punished the slaughterers, persecutors, predators! How it cleansed Prague of evil and infamy, of degeneracy and murder, of vice and perfidy! But when at last the Great Rabbi Judah Loew wished the golem to subside, he climbed a ladder (a golem grows bigger every day), reached up to the golem's forehead, and erased the letter *aleph*. Instantly the golem fell lifeless, given back to spiritless clay: lacking the *aleph*, the remaining letters, *mem* and *tav*, spelled *met*—dead. The golem's body was hauled up to the attic of the Altneuschul, where it still rests among ever-thickening cobwebs. "No one may touch the cobwebs," ran one of the stories, "for whoever touches them dies."

For Puttermesser, the wonder of this tale was not in any of its remarkable parts, familiar as they were, and not even in its recurrence. The golem recurred, of course. It moved from the Exile of Babylon to the Exile of Europe; it followed the Jews. In the third century Rabbi Rava created a golem, and sent it to Rabbi Zera, who seemed not to know it was a golem until he discovered that it could not speak. Then realization of the thing's true nature came to him, and he rebuked it: "You must have been made by my comrades of the Talmudic Academy; return to your dust." Rabbi Hanina and Rabbi Oshaya were less successful than Rabbi Rava; they were only able to produce a very small calf, on which they dined. An old kabbalistic volume, the Book of Creation, explains that Father Abraham himself could manufacture human organisms. The Book of Raziel contains a famous workable prescription for golem-making: the maker utilizes certain chants and recitations, imprinted medals, esoteric names, efficacious shapes and totems. Ben Sira and his father, the prophet Jeremiah, created a golem, in the logical belief that Adam himself was a golem; their golem, like Adam, had the power of speech. King Nebuchadnezzar's own idol turned into a living golem when he set on its head the diadem of the High Priest, looted out of the Temple in Jerusalem; the jeweled letters of the Tetragrammaton were fastened into the diadem's silver sockets. The prophet Daniel, pretending to kiss the king's golem, swiftly plucked out the gems that spelled the Name of God, and the idol was again lifeless. Even before that, thieves among the wicked generation that built the Tower of Babel swiped some of the contractor's materials to fashion idols, which were made to walk by having the Name shoved into their mouths; then they were taken for gods. Rabbi Aharon of Baghdad and Rabbi Hananel did not mold images; instead, they sewed parchments inscribed with the Name into the right arms of corpses, who at once revived and became members of the genus golem. The prophet Micah made a golden calf that could dance, and Bezalel, the designer of the Tabernacle, knew how to combine letters of the alphabet so as to duplicate Creation, both Heaven and earth. Rabbi Elazar of Worms had a somewhat similar system for golem-making: three adepts must gather up "virginal mountain earth," pour running water over it, knead it into a man, bury it, and recite two hundred and twenty-one alphabetical combinations, observing meticulously the prescribed order of the vowels and consonants. But Abraham Abulafia could make a man out of a mere spoonful of earth by blowing it over an ordinary dish of water; undoubtedly this had some influence on Paracelsus, the sixteenth-century Swiss alchemist, who used a retort to make a homunculus: Paracelsus's manikin, however, was not telluric, being composed of blood, sperm, and urine, from which the Jewish golem-makers recoiled. For the Jews, earth, water, and the divine afflatus were the only permissible elements—the afflatus being summoned through the holy syllables. Rabbi Ishmael, on the other hand, knew another way of withdrawing that life-conferring holiness and rendering an active golem back into

dust: he would recite the powerful combinations of sacred letters backward, meanwhile circling the creature in the direction
opposite to the one that had quickened it.

There was no end to the conditions of golem-making, just as
there was no end to the appearance of one golem after another
in the pullulating procession of golem-history; but Puttermesser's brain, crowded with all these acquisitions and rather a
tidy store of others (for instance, she had the noble Dr. Gershom
Scholem's bountiful essay "The Idea of the Golem" virtually by
heart), was unattracted either to number or to method. What
interested Puttermesser was something else: it was the plain fact
that the golem-makers were neither visionaries nor magicians
nor sorcerers. They were neither fantasists nor fabulists nor
poets. They were, by and large, scientific realists—and, in nearly
every case at hand, serious scholars and intellectuals: the plausible forerunners, in fact, of their great-grandchildren, who are
physicists, biologists, or logical positivists. It was not only the
Great Rabbi Judah Loew, the esteemed golem-maker of Prague,
who had, in addition, a reputation as a distinguished Talmudist,
reasoner, philosopher; even Rabbi Elijah, the most celebrated
Jewish intellect of Eastern Europe (if Spinoza is the most celebrated on the Western side), whose brilliance outstripped the
fame of every other scholar, who founded the most rigorous rab-
binical academy in the history of the cold lands, who at length
became known as the Vilna Gaon (the Genius of the city of
Vilna, called, on his account, the Jerusalem of the North)—even
the Vilna Gaon once attempted, before the age of thirteen, to
make a golem! And the Vilna Gaon, with his stern refinements
of exegesis and analysis, with his darting dazzlements of logical
penetration, was—as everyone knows—the scourge of mystics,
protester (*mitnagid*) against the dancing hasidim, scorner of
those less limber minds to the Polish south, in superstitiously
pious Galicia. If the Vilna Gaon could contemplate the making
of a golem, thought Puttermesser, there was nothing irrational

in it, and she would not be ashamed of what she herself had concocted.

She asked Xanthippe: "Do you eat?"

The golem wrote, *"Vivo, ergo edo.* I live, therefore I eat."

"Don't pull that on me—my Latin is as good as yours. Can you cook?"

"I can do what I must, if my mother decrees it," the golem wrote.

"All right," Puttermesser said. "In that case you can stay. You can stay until I decide to get rid of you. Now make lunch. Cook something I like, only better than I could do it."

III. THE GOLEM COOKS, CLEANS, AND SHOPS

he golem hurried off to the kitchen. Puttermesser heard the smack of the refrigerator, the clatter of silver, the faucet turned on and off; sounds of chopping in a wooden bowl; plates set out, along with an eloquent tinkle of glassware; a distant whipping, a distant sizzling; mushroom fragrances; coffee. The golem appeared at the bedroom door with a smug sniff, holding out her writing pad:

"I can have uses far beyond the mere domestic."

"If you think you're too good for kitchen work," Puttermesser retorted, "don't call yourself Xanthippe. You're so hot on aspiration, you might as well go the whole hog and pick Socrates."

The golem wrote: "I mean to be a critic, even of the highest philosophers. Xanthippe alone had the courage to gainsay Socrates. Nay, I remain Xanthippe. Please do not allow my

Swedish mushroom soufflé to sink. It is best eaten in a steaming condition."

Puttermesser muttered, "I don't like your prose style. You write like a translation from the Middle Finnish. Improve it," but she followed the golem into the little kitchen. The golem's step was now light and quick, and the kitchen too seemed transformed—a floating corner of buoyancy and quicksilver: it was as if the table were in the middle of a Parisian concourse, streaming, gleaming: it had the look of a painting, both transient and eternal, a place where you sat for a minute to gossip, and also a place where the middle-aged Henry James came every day so that nothing in the large world would be lost on him. "You've set things up nicely enough," Puttermesser said; "I forgot all about these linen placemats." They were, in fact, part of her "trousseau"; her mother had given her things. It was expected, long ago, that Puttermesser would marry.

The golem's soufflé was excellent; she had also prepared a dessert that was part mousse, part lemon gelatin. Puttermesser, despite her periodontic troubles, took a greedy second helping. The golem's dessert was more seductive even than fudge; and fudge for Puttermesser was notoriously paradisal.

"First-rate," Puttermesser said; the golem had been standing all the while. "Aren't you having any?"

Immediately the golem sat down and ate.

"Now I'm going for a walk," Puttermesser announced. "Clean all this up. Make the bed. Be sure to mop under it. Look in the hamper, you'll find a heap of dirty clothes. There's a public washing machine in the basement. I'll give you quarters."

The golem turned glum.

"Well, look," Puttermesser argued, "I can use you for anything I please, right?"

The golem wrote, "The Great Rabbi Judah Loew's wife sent the golem of Prague to fetch water, and he fetched, and he fetched, until he flooded the house, the yard, the city, and finally the world."

"Don't bother me with fairy tales," Puttermesser said.

The golem wrote, "I insist I am superior to mere household use."

"No one's superior to dirty laundry," Puttermesser threw back, and went out into the great city. She intended to walk and brood; though she understood at last how it was that she had brought the golem to life, it disturbed her that she did not recall *making* her—emptying all the plant pots, for instance. Nor was Puttermesser wise to her own secret dictates in creating the golem. And now that the golem was actually in the house, what was to be done with her? Puttermesser worried about the landlord, a suspicious fellow. The landlord allowed no dogs or—so the lease read—"irregular relationships." She thought of passing Xanthippe off as an adopted daughter—occasionally she would happen on an article about single parents of teen-age foster children. It was not so unusual. But even that would bring its difficulty, because—to satisfy the doorman and the neighbors—such a child would have to be sent to school; and it was hardly reasonable, Puttermesser saw, to send the golem to an ordinary high school. They would ship her off to an institution for deaf-mutes, to learn sign language—and it would become evident soon enough, wouldn't it, that the golem was not the least bit deaf? There was really no place for her in any classroom; she probably knew too much already. The erratic tone of her writing, with its awful pastiche, suggested that she had read ten times more than any other tenth-grader of the same age. Besides, did the golem *have* an age? She had the shape of a certain age, yes; but the truth was she was only a few hours old. Her public behavior was bound to be unpredictable.

Puttermesser was walking northward. Her long introspective stride had taken her as far as Eighty-sixth Street. She left Madison and veered up Lexington. She had forgotten her gloves; her fingers were frozen. February's flying newspapers scuttled over broken bottles and yogurt cups squashed in the gutter. A bag lady slept in a blue-black doorway, wrapped in a pile of ragged coats. Dusk was coming down; all the store windows, without exception, were barred or shuttered against the late-afternoon Sunday emptiness. Burglars, addicts, marauders, the diverse criminal pestilences of uptown and downtown, would have to find other ways of entry: breaking through a roof; a blowtorch on a steel bar; a back toilet window with a loose grill. Ingenuity. Puttermesser peered around behind her for the mugger who, in all logic, should have been stalking her; no one was there. But she was ready: she had left her wallet at home on purpose; a police whistle dangled on a cord around her neck; she fondled the little knife in her pocket. New York! All the prisons in the metropolitan area were reputed to be hopelessly overcrowded.

At Ninety-second Street she swung through the revolving doors of the Y to warm up. The lobby was mostly uninhabited; a short line straggled toward the ticket office. Puttermesser read the poster: a piano concert at eight o'clock. She headed downtown. It was fully dark now. She reflected that it would be easy enough to undo, to reverse, the golem; there was really no point in keeping her on. For one thing, how would the golem be occupied all day while Puttermesser was at work? And Puttermesser was nervous: she had her demotion to think about. Stripped. Demoralized. That pest Cracow. Turtelman and Marmel. The Civil Service, founded to eradicate patronage, nepotism, favoritism, spoils, payoffs, injustice, corruption! Lost, all lost. The Mayor had no intention of answering Puttermesser's urgent letter.

Taking off her coat, Puttermesser called to the golem, "What's going on in there?" An unexpected brilliance spilled out of the bedroom: a lamp in the form of the Statue of Liberty stood on the teak desk. "What's this?"

"I bought it," the golem wrote. "I did everything my mother instructed. I cleaned up the kitchen, made the bed"—a new blue bedspread, with pictures of baseball mitts, covered it—"mopped the whole house, did the laundry, ironed everything, hung my mother's blouses and put my mother's panty-hose into the drawer—"

Puttermesser grabbed the sheet of paper right off the golem's pad and tore it up without reading the rest of it. "What do you mean you bought it? What kind of junk is this? I don't want the Statue of Liberty! I don't want baseball mitts!"

"It was all I could find," the golem wrote on a fresh page. "All the stores around here are closed on Sunday. I had to go down to Delancey Street on the Lower East Side. I took a taxi."

"Taxi! You'll shop when I tell you to shop!" Puttermesser yelled. "Otherwise you stay home!"

"I need a wider world," the golem wrote. "Take me with you to your place of employment tomorrow."

"My foot I will," Puttermesser said. "I've had enough of you. I've been thinking"—she looked for a euphemism—"about sending you back."

"Back?" the golem wrote; her mouth had opened all the way.

"You've got a crooked tooth. Come here," Puttermesser said, "I'll fix it."

The golem wrote, "You can no longer alter my being or any part of my being. The speaking of the Name fulfills; it precludes alteration. But I am pleasant to look on, am I not? I will not again gape so that my crooked tooth can offend my mother's eye. Only use me."

"You've got rotten taste."

The golem wrote, "It was my task to choose between baseball mitts and small raccoons intermingled with blue-eyed panda bears. The baseball mitts struck me as the lesser evil."

"I never *wanted* a bedspread," Puttermesser objected. "When I said to make the bed I just meant to straighten the blankets, that's all. And my God, the Statue of Liberty!"

The golem wrote, "A three-way bulb, 150 watts. I thought it so very clever that the bulb goes right into the torch."

"Kitsch. And where'd you get the money?"

"Out of your wallet. But see how pleasantly bright," the

golem wrote. "I fear the dark. The dark is where pre-existence abides. It is not possible to think of pre-existence, but one dreads its facsimile: post-existence. Do not erase, obliterate, or annihilate me. Mother, my mother. I will serve you. Use me in the wide world."

"You stole my money right out of my wallet, spent a fortune on a taxi, and brought home the cheapest sort of junk. If you pull this kind of thing in the house, don't talk to me about the wide world!"

IV. XANTHIPPE AT WORK

But the next morning the golem was in Puttermesser's office.

"Who's the kid?" Cracow asked.

"Marmel's letting me have a typist," Puttermesser said.

"Marmel? That don't make sense. After demoting you?"

"I was reassigned," Puttermesser said; but her cheeks stung.

"Them's the breaks," Cracow said. "So how come the royal treatment? You could use the typing pool like the rest of us."

"Turtelman's put me on a special project."

"Turtelman? Turtelman kicked you in the head. What special project?"

"I'm supposed to check out any employee who broods about lawsuits on City time," Puttermesser said.

"Oh come on, Ruth, can the corn. You know damn well I've been maligned. My lawyer says I have a case. I damn well have a case. What's the kid's name?"

"Leah."

"Leah." Cracow pushed his face right into the golem's. "Do they hire 'em that young? What are you, Leah, a high-school dropout?"

"She's smart enough as is," Puttermesser said.

"Whyn't you let the kid answer for herself?"

Puttermesser took Cracow by the elbow and whispered, "They cut out her throat. Malignancy of the voicebox."

"Whew," Cracow said.

"Get going," Puttermesser ordered the golem, and led her to the ladies' room. "I told you not to come! I'm in enough hot water around here, I don't need you to make trouble."

The golem plucked a paper towel from the wall, fetched Puttermesser's ballpoint pen from the pocket of Puttermesser's cardigan (the golem was still wearing it), and wrote: "I will ameliorate your woe."

"I didn't say woe, I said hot water. *Trouble*. First kitsch, now rococo. Observe reality, can't you? Look, you're going to sit in front of that typewriter and that's it. If you can type half as well as you cook, fine. I don't care *what* you type. Stay out of my way. Write letters, it doesn't matter, but stay out of my way."

The golem wrote, "I hear and obey."

All day the golem, a model of diligence, sat at the typewriter and typed. Puttermesser, passing en route from one fruitless meeting to another, saw the sheets accumulating on the floor. Was Xanthippe writing a novel? a memoir? To whom, after all, did she owe a letter? The golem looked abstracted, rapt. Puttermesser was hoping to patch together, bit by bit, her bad fortune. The gossips ran from cubicle to cubicle, collecting the news: Turtelman's niece, an actress—she had most recently played a medieval leper, with a little bell, in a television costume drama—was engaged to the Mayor's cousin. Marmel's aunt had once stayed in the same hotel in Florida with Mrs. Minnie Mavett, the Mayor's elderly widowed adoptive mother. (The Mayor had been an adopted child, and campaigned with his wife and four natural children as a "lucky orphan.") Marmel and Turtelman were said to have married twin sisters; surely this was a symbolic way of marrying each other? Or else Marmel was married to a Boston blueblood, Turtelman to a climber from Great Neck. On the other hand, only Marmel was married; Turtelman was an austere bachelor. One of the secretaries in the Administrative Assistant's office had observed that Marmel, Turtelman, and the Mayor all wore identical rings; she denied they were school rings. Turtelman's "restructuring," moreover, had begun (according to Polly in Personnel) to assume telltale forms. He was becoming bolder and bolder. He was like some crazed plantation owner at harvest time, who, instead of cutting down the standing grain, cuts down the conscientious reapers. Or he was like a raving chessmaster who throws all the winning pieces in the fire. Or he was like a general who leads a massacre against his own best troops. All these images failed. Turtelman was destroying the Department of Receipts and Disbursements. What he looked for was not performance but loyalty. He was a mayoral appointee of rapacious nature conniving at the usual outrages of patronage; he was doing the Mayor's will. He did not love the democratic polity as much as he feared the Mayor. Ah, Walt Whitman was not in his kidneys. Plunder was.

Cracow, meanwhile, reported that several times Adam Marmel had telephoned for Puttermesser. It was urgent. "That new girl's no good, Ruth. I'm all in favor of hiring the handicapped, but when it comes to answering the telephone what's definitely needed is a larynx. I had to pick up every damn time. You think Marmel wants to put you back up there in the stratosphere?"

Puttermesser said nothing. Cracow thought women ought to keep their place; he took open satisfaction in Puttermesser's flight downward. He nagged her to tell him what Turtelman's special project was. "You'd rather do special projects for the higher-ups than date a nice guy like me," he complained. "At least let's have lunch." But Puttermesser sent the golem out to a delicatessen for sandwiches; it was a kosher delicatessen— Puttermesser thought the golem would care about a thing like that. By the middle of the afternoon the golem's typed sheets were a tall stack.

At a quarter to five Turtelman's bony acolyte came puffing in. "Mr. Turtelman lent me to Mr. Marmel just to give you this. I hope you appreciate I'm not normally anyone's delivery boy. You're never at your desk. You can't be reached by phone. You're not important enough to be incommunicado, believe me. Mr. Marmel wants you to prepare a portfolio for him on these topics toot sweet."

Marmel's memo:

> Dear Ms. Puttermesser:
> Please be good enough to supply me with the fol-
> lowing at your earliest convenience. A list of the
> City's bank depositories. Average balance in each
> account for the last three years. List of contact
> people at banks—names, titles, telephone numbers.
> List of contacts for Department of Receipts and Dis-
> bursements (referred to below as "we," "our," and
> "us") in Office of Mayor, Department of Budget,
> relevant City Council committees, Office of Comp-
> troller. Copies of all evaluation reports published
> during past year. Current organization chart show-
> ing incumbent, title, and salary for each of our
> Office Heads. Why do we not have any window
> poles? Where have all the window poles gone? How
> to get toilet paper and soap regularly replaced in
> executive washroom? What kind of Management
> Information System files do we have on the assessed
> value of City real estate? How effective was our last
> Investors' Tour? Old notes disclose visit to sewage
> disposal plant, helicopter ride, fireboat demonstra-
> tion, lunch and fashion show for the ladies—how to
> win goodwill this year from these heavy pockets?
> What hot litigation should I know about in re our
> Quasi-Judicial Division?

It was the old story: the floundering new official perplexed and beleaguered. Puttermesser felt a touch of malicious pleasure in Marmel's memo; she had known it would come to this— Turtelman, having thrown her out, now discovered he could not clear a space for himself without the stirring of Puttermesser's little finger. Marmel, spurred by Turtelman (too high-and-mighty to ask on his own), had set out to pick Puttermesser's brain. He was appealing to Puttermesser to diaper him. Each item in Marmel's memo would take hours and hours to answer! Except for the window poles. Puttermesser could explain about the window poles in half a second.

"Stand by," she said to the bony acolyte. And to Xanthippe: "Take a letter!"

> Mr. Adam Marmel
> First Bursary Officer
> Bureau of Summary Sessions
> Department of Receipts and Disbursements
> Municipal Building
>
> Dear Mr. Marmel:
> Window poles are swiped by the hottest and sweatiest secretaries. The ones located directly above the furnace room, for instance. Though lately the ones who jog at lunchtime are just as likely to pinch poles. When they get them they hide them. Check out the second-floor ladies' room.
> The fresh air of candor is always needed whenever the oxygen of honest admission has been withdrawn. Precisely WHY ["Make that all capitals," Puttermesser said, dictating] have I been relieved of my position? Precisely WHY have you stepped into my job? Let us have some fresh air!
> > Yours sincerely,
> > R. Puttermesser, Esq.

The bony acolyte snatched the sheet directly from the golem's typewriter. "There's a lot more he wants answers to. You've left out practically everything."

"Window poles are everything," Puttermesser said. "The

fresh air of candor is all." She observed—it was a small shock—that the golem's style had infected her.

The bony acolyte warned, "Fresh is right. You better answer the rest of what he wants answered."

"Go home," Puttermesser told the golem. "Home!"

During dinner in the little kitchen Puttermesser was nearly as silent as the golem. Injustice rankled. She paid no attention to the golem's scribblings. The nerve! The nerve! To throw her out and then come and pick her brain! "No more Swedish soufflé," she growled. "Cook something else for a change. And I'm getting tired of seeing you in my old sweater. I'll give you money, tomorrow go buy yourself some decent clothes."

"Tomorrow," the golem wrote, "I will again serve you at your place of employment."

But in the morning Puttermesser was lackadaisical; ambition had trickled away. What, after so much indignity, was there to be ambitious *for*? For the first time in a decade she came to the office late. "What's the special project, Ruth?" Cracow wanted to know right away. "The kid was burning up the typewriter yesterday. What is she anyhow, an illegal alien? She don't look like your ordinary person. Yemenite Israeli type? What is this, already she don't show up, it's only the second day on the job? The phone calls you missed! Memos piled up! That gal from Personnel back and forth two, three times! They're after you today, Ruth! The higher-ups! What's the special project, hah? And the kid leaves you high and dry!"

"She'll turn up." Puttermesser had given the golem a hundred and twenty dollars and sent her to Alexander's. "No taxis or else," Puttermesser said; but she knew the golem would head downtown to Delancey Street. The thronged Caribbean faces and tongues of the Lower East Side drew her; Xanthippe, a kind of foreigner herself, as even Cracow could see, was attracted to immigrant populations. Their tastes and adorations were hers. She returned with red and purple blouses, narrow skirts and flared pants of parrot-green and cantaloupe-orange, multicolored high-heeled plastic shoes, a sunflower-yellow plastic shoulder bag with six double sets of zippers, a pocket mirror, and a transparent plastic comb in its own peach tattersall plastic case.

"Hispanic absolutely," Cracow confirmed—Cracow the bigot—watching Xanthippe lay open boxes and bags.

But Puttermesser was occupied with a trio of memos. They appeared to originate with Marmel but were expressed through Polly, the Atropos of Personnel, she who had put aside her shears for the flurry of a thousand Forms, she who brooded like Shiva the Destroyer on a world of the lopped.

Memo One:

> You are reported as having refused to respond to requests for information relating to Bureau business. You now are subject to conduct inquiry. Please obtain and fill out Form 10V, Q17, with particular reference to Paragraph L, and leave it *immediately* with Polly in Personnel.

Memo Two:

> In consideration of your seniority, Commissioner Alvin Turtelman, having relieved you of Level Eleven status in the Bureau of Summary Sessions, Department of Receipts and Disbursements, due to insufficient control of bursary materials, weak administrative supervision as well as output insufficiency, has retained you at Level Four. However, your work shows continued decline. Lateness reported as of A.M. today. Fill out Below-Level-Eight Lateness Form 14TG. (Submit Form to Polly in Personnel.)

Memo Three:

> As a result of a determination taken by Commissioner Alvin Turtelman in conjunction and in consultation with First Bursary Officer Adam Marmel, your Level Four appointment in the Department of

Receipts and Disbursements is herewith terminated. Please submit Below-Level-Six Severance Form A97, Section 6, with particular reference to Paragraph 14b, to Polly in Personnel.

Severed! Sacked! Dismissed! Let go! Fired! And all in the space of three hours! "Output insufficiency," a lie! "Decline," a fiction! "Conduct inquiry"—like some insignificant clerk or window-pole thief! Late once in ten years and Cracow, litigious would-be lover, snitches to Polly, the Atropos, the Shiva, of Personnel! Who else but Cracow? Lies. Fabrications. Accusations. Marmel the hollow accuser. Absence of due process!

The Honorable Malachy Mavett
Mayor, City of New York
City Hall

Dear Mayor Mavett:
Where is your pride, to appoint such men? Men who accuse without foundation? An accuser who seizes the job of the accused? Suspect! Turtelman wanted me out in order to get Marmel in! I stand for Intellect and Knowledge, they stand for Politics and Loyal Cunning. Hart Crane, poet of New York, his harp the Brooklyn Bridge, does that harp mean nothing to you? Is Walt Whitman dead in your kidneys? Walt Whitman who cried out "numberless crowded streets, high growths of iron, slender, strong, light, splendidly uprising toward clear skies," who embraced "a million people—manners free and superb—open voices—hospitality . . ." Oh, Mayor Mavett, it is Injustice you embrace! You have given power to men for whom Walt Whitman is dead in their kidneys! This city of masts and spires opens its breast for Walt Whitman, and you feed it with a Turtelman and a Marmel! Ruth Puttermesser is despised, demoted, thrown away at last! Destroyed. Without work. Doer of nought, maker of nothing.

This letter remained locked inside Puttermesser's head. Cracow was trying hard not to look her way. He had already read Marmel's memos manifested through Polly the Destroyer; he had surely read them. He stood behind the golem's chair, attentive to her fingers galloping over the typewriter keys— including the newly lengthened one; how glad Puttermesser was that she had fixed it! "Hey Ruth, take a gander at this stuff. What's this kid *doing*? That's some so-called special project for Turtelman."

"The special project for Turtelman," Puttermesser said coldly, "is my vanquishment. My vanishing. My send-off and diminishment. So long, Leon. May you win your case against the mediocre universality of the human imagination."

"You been canned?"

"You know that."

"Well, when Polly walks in you figure what's up. You figure who's out."

"Beware of *Schadenfreude*, Leon. You could be next."

"Not me. I don't look for trouble. You look for trouble. I knew right away this whole setup with the kid was phony. She's typing up a craziness—whatever it is, Bureau business it isn't. You let in the crazies, you get what you expect."

At that moment—as Cracow's moist smile with its brown teeth turned and turned inside Cracow's dark mouth—a clarification came upon Puttermesser: no: a clarity. She was shut of a mystery. She understood; she saw.

"Home!" Puttermesser ordered the golem. Xanthippe gathered up her clothes and shoved the typewritten sheets into one of the blouse bags.

V. WHY THE GOLEM WAS CREATED; PUTTERMESSER'S PURPOSE

hat night the golem cooked spaghetti. She worked barefoot. The fragrance of hot buttered tomato sauce and peppers rushed over a mound of shining porcelain strands. "What are you doing?" Puttermesser demanded; she saw the golem heaping up a second great batch. "Why are you so hungry?"

The golem looked a little larger today than she had yesterday.

Then Puttermesser remembered that it was in the nature of a golem to grow and grow. The golem's appetite was nevertheless worrisome—how long would it take for Xanthippe to grow out of over one hundred dollars' worth of clothes? Could only a Rothschild afford a golem? And what would the rate of growth be? Would the golem eventually have to be kept outdoors, so as not to crash through the ceiling? Was the golem of Prague finally reversed into lifelessness on account of its excessive size, or because the civic reforms it was created for had been accomplished?

Ah, how this idea glowed for Puttermesser! The civic reforms of Prague—the broad crannied city of Prague, Prague distinguished by numberless crowded streets, high growths of iron, masts and spires! The clock-tower of the Jewish Community House, the lofty peaked and chimneyed roof of the Altneuschul! Not to mention Kafka's Castle. All that manifold urban shimmer choked off by evil, corruption, the blood libel, the strong dampened hearts of wicked politicos. The Great Rabbi Judah Loew had undertaken to create his golem in an unenlightened year, the dream of America just unfolding, far away, in all its spacious ardor; but already the seed of New York was preparing in Europe's earth: inspiration of city-joy, love for the comely, the cleanly, the free and the new, mobs transmuted into troops of the blessed, citizens bursting into angelness, sidewalks of alabaster, buses filled with thrones. Old delicate Prague, swept and swept of sin, giving birth to the purified daylight, the lucent genius, of New York!

By now Puttermesser knew what she knew.

"Bring me my books," she ordered the golem. And read:

> A vision of Paradise must accompany the signs. The sacred formulae are insufficient without the trance of ecstasy in which are seen the brilliance of cities and their salvation through exile of heartlessness, disorder, and the desolation of sadness.

A city washed pure. New York, city (perhaps) of seraphim. Wings had passed over her eyes. Her arms around Rappoport's heavy *Times*, Puttermesser held to her breast heartlessness, disorder, the desolation of sadness, ten thousand knives, hatred painted in the subways, explosions of handguns, bombs in the cathedrals of transportation and industry, Pennsylvania Station, Grand Central, Rockefeller Center, terror in the broadcasting booths with their bustling equipment and seductive provincial voices, all the metropolitan airports assaulted, the decline of the Civil Service, maggots in high management. Rappoport's *Times*, repository of a dread freight! All the same, carrying Rappoport's *Times* back to bed, Puttermesser had seen Paradise.

New York washed, reformed, restored.

"Xanthippe!"

The golem, who had been scrubbing spaghetti sauce off the dishes in a little cascade of water-thunder under the kitchen faucet, wiped her hands on her new purple blouse, snatched up ballpoint pen and notepad, and ran to Puttermesser.

Puttermesser asked, "When you woke into life what did you feel?"

"I felt like an embryo," the golem wrote.

"What did you know?"

"I knew why I was created," the golem wrote.

"Why were you created?"

"So that my mother should become what she was intended to become," the golem wrote.

"Bring me that sack of stuff you were fooling around with in the office," Puttermesser ordered, but the golem had already scampered off to the bedroom closet to rummage among her boxes and bags of new clothes.

So Puttermesser set aside her books about the history and nature of the genus golem and settled down to contemplate all the pages the golem had typed for two days in Puttermesser's sorrowful cubicle, shared with Cracow—the cubicle of her demotion, denigration, disgrace—in the Taxation Section of the Bureau of Summary Sessions of the Department of Receipts and Disbursements of the City of New York.

What the golem had composed was a *PLAN*. Puttermesser recognized everything in it. It was as if she had encountered this *PLAN* before—its very language. It was as if, in the instant it had occurred to her to make the golem, she had read the *PLAN* in some old scroll. Ah, here was a stale and restless truth: that she did not recollect the actual fabrication of the golem, that she had helplessly, without volition, come upon Xanthippe in her bed as if the golem were some transient mirage, an aggressive imagining, or else a mere forward apparition—this had, with a wearisome persistence, been teasing at the edge of Puttermesser's medulla oblongata all along, ever since the first mulling of it on her desolate walk to the Y. It was like a pitcher that will neither fill nor pour out. But it was now as plain as solid earth itself that the golem was no apparition. Apparitions do not, in hideous public jargon, type up exhaustive practical documents concerning civic reform! Puttermesser knew what she knew—it unraveled before her in the distance, the *PLAN*, approaching, approaching, until it crowded her forebrain with its importuning force: how she had set Rappoport's *Times*, record of multiple chaos and urban misfortune, down on the floor beside the bed, where the *Theaetetus* already lay. How, with a speed born of fever and agitation, she had whirled from window sill to window sill, cracking open clay plant pots as though they were eggs, and scooping up the germinative yolks of spilling earth. How she had fetched it all up in her two palms and dumped it into the bathtub. How only a half-turn of the tap stirred earth to the consistency of mud—and how there then began the blissful shudder of Puttermesser's wild hands, the molding and the shaping, the caressing and the smoothing, the kneading and the fingering, the straightening and the rounding, but quickly, quickly, with detail itself (God is in the details) unachieved, blurred, completion deferred, the authentic pleasure of the precise final form of nostril and eyelid and especially mouth left for afterward. Into the hole of the unfinished face of clay Puttermesser pressed a tag of paper, torn from the blank upper margin of Rappoport's *Times*, on which she had written in her own spittle two oracular syllables. The syllables adhered and were as legible as if inscribed in light. Then Puttermesser raised up out of the tub the imponderous damp relentless clay of a young girl—a lifeless forked creature in the semblance of a girl—and smelled the smell of mud, and put her down in her own bed to dry. The small jar to that small weight loosened crumbs of earth wherever a limb was joined to the trunk, and where the neck was joined, and where the ears had their fragile connecting stems. The crumbs sprinkled down. They crept under Puttermesser's fingernails.

And all this Puttermesser performed (aha, now it beat in hindbrain and in forebrain, she saw it, she knew it again!) because of agitation and fever: because of the wilderness inside Rappoport's *Times*. Why should the despoiled misgoverned miscreant City not shine at dawn like washed stones? Tablets of civilization, engraved with ontological notations in an ancient tongue. Puttermesser craved. Her craving was to cleanse the wilderness; her craving was to excise every black instance of injustice; her craving was to erase outrage. In the middle of her craving—out of the blue—she formulated the *PLAN*.

She was thumbing it now, it was in her hands:

PLAN
FOR THE
RESUSCITATION,
REFORMATION,
REINVIGORATION
& REDEMPTION
OF THE
CITY OF NEW YORK

"Where did you get this?" Puttermesser demanded.

"I am your amanuensis," the golem wrote. "I express you. I copy and record you. Now it is time for you to accomplish your thought."

"Everyone has funny thoughts," Puttermesser croaked; an uneasiness heated her. She was afraid of the last page.

"No reality greater than thought," the golem wrote.

"Lay off the Middle Finnish. I want to hear the truth about all this. Where'd this stuff come from? You *couldn't* copy it, I never put any of it down."

The golem wrote: "Two urges seeded you. I am one, this is the other. A thought must claim an instrument. When you conceived your urge, simultaneously you conceived me."

"Not simultaneously," Puttermesser objected; perhaps the golem could not be trusted with chronology. She breathed outside history. Puttermesser reimagined the electric moment exactly: the *PLAN* swimming like an inner cosmos into being, the mere solid golem an afterthought.

"No matter; I will serve your brain. I am your offspring, you are my mother. I am the execution of the grandeur of your principles. Grand design is my business. Leave visionary restoration to me." After which the golem put the ballpoint pen in her mouth and patiently sucked.

A fatigue seeped into Puttermesser; a tedium. It struck her

that the golem was looking sly. She noticed that the seams along the armholes in the golem's purple blouse had begun to open. Growth. Enlargement. Swelling. Despite distraction Puttermesser read on. The *PLAN*, though it had originated in her own mind, nevertheless smacked of Marmel's lingo, Turtelman's patois. It appeared to derive, in truth, from the Form-language of Polly the Destroyer. A starkness penetrated Puttermesser; the dead words themselves depressed her. Her wrists shook. Was it not possible to dream a dream of City without falling into the mouth of the Destroyer? Behold the conservation of residential property through the exclusion of depreciating factors. Compute twelve hundred and fifty zoning codes. Note physical aspects. Social aspects. Retail and wholesale business. Manufacturing. Shipping. Single and multiple residences. Cultural institutions. Parks, public buildings, amusements, schools, universities, community objectives, rapidity and feasibility of transportation via streets and transit lines. Health, traffic, safety, public assembly conveniences. Sanitation. Prevention of slums. Transformation of slums. Eradication of poverty. Morality and obedience to law. Ordinances. Trust and pension funds. Treasury, public works, water. Public library. Police. Inspection. Councils and commissions. Welfare. Trustees. Revenue forecasting. Remote teleprocessing systems, computerized key-entry, restructuring of assessment districts, liens, senior-citizen rent-increase exemptions, delinquency centralization, corporate billings!

"My God," Puttermesser said.

"My mother has mastered and swallowed all of it," the golem wrote. "All of it is inside my mother's intelligence."

"I only meant—" Weak, Puttermesser wondered what it was she had meant. "Gardens and sunlight. Washed stones. Tablets. No; tables. Picnic tables."

Xanthippe stood nodding. The slyness powered her eyes. "My mother will become Mayor," she wrote.

The golem took the stack of typed sheets from Puttermesser's unquiet hands and held out the last page:

BY ORDER OF
RUTH PUTTERMESSER,
MAYOR
OF THE
CITY OF NEW YORK

"Drivel. Now you've gone too far. *I* never thought of that."

"Sleep on it," the golem wrote.

"That's *your* idea. You're the one who put that one in."

"Creator and created," the golem wrote, "merge," scribbling this with a shrug; the shrug made the ripped seams in her purple blouse open a little more.

> The Honorable Malachy Mavett
> Mayor
> City Hall
>
> Dear Mayor Mavett:
> It is not respectful of a citizen's conception of the Mayor's office as "responsive" that you ignore my letter about possible spoils and other abuses. Still less is it respectful of me as a living human being and as a (former, now dismissed) Civil Servant. Shame! Shame!
> Very sincerely yours,
> THE HONORABLE RUTH PUTTERMESSER

This letter too remained locked inside Puttermesser's head. The signature was experimental—just to see what it looked like.

"No use, no use," the golem wrote on her notepad. "Mayor Puttermesser, by contrast, will answer all letters."

VI. MAYOR PUTTERMESSER

nd so Puttermesser becomes Mayor of New York. The "and so" encloses much—but not so much as one might think. It is only a way of hastening Puttermesser's blatant destiny, of avoiding—never mind that God is in the details!—a more furrowed account of how the golem, each day imperceptibly enlarging, goes about gathering signatures for a citizens' petition. The golem is above all a realist; Puttermesser will run as an independent. There is not the minutest hope that the county leaders of either the Democratic or the Republican party will designate, as preferred candidate for Mayor of the City of New York, Ruth Puttermesser, Esq., a currently unemployed attorney put out in the street, so to speak, by Commissioner Alvin Turtelman of the Department of Receipts and Disbursements, in conjunction and in consultation with First Bursary Officer Adam Marmel. The golem is Puttermesser's campaign manager. She has burst out of all her new clothes, and has finally taken to extra-large men's denim overalls bought in the Army-Navy store on the corner of Suffolk and Delancey. The golem's complexion has coarsened a little. It is somehow redder, and the freckles on her forehead, when gazed at by an immobile eye, appear to have the configuration of a handful of letters from a generally unrecognizable alphabet:

$$\dagger \; \S \; K$$

Puttermesser has not failed to take note of how these letters, *aleph, mem,* and *tav,* in their primal North Semitic form, read from right to left, have extruded themselves with greater and greater clarity just below the golem's hairline. Puttermesser attributes this to pressure of the skin as the golem gains in height and thickness. She orders the golem to cut bangs. Though she is periodically alarmed at what a large girl Xanthippe is growing into, otherwise Puttermesser is pleased by her creation. Xanthippe is cheerful and efficient, an industrious worker. She continues to be a zealous cook. She remains unsure about time (occasionally she forgets that Wednesday intrudes between Tuesday and Thursday, and she has not quite puzzled out the order of all the months, though she has it splendidly fixed that November will embrace what has now become the sun of Puttermesser's firmament—Election Day); she is sometimes cocky; often intrepid; now and then surly; mainly she smiles and smiles. She can charm a signature out of anyone. At her own suggestion she wears around her neck a card that reads DEAF-MUTE, and with this card dangling on her bosom, in overalls, she scrambles up and down tenement steps as far away as Bensonhurst and Canarsie, in and out of elevators of East Side and West Side apartment buildings. She churns through offices, high schools and universities (she has visited Fordham, LIU, Pace, NYU, Baruch College, Columbia; she has solicited the teaching staffs of Dalton, Lincoln, Brearley, John Dewey, Julia Richman, Yeshiva of Flatbush, Fieldston, Ramaz, as well as Puttermesser's own alma mater, Hunter High), supermarkets, cut-rate drugstores, subway stations, the Port Authority bus terminal. Wherever there are signers to be found, the golem appears with her ballpoint pen.

The petition is completed. The golem has collected fourteen thousand five hundred and sixty-two more signatures than the law calls for.

All this must be recorded as lightly and swiftly as possible; a dry patch to be gotten through, perhaps via a doze or a skip. For Puttermesser herself it is much more wretched than a mere dry patch. She suffers. Her physiological responses are: a coldness in the temples, blurring of the eyes, increased periodontic difficulties. She is afflicted with frequent diarrhea. Her spine throbs. At night she weeps. But she keeps on. Xanthippe gives her no peace, urges her to rephrase her speeches with an ear for the lively, insists that she sport distinctive hats, glossy lipstick, even contact lenses (Puttermesser, edging into middle age, already owns reading glasses).

The golem names Puttermesser's party as follows: Independents for Socratic and Prophetic Idealism—ISPI for short. A graphic artist is hired to devise a poster. It shows an apple tree with a serpent in it. The S in ISPI is the serpent. Puttermesser has promised to transform the City of New York into Paradise. She has promised to cast out the serpent. On Election Day, Malachy ("Matt") Mavett, the incumbent, is routed. Of the three remaining candidates, two make poor showings. Puttermesser is triumphant.

Puttermesser is now the Mayor of the City of New York!

Old ardors and itches wake in her. She recites to herself: Justice, justice shalt thou pursue. Malachy ("Matt") Mavett takes his wife and family to Florida, to be near Mrs. Minnie Mavett, his adoptive mother. He is no longer a lucky orphan. He gets a job as a racetrack official. It is a political job, but he is sad all the same. His wife bears his humiliation gracelessly. His children rapidly acquire accents that do not mark them as New Yorkers. Turtelman and Marmel vanish into rumor. They are said to be with the FBI in Alaska, with the CIA in Indonesia. They are said to have relocated at Albany. They are said to be minor factotums in the Federal Crop Insurance Corporation, with offices in Sourgrass, Iowa. They are said to have mediocre positions in the Internal Revenue Service, where they will not be entitled to Social Security. They are said to have botched a suicide pact. No one knows what has become of Turtelman and Marmel. But Puttermesser is relieved; she herself, by means of a memo from City Hall, has dismissed them. Turtelman and Marmel are sacked! Let go! Fired!

Malachy ("Matt") Mavett, following protocol, telephones to congratulate Puttermesser on her victory. But he confesses to bafflement. Where has Puttermesser come from? An ordinary drone from the Bureau of Summary Sessions of the Department of Receipts and Disbursements! How can she, "an unknown," he asks, "a political nonentity," have won the public over so handily? Puttermesser reminds him that some months ago she wrote him a letter asking for justice, condemning patronage and spoils. "You did not reply," she accused him in a voice hoarse from speechmaking. The ex-Mayor does not remember any letter.

Though Puttermesser is disconcerted by the move to Gracie Mansion (in her dreams her mother is once again rolling up winter rugs and putting down summer rugs in the wide sun-periled apartment on the Grand Concourse), the golem immediately chooses the most lavish bedroom in the Mayor's residence for herself. It contains an antique dresser with gryphon feet and a fourposter arched by a lofty tester curtained in white velvet. Old brass bowls glint on the dresser-top. The golem fills one whole closet with fresh overalls. She wanders about studying the paintings and caressing the shining banister. She exhorts Puttermesser to rejoice that she no longer has her old suspicious landlord on East Seventy-first Street to worry about. Millions of citizens are her landlord now!

Puttermesser cannot pay attention to the golem's sprightliness. She is in a frenzy over the job of appointing commissioners and agency heads. She implores Xanthippe to keep away from City Hall—the campaign is over, she will only distract from business. The new Mayor intends to recruit noble psyches and visionary hearts. She is searching for the antithesis of Turtelman and Marmel. For instance: she yearns after Wallace Stevens— insurance executive of probity during office hours, enraptured poet at dusk. How she would like to put Walt Whitman himself in charge of the Bureau of Summary Sessions, and have Shelley take over Water Resource Development—Shelley whose principle it is that poets are the legislators of mankind! William Blake in the Fire Department. George Eliot doing Social Services. Emily Brontë over at Police, Jane Austen in Bridges and Tunnels, Virginia Woolf and Edgar Allan Poe sharing Health. Herman Melville overseeing the Office of Single Room Occupancy Housing. *"Integer vitae scelerisque purus,"* the golem writes on her notepad, showing off. "That's the ticket," Puttermesser agrees, "but what am I supposed to do, chase around town like Diogenes with a lantern looking for an honest man?" Xanthippe writes philosophically, "The politics of Paradise is no longer politics." "The politics of Paradise is no longer Paradise," Puttermesser retorts; "don't annoy me anyhow, I have to get somebody fast for Receipts and Disbursements." "You could promote Cracow," the golem writes. "I already have. I moved him over to Bronx Landfill and Pest Control. That's two levels up. He's got a good idea for winter, actually—wants to convert that garbage mountain out near the bay to a ski jump. And he's stopped asking me out. Thank God he's scared of dating the Mayor." "If you would seek commissioners of integrity and rosy cleverness," the golem writes, "fashion more of my kind." Fleetingly, Puttermesser considers this; she feels tempted. The highest echelons of City management staffed by multiple members of the genus golem! Herself the creator, down to the last molecule of ear-wax, of every commissioner, deputy, bureau chief, executive director! Every mayoral assistant, subordinate, underling, a golem! She looks over at Xanthippe. Twice already Xanthippe has quarreled with the Mansion's official cook. The cook has refused to follow the golem's recipes. "One is enough," Puttermesser says, and hurries down the subway and off to City Hall.

Despite its odious language reminiscent of Turtelman and Marmel, Puttermesser repeatedly consults the

PLAN

FOR THE

RESUSCITATION,

REFORMATION,
REINVIGORATION
& REDEMPTION
OF THE
CITY OF NEW YORK.

She blames Xanthippe for such a preposterous text: only two days spent in the Bureau of Summary Sessions, and the golem has been infected by periphrasis, pleonasm, and ambagious tautology. But behind all that there glimmers a loveliness. To Puttermesser's speeding eye, it is like the spotted sudden flank of a deer disturbing a wood. There *will* be resuscitation! There *will* be redemption!

And it begins. Mayor Puttermesser sends the golem out into the City. At first she tends to hang out among the open-air stalls of Delancey Street, but Puttermesser upbraids her for parochialism; she instructs the golem to take subways and buses—no taxis—out to all the neighborhoods in all the boroughs. It goes without saying that a robust reformist administration requires a spy. The golem returns with aching tales of what she has seen among the sordid and the hopeless; sometimes she even submits a recommendation on a page of her notepad. Puttermesser does not mind. Nothing the golem reports is new to Mayor Puttermesser. What is new is the discovery of the power of office. Wrongdoing and bitterness can be overturned: it is only a matter of using the power Puttermesser owns.

Crowds of self-seeking importuners float up the steps of City Hall; Mayor Puttermesser shoos them away. She admits visionary hearts only. She tacks signs up all around her desk: NO MORE SPOILS QUOTA. MERIT IS SWEETER THAN GOLD. WHAT YOU ARE, NOT WHOM YOU KNOW.

Lost wallets are daily being returned to their owners. Now it is really beginning—the money and credit cards are always intact. The golem ascends from the subway at Sixty-eighth and Lexington (this is the very corner where Puttermesser's alma mater, Hunter High, used to stand), looking slightly larger than the day before, but also irradiated. The subways have been struck by beauty. Lustrous tunnels unfold, mile after mile. Gangs of youths have invaded the subway yards at night and have washed the cars clean. The wheels and windows have been scrubbed by combinations of chemicals; the long seats have been fitted with velour cushions of tan and blue. Each car shines like a bullet. The tiles that line the stations are lakes of white; the passengers can cherish their own reflections in the walls. Every Thursday afternoon the youths who used to terrorize the subways put on fresh shirts and walk out into Central Park, reconnoitering after a green space; then they dance. They have formed themselves into dancing clubs, and crown one another's heads with clover pulled up from the sweet ground. Foliage is browning, Thursday afternoons grow cold and dusky. But the youths who used to terrorize the subways are whirling in rings over darkening lawns.

The streets are altered into garden rows: along the curbs, between sidewalk and road, privet hedges shake their little leaves. The open sanitation carts are bright, like a string of scarlet chariots. They are drawn by silent horses who sniff among the new hedges. Flutes and clarinets announce the coming of the cart procession every day at noon, and children scramble to pick up every nub of cigarette or scrap of peel or paper wrapper, pressing with fistfuls toward the singing flutes and gravely marching horses, whose pairs of high nostrils flare outward like trumpets.

The great cargo trucks still spill into the intersections, carrying bolts of cloth, oranges, fowl, refrigerators, lamps, pianos, cards of buttons, lettuces, boxes of cereal, jigsaw puzzles, baby carriages, pillowcases with peacocks imprinted on them; some deliver uptown, others downtown; they pant and rumble freely, unimpeded; buses and taxis overtake them effortlessly. Except for fire engines and ambulances, there are no other motored vehicles. Little girls dare, between buses, to jump rope in the middle of the street. Some roads, though, have been lushly planted, so that lovers seek them out to hide in one another's breast. The tall grasses and young maples of the planted roads are haunted by pretzel sellers, hot-chestnut peddlers, hawkers of books in wheelbarrows. The children are often indoors after school, carpentering bookshelves. The libraries are lit all night, and the schools are thronged in the evenings by administrative assistants from the great companies, learning Spanish, Portuguese, Russian, Hebrew, Korean, and Japanese. There are many gardeners now, and a hundred urban gardening academies. There is unemployment among correction officers; numbers of them take gardening jobs. No one bothers to drag the steel shutters down over storefronts after closing. The Civil Service hums. Intellect and courtliness are in the ascendancy. Mayor Puttermesser has staffed the Department of Receipts and Disbursements with intelligent lawyers, both women and men, who honor due process. Turtelman and Marmel are replaced by visionary hearts. Never again will an accuser take the job of the accused, as Marmel did with Puttermesser! There is no more rapaciousness in the Bureau of Summary Sessions.

A little-known poet who specializes in terza rima is put in charge of Potter's Field. For each sad burial there, she composes a laudatory ode; even the obscure dead are not expendable or forlorn. The parks, their arbors and fields, are speckled with wide-mouthed terra-cotta urns; no one injures them. Far away in the Bronx, the grape-wreathed heads of wine gods are restored to the white stelae of the Soldiers' Monument, and the bronze angel on top of the Monument's great stone needle glistens. Nothing is broken, nothing is despoiled. No harm comes to anything or anyone. The burnt-out ruins of Brownsville and the South Bronx burst forth with spinneys of pines and thorny locusts. In their high secret pride, the slums undo themselves: stoops sparkle, new factories and stores buzz, children gaze down in gladness at shoes newly bought, still unscratched; the shoe stores give away balloons, and the balloons escape to the sky. Everywhere former louts and loiterers, muggers and thieves, addicts and cardsharps are doing the work of the world, absorbed, transformed. The biggest City agency is what used to be called Welfare; now it is the Department of Day Play, and delivers colored pencils and finger paints and tambourines to nurseries clamorous as bee-loud glades, where pianos shake the floors, and storytellers dangle toddlers in suspense from morning to late afternoon, when their parents fetch them home to supper. Everyone is at work. Lovers apply to the City Clerk for marriage licenses. The Bureau of Venereal Disease Control has closed down. The ex-pimps are learning computer skills.

Xanthippe's heels have begun to hang over the foot of her fourposter bed in Gracie Mansion. The golem is worn out. She lumbers from one end of the City to the other every day, getting ideas. Mayor Puttermesser is not disappointed that the golem's ideas are mainly unexciting. The City is at peace. It is in the nature of tranquility—it is in the nature of Paradise—to be pacific; tame; halcyon. Oh, there is more to relate of how Mayor Puttermesser, inspired by the golem, has resuscitated, reformed, reinvigorated and redeemed the City of New York! But this too must be left to dozing and skipping. It is essential to record only two reflections that especially engage Mayor Puttermesser. The first is that she notices how the City, tranquil, turns toward the conventional and the orderly. It is as if tradition, continuity, propriety blossom of themselves: old courtesies, door-holding, hat-tipping, a thousand pleases and pardons and thank-yous. Something in the grain of Paradise is on the side of the expected. Sweet custom rules. The City in its redeemed state wishes to conserve itself. It is a rational daylight place; it has shut the portals of night.

Puttermesser's second reflection is about the golem. The coming of the golem animated the salvation of the City, yes—but who, Puttermesser sometimes wonders, is the true golem? Is it Xanthippe or is it Puttermesser? Puttermesser made Xanthippe; Xanthippe did not exist before Puttermesser made her: that is clear enough. But Xanthippe made Puttermesser Mayor, and Mayor Puttermesser too did not exist before. And that is just as clear. Puttermesser sees that she is the golem's golem.

In the newborn peaceable City, Xanthippe is restless. She is growing larger. Her growth is frightening. She can no longer fit into her overalls. She begins to sew together pairs of sheets for a toga.

VII. RAPPOPORT'S RETURN

n a late spring afternoon about halfway through her mayoral term, and immediately after a particularly depressing visit to the periodontist (she who had abolished crime in the subways was unable to stem gum disease in the hollow of her jaw), Puttermesser came home to Gracie Mansion to find Rappoport waiting in her private sitting room.

"Hey, you've got some pretty tough security around here. I had a hell of a time getting let in," Rappoport complained.

"Last time I saw you," Puttermesser said, "you had no trouble letting yourself out."

"How about we just consider that water under the bridge, Ruth, what do you say?"

"You walked out on me. In the middle of the night."

"You were liking Socrates better than me," Rappoport said.

"Then why are you back?"

"My God, Ruth, look who you've become! I can't pass through New York without seeing the Mayor, can I? Ruth," he said, spreading his impressive nostrils, "I've thought about you a lot since the election. We read all about you up in Toronto."

"You and Mrs. Rappoport?"

"Oh come on, let's give it another try. Not that I don't understand you have to be like Caesar's wife. Above susp—"

"I have to be Caesar," Puttermesser broke in.

"Well, even Caesar gives things another try."

"You're no Cleopatra," Puttermesser said.

There was a distant howl; it was the cook. She was fighting with the golem again. In a moment Xanthippe stood in the doorway, huge and red, weeping.

"Leave that woman alone. She'll cook what she'll cook, you can't tell her anything different," Puttermesser scolded. "She runs a strictly kosher kitchen and that's enough. Go and wash your face."

"Plump," Rappoport said, staring after Xanthippe in her toga. "Rubenesque."

"A growing girl. She wears what she pleases."

"Who is she?"

"I adopted her."

"I like a big girl like that." Rappoport stood up. "The town looks terrific. I came to congratulate you, Ruth."

"Is that why you came?"

"It turns out. Only I figured if you could bring a whole city back to life—"

"There are some things, Morris, that even the Mayor can't revive."

Rappoport, his briefcase under his arm, wheeled and hesitated. "It didn't make it through the move? My avocado tree that I grew from a pit in Toronto? It was doing fine in your old apartment."

"I don't have it any more."

"Aha, you wanted to dispose of me lock, stock, and barrel. You got rid of every symptom and sign. The least bit of green leaf—"

"All my plants are gone."

"No kidding. What happened?"

"I took their earth and made a golem."

Rappoport, flaunting his perfect teeth under his mustache, laughed out loud. In the middle of his laughter his head suddenly fell into the kind of leaning charm Puttermesser recalled from long ago, when they had first become lovers; it almost made her relent.

"Goodbye, Ruth. I really do congratulate you on civic improvement." Rappoport held out his hand. "It's one terrific town, I mean it. Utopia. Garden of Eden. In Toronto they run articles on you every day."

"You can stay for dinner if you like," Puttermesser offered. "Though I've got a meeting right after—municipal bonds. Myself, it's eat and get on down to City Hall."

Someone had seized Rappoport's outstretched hand and was shaking it; it was not Puttermesser. Xanthippe, practiced politician, her wide cheeks refreshed and soap-fragrant, had sped forward out of nowhere. Rappoport looked stunned; he looked interested. He slipped his fingers out of the golem's grasp and moved them upward against her chest, to catch hold of the card that twirled there: DEAF-MUTE.

"That's awfully generous of you, Ruth, adopting someone like that. You're a wonderful person. We really ought to get together again. I *will* stay for a bite, if you don't mind."

The golem did not bring her ballpoint to the table. She dealt with her soup spoon as if it were her enemy, the cook. Disgruntled, she heaped a fourth helping of mashed potatoes onto her plate. But her eye was on Rappoport, and her mouth was round with responsiveness: was it his teeth? was it his reddish mustache, turning gray? was it his wide welcoming nostrils? was it his briefcase bulging with worldly troubles?

Rappoport was talkative. His posture was straight-backed and heroic: he told of his last clandestine trip to Moscow, and of the turmoil of the oppressed.

When Puttermesser returned at midnight from the meeting

on municipal bonds, the golem was asleep in her fourposter bed, her heels thrust outward in their pink socks over the footboard, and Rappoport was snoring beside her.

Eros had entered Gracie Mansion.

VIII. XANTHIPPE LOVESICK

Consider now Puttermesser's situation. What happens to an intensely private mind when great celebrity unexpectedly invades it? Absorbed in the golem's *PLAN* and its consequences—consequences beyond the marveling at, so gradual, plausible, concrete, and sensible are they, grounded in a policy of civic sympathy and urban reasonableness—Puttermesser does not readily understand that she induces curiosity and applause. She has, in fact, no expectations; only desires as strong and as strange as powers. Her desires are pristine, therefore acute; clarity is immanent. Before this inward illumination of her desires (rather, of the *PLAN*'s desires), everything else—the clash of interests that parties, races, classes, are said to give rise to—falls away into purposelessness. Another way of explaining all this is to say that Mayor Puttermesser finds virtue to be intelligible. Still another way of explaining it is to say that every morning she profoundly rejoices. There is fruitfulness everywhere. Into the chaos of the void (defeat, deception, demoralization, loss) she has cast a divinely clarifying light. Out of a dunghill she has charmed a verdant citadel. The applause that reaches her is like a sea-sound at the farthest edge of her brain; she both hears it and does not hear it. Her angelic fame— the fame of a purifying angel—is virtue's second face. Fame makes Puttermesser happy, and at the same time it brings a forceful sense of the penultimate, the tentative, the imperiled.

It is as if she is waiting for something else: for some conclusion, or resolution, or unfolding.

The golem is lovesick. She refuses to leave the Mansion. No more for her the daily voyage into the broad green City as the Mayor's ambassador and spy. She removes the DEAF-MUTE card and substitutes another: CONTEMPLATIVE. Puttermesser does not smile at this: she is not sure whether it is meant to be a joke. There is too much gloom. There are hints of conspiracy. Anyhow the golem soon takes off the new sign. In the intervals between Rappoport's appearances Xanthippe languishes. Rappoport comes often—sometimes as often as three or four times a week. Xanthippe, moping, thumps out to greet him, trailing a loose white tail of her toga; she escorts him straight into her bedroom. She turns on the record player that Rappoport has brought her as a birthday gift. She is two years old and insatiable. God knows what age she tells her lover.

Rappoport steals out of the golem's bedroom with the dazzled inward gaze of a space traveler.

The Mayor upbraids Xanthippe: "It's enough. I don't want to see him around here. Get rid of him."

Xanthippe writes: "Jealousy!"

"I'm tired of hearing complaints from the cook. This is Gracie Mansion, it's not another kind of house."

"Jealousy! He used to be yours."

"You're stirring up a scandal."

"He brings me presents."

"If you keep this up, you'll spoil everything."

"My mother has purified the City."

"Then don't foul it."

"I am in contemplation of my future."

"Start contemplating the present! Look out the window! Fruitfulness! Civic peace! You saw it happening. You caused it."

"I can tear it all down."

"You were made to serve and you know it."

"I want a life of my own. My blood is hot."

The Mansion thickens with erotic airs. Heavy perfumes float. Has Rappoport journeyed to mysterious islands to offer the golem these lethargic scents, these attars of weighty drooping petals? The golem has discarded her sewn-together sheets and looms with gemlike eyes in darkling passageways, wrapped in silks, vast saris that skim the carpets as she goes; each leg is a pillar wound in a bolt of woven flowers.

The summer deepens. A dry dust settles on the leaves in the Bronx Botanical Gardens, and far away the painted carousels of Brooklyn cry their jollities.

The Mayor: "I notice Rappoport hasn't been around lately."

Xanthippe writes: "He left."

"Where?"

"He clouded over his destination. Vienna. Rome. Jerusalem. Winnipeg. What do I care? A man of low position. Factotum of refugee philanthropy, twelve bosses over him."

"What happened?"

"I wore him out."

"I need you right away," Puttermesser urges. "We're putting in new tiles on the subway line out toward Jamaica Avenue. With two-color portraits baked right into the glaze—Thoreau, Harriet Beecher Stowe, Emerson, so far. You can decide who else."

"No."

"You haven't been anywhere in months."

"My mother speaks the truth. I thirst for the higher world. Office and rank. Illustrious men."

Puttermesser is blighted with melancholy. She fears. She foresees. In spite of fruitfulness and civic peace (rather, on their account), it is beginning to be revealed to her what her proper mayoral duty directs.

She does nothing.

In pity, she waits. Sometimes she forgets. How long did the

Great Rabbi Judah Loew of Prague wait, how often did he forget? There are so many distinguished visitors. The Emperor of Japan takes the elevator to the top of the Empire State Building. Puttermesser gives an astronaut a medal on the steps of City Hall; he has looked into the bosom of Venus. The mayors of Dublin, San Juan, and Tel Aviv arrive. In the Blue Room, Puttermesser holds a news conference about interest rates. She explains into the television cameras that the City of New York, in its abundance, will extend interest-free loans to the Federal government in Washington.

Now and then Xanthippe disappears. She does not return to the Mansion at night. Frequently her fourposter stands empty.

Early one morning, the golem, her eyes too polished, her cheeks too red, her silk windings torn, the tiny letters on her forehead jutting like raw scars, thumps home.

"Four days gone without a word!" Puttermesser scolds.

Xanthippe writes impatiently: "Been down to Florida."

"Florida!"

"Been to visit ex-Mayor Malachy ('Matt') Mavett."

"What for?"

"Remember Marmel?"

"What's this about?"

"Been out West to visit him. Him and Turtelman."

"What *is* this?"

But Puttermesser knows.

There are curious absences, reports of exhaustion, unexplained hospitalizations. The new Commissioner of Receipts and Disbursements whispers to Puttermesser, in confidence, that he will divorce his wife. His eyeballs seem sunken, his lips drop back into a hollow face. He has lost weight overnight. He will not say what the trouble is. He resigns. The Executive Director of the Board of Education resigns. It is divulged that he suffers from catarrh and is too faint to stand. The Commissioner of the Department of Cultural Affairs has been struck stone-deaf by a horrible sound, a kind of exultant hiss; he will not say what it was. The City's managers and executives all appear to sicken together: commissioner after commissioner, department after department. Puttermesser's finest appointments—felled; depleted. There is news of an abortion in Queens. A pimp sets himself up in business on Times Square again, in spite of the cherry trees the Department of Sanitation has planted there; the Commissioner of Sanitation himself stalks under the hanging cherries, distracted, with a twisted spine and the start of a hunch. Two or three of the proud young men of the dancing clubs defect and return to mugging in the subways. The City's peace is unraveling. The commissioners blow their noses into bloody tissues, drive their little fingers into their ears, develop odd stammers, instigate backbiting among underlings.

The golem thirsts.

"Stay home," the Mayor pleads. "Stay out of the City."

The golem will no longer obey. She cannot be contained. "My blood is hot," Xanthippe writes; she writes for the last time. She tosses her ballpoint pen into the East River, back behind the Mansion.

IX. THE GOLEM DESTROYS HER MAKER

ayor Puttermesser's reputation is ebbing. The cost of municipal borrowing ascends. A jungle of graffiti springs up on the white flanks of marble sculptures inside museums; Attic urns are smashed. Barbarians cruise the streets. O New York! O lost New York!

Deputy commissioners and their secretaries blanch at the sound of a heavy footstep. Morning and afternoon the golem lumbers from office to office, searching for high-level managers. In her ragged sari brilliant with woven flowers, her great head garlanded, drenched in a density of musky oils, Xanthippe ravishes prestigious trustees, committee chairmen, council members, borough presidents, the Second Deputy Comptroller's three assistants, the Director of the Transit Authority, the Coordinator of Criminal Justice, the Chief of the Office of Computer Plans and Controls, the Head of Intergovernmental Relations, the Chancellor of the City University, the Rector of the Art Commission, even the President of the Stock Exchange! The City is diseased with the golem's urge. The City sweats and coughs in her terrifying embrace. The City is in the pincer of the golem's love, because Xanthippe thirsts, she thirsts, she ravishes and ravages, she ambushes management level after management level. There is no Supervising Accountant or Secretary to the Minority Leader who can escape her electric gaze.

Sex! Sex! The golem wants sex! Men in high politics! Lofty officials! Elevated bureaucrats!

Mayor Puttermesser is finished. She can never be re-elected. She is a disgrace; her Administration is wrecked. Distrust. Desolation. It is all over for Mayor Puttermesser and the life of high politics. The prisons are open again. The press howls. Mayor Puttermesser is crushed. The golem has destroyed her utterly.

X. THE GOLEM SNARED

Puttermesser blamed herself. She had not forestalled this devastation. She had not prepared for it; she had not acted. She had seen what had to be done, and put it off and put it off. Dilatory. She could not say to herself that she was ignorant; hadn't she read in her books, a thousand times, that a golem will at length undo its creator? The turning against the creator is an attribute of a golem, comparable to its speechlessness, its incapacity for procreation, its soullessness. A golem has no soul, therefore cannot die—rather, it is returned to the elements of its making.

Xanthippe without a soul! Tears came to Puttermesser, her heart in secret shook. She was ready to disbelieve. A golem cannot procreate? Ah, but its blood is as hot as human blood. Hotter! A golem lusts tremendously, as if it would wrest the flame of further being from its own being. A golem, an earthen thing of packed mud, having laid hold of life against all logic and natural expectation, yearns hugely after the generative, the fructuous. Earth is the germ of all fertility: how then would a golem not dream itself a double? It is like a panting furnace that cries out for more and more fuel, that spews its own firebrands to ignite a successor-fire. A golem cannot procreate! But it has the will to; the despairing will; the violent will. Offspring! Progeny! The rampaging energies of Xanthippe's eruptions, the furious bolts and convulsions of her visitations—Xanthippe, like Puttermesser herself, longs for daughters! Daughters that can never be!

Shall the one be condemned by the other, who is no different?

Yet Puttermesser weeps. The golem is running over the City. She never comes home at all now. A ferry on its way from the Battery to Staten Island is terrorized; some large creature, bat or succubus, assaults the captain and causes him to succumb. Is it Xanthippe? Stories about "a madwoman on the loose, venomous against authority" ("unverifiable," writes the City Hall Bureau of the *Times*) wash daily over Mayor Puttermesser's desk. The secret chamber where sleeps the President of the Chase Manhattan Bank has had its windows brutally smashed; a bit of flowered silk clings to the jagged glass.

Xanthippe! Xanthippe! Puttermesser calls in her heart.

Every night pickets parade in front of Grace Mansion, with torches and placards:

> MAYOR PUTTERMESSER WHAT HAS HAPPENED
>   TO THE SUBWAYS?
> HIGH HOPES THE HIGH ROAD TO HELL.
> SHE WHO SPARKED SNUFFED.
> PUTTERMESSER'S BITTER MESSES.
> RUTHIE WITH SUCH A DOWN WE NEEDED YOUR UP?
> FROM SMASH HIT TO SMASH.
> KAPUT-TERMESSER!

Every day there are speakers on the steps of City Hall, haranguing; when the police chase them, they vanish for ten minutes and reappear. Mobs bubble, hobble, guffaw.

Puttermesser composes a letter to ex-Mayor Malachy ("Matt") Mavett:

> Gracie Mansion
> City of New York
>
> Dear Matt [she permits herself this liberty]:
>   My campaign manager's recent Florida visit may have caused you some distress. I did not authorize it. Your defeat via the ballot box, which eliminated the wrongdoers Turtelman and Marmel from City officialdom, was satisfaction enough. Please excuse any personal indignities my campaign manager (who is now on my personal staff) may have in-

flicted. She expresses her nature but cannot assume responsibility for it.

Dilatory! Procrastinator! Imaginary letters! Puttermesser's tears go on falling.

> Gracie Mansion
> City of New York

> Dear Morris:
>   Please come.
>   In friendship
>   Ruth

She hands this to one of the window-pole thieves to mail. In a few days it brings Rappoport, out of breath, his once-pouting briefcase hollow, caved in; Rappoport himself is hollow, his stout throat caved in, as if he had ejected his Adam's apple. His nose and chin, and the furless place between his eyebrows, have a papery cast. His beautiful teeth are nicked. His mustache looks squirrelly, gray.

"Xanthippe's left home," Puttermesser announces.

"You're the Mayor. Call the Missing Persons Bureau."

"Morris. Please."

"What do you want?"

"Bring her back."

"Me?"

"You can do it."

"How?"

"Move in."

"What? Here? In Gracie Mansion?"

"In Xanthippe's bed. Morris. Please. She likes you. You're the one who started her off."

"She got too big for her britches. In more than a manner of speaking, if you don't mind my saying so. What d'you mean, started her off?"

"You excited her."

"That's not my fault."

"You created desire. Morris, bring her back. You can do it."

"What for? I've had enough. No more. Drained. Drained, believe me, Ruth."

"Lie in her bed. Just once."

"What's in it for me? I didn't come back to this rotten town for the sake of a night's sleep in Gracie Mansion. The novelty's worn off. The bloom is no longer on the rose, you follow? Besides, you've gone downhill, Ruth, did you see those pickets out there?" He shows her his sleeve—two buttons ripped off. "They treated me like a scab, walking in here—"

"Just lie down in her bed, Morris. That's all I'm asking."

"No."

"I'll make it worth your while."

"What're you getting at? You're getting at something."

"You're a fund-raiser by profession," Puttermesser says meditatively; a strangeness rises in her. A noxious taste.

"Something like that. There's a lot of different things I do."

"That's right. Plenty of experience. You're qualified for all sorts of fine spots."

"I'm qualified for what?"

"The truth is," Puttermesser says slowly, "I'm in possession of a heap of resignations. Several of my commissioners," Puttermesser says slowly, "have fallen ill."

"I hear there's typhoid in some of those buildings along Bruckner Boulevard. What've you got, an epidemic? I heard cholera in Forest Hills."

"Rumors," Puttermesser spits out. "People love to badmouth. That's what makes the City go down. The banks are leaving, nobody worries about *that*. I'm talking resignations. *Openings*, Morris. You can take your pick, in fact. How about the Department of Investigation? Run the Inspectors General. Or I can appoint you judge. How about Judge of the Criminal Court? Good spot, good pay. Prestige, God knows. Look, if you like you can take over Receipts and Disbursements."

Rappoport stared. "Commissioner of Receipts and Disbursements?"

"I can go higher if you want. Fancier. Board of Water Supply's a dandy. Nice remuneration, practically no show."

"Ruth, Ruth, what is this?"

Justice, justice shalt thou pursue!

It is Mayor Puttermesser's first political deal.

"Stay a night in Xanthippe's bed and any job you want is yours. The orchard's dropping into your lap, Morris, I'm serious. Plums."

"A spot in your Administration actually?"

"Why not? Choose."

"Receipts and Disbursements," Rappoport instantly replies.

Puttermesser says sourly, "You're at least as qualified as Turtelman."

"What about my wife?"

"Keep her in Toronto."

Standing in solitude in the night fragrance behind Gracie Mansion, Puttermesser catches river-gleams: the Circle Line yacht with its chandelier decks; a neon sign pulsing; the distant caps of little waves glinting in moonwake, in neonwake. White bread baking on the night shift casts its faintly animal aroma on the waters: rich fumes more savory than any blossom. It is so dark in the back garden that Puttermesser imagines she can almost descry Orion's belt buckle. One big moving star twins as it sails: the headlights of an airliner nosing out toward Europe. Plane after plane rises, as if out of the black river. Puttermesser counts them, each with its sharp beams like rays scattered from the brow of Moses, arching upward into the fathomless universe. She counts planes; she counts neon blinks; she counts the silhouettes of creeping scows; she counts all the mayors who have preceded her in the City of New York. Thomas Willett, Thomas Delavall . . . William Dervall, Nicholas De Meyer, Stephanus Van Cortlandt . . . Francis Rombouts . . . Isaac de Reimer, Thomas Noell, Philip French, William Peartree, Ebenezer

Wilson . . . DeWitt Clinton . . . Gideon Lee . . . Smith Ely . . . Jimmy Walker . . . John P. O'Brien, Fiorello H. LaGuardia . . . Robert F. Wagner, John V. Lindsay, Abraham D. Beame, Edward I. Koch! She counts and waits. She is waiting for the golem to be lured homeward, to be ensnared, to lumber groaning with desire into her fourposter bed.

In the golem's fourposter, Commissioner Morris Rappoport, newly appointed chief of the Department of Receipts and Disbursements, lies in sheets saturated with a certain known pungency. He has been here before. He recoils from the familiar scented pillows.

Indoors and out, odors of what has been and what is about to be: the cook's worn eggplant au gratin, river smells, the garden beating its tiny wings of so many fresh hedge-leaves, airplane exhaust spiraling downward, the fine keen breath of the bread ovens, the golem's perfumed pillows—all these drifting smokes and combinations stir and turn and braid themselves into a rope of awesome incense, drawing Xanthippe to her bed. Incense? Fetor and charged decay! The acrid signal of dissolution! Intimations of the tellurian elements! Xanthippe, from wherever she has hurtled to in the savage City (savage once again), is pulled nearer and nearer the Mansion, where the portraits of dead mayors hang. Scepter and status, all the enchantments of influence and command, lead her to her undoing: in her bed lies the extremely important official whose job it is to call the tune that makes the City's money dance. She will burst on him her giant love. On the newly appointed Commissioner of Receipts and Disbursements the golem will spend her terrible ardor. Then she will fall back to rest, among the awful perfumes of her cleft bed.

Whereupon Mayor Puttermesser, her term of office blighted, her comely *PLAN* betrayed, will dismantle the golem, according to the rite.

XI. THE GOLEM UNDONE, AND THE
BABBLING OF RAPPOPORT

The City was ungovernable; the City was out of control; it was no different now for Mayor Puttermesser than it had ever been for any mayor. In confusion and hypocrisy, Puttermesser finished out what was left of her sovereign days.

One thing was different: a certain tumulus of earth introduced by the Parks Commissioner in the mournful latter half of Mayor Puttermesser's Administration.

Across the street from City Hall lies a little park, crisscrossed by paths and patches of lawn fenced off by black iron staves. There are benches set down here and there with a scattered generosity. There is even an upward-flying fountain. Perhaps because the little park is in the shadow of City Hall and, so to speak, under its surveillance, the benches have not been seriously vandalized, and the lawns not much trampled on. Best of all, and most alluring, are the flower beds, vivid rectangles of red geraniums disposed, it must be admitted, in the design of a miniature graveyard. Civil servants peering down from high windows of the elephant-gray Municipal Building can see the crimson slash that with wild brilliance cuts across the concrete bitterness below. Some distance behind the flower beds rise those great Stonehenge slabs of the Twin Towers; eastward, the standing zither that is Brooklyn Bridge.

From the Mayor's office inside City Hall the park is not visible, and for Puttermesser this is just as well. It would not have done for her to be in sight of Xanthippe's bright barrow while engaged in City business. Under the roots of the flower beds lay fresh earth, newly put down and lightly tamped. Mayor Puttermesser herself, in the middle of the night, had telephoned the Parks Commissioner (luckily just back from Paris) and ordered the ground to be opened and a crudely formed and crumbling mound of special soil to be arranged in the cavity, as in an envelope of earth. The Parks Commissioner, urgently summoned, thought it odd, when he arrived at Gracie Mansion with his sleepy diggers, that the Mayor should be pacing in the back garden behind the Mansion under a veined half-moon; and odder yet that she should be accompanied by a babbling man with a sliding tongue, who identified himself as the newly appointed Commissioner of Receipts and Disbursements, Morris Rappoport.

"Did you bring spades? And a pickup truck?" the Mayor whispered.

"All of that, yes."

"Well, the spades won't do. At least not yet. You don't shovel up a floor. You can use the spades afterward, in the park. There's some dried mud spread out on a bedroom floor in the Mansion. I want it moved. With very great delicacy. Can you make your men understand that?"

"Dried mud?"

"I grant you it's in pieces. It's already falling apart. But it's got a certain design. Be delicate."

What the Parks Commissioner saw was a very large and shapeless, or mainly shapeless, mound of soil, insanely wrapped (so the Parks Commissioner privately judged) in a kind of velvet shroud. The Parks Commissioner had been on an official exchange program in France, and had landed at Kennedy Airport less than two hours before the Mayor telephoned. The exchange program meant that he would study the enchanting parks of Paris, while his Parisian counterpart was to consider the gloomier parks of New York. The Parks Commissioner, of course, was Puttermesser's own appointee, a botanist and city planner, an expert on the hardiness of certain shade trees, a specialist in filigreed gazebos, a lover of the urban nighttime. All the same, he was perplexed by the Mayor's caprice. The mound of dirt on the bedroom floor did not suggest to him his own good fortune and near escape. In fact, though neither would ever learn this, the Parks Commissioner and his Parisian counterpart were both under a felicitous star—the Parisian because his wife's appendectomy had kept him unexpectedly and rather too lengthily in Paris so that he never arrived in New York at all (he was an anxious man), and the Parks Commissioner because he had not been at home in his lower Fifth Avenue bed when the golem came to call. Instead, he had been out inspecting the Bois de Boulogne—consequently, the Parks Commissioner was in fine mental health, and was shocked to observe that the newly appointed Commissioner of Receipts and Disbursements was not.

Rappoport babbled. He followed after Puttermesser like a dog. He had performed exactly as she had instructed, it seemed, but then her instructions became contradictory. First he was to circle. Then he was not to circle. Rather, he was to scrape with his penknife. There he was, all at once a satrap with a title; the title was as palpable as a mantle, and as sumptuous; overhead drooped the fourposter's white velvet canopy with its voluptuous folds and snowy crevices—how thickly warm his title, how powerful his office! Alone, enclosed in the authority of his rank, Rappoport awaited the visitation of the golem. Without a stitch, not a shred of sari remaining, her burnished gaze on fire with thirst for his grandeur, she burst in, redolent of beaches, noisy with a fiery hiss; Rappoport tore the white velvet from the tester and threw it over burning Xanthippe.

Rappoport babbled. He told all the rest: how they had contended; how he had endured her size and force and the horror of her immodesty and the awful sea of her sweat and the sirocco of her summer breath; and how he—or was it she?—had chanted out the hundred proud duties of his new jurisdiction: the protocol and potency of the City's money, where it is engendered, where it is headed, where it lands: it could be said that she was teaching him his job. And then the Mayor, speaking through the door, explaining the depth of tranquility after potency that is deeper than any sleep or drug or anesthesia, directing him to remove Xanthippe in all her deadweight mass from the four-poster down to the bare floor, and to wind her in the canopy.

Rappoport babbled: how he had lifted Xanthippe in her trance, the torpor that succeeds ravishment, down to the bare floor; how he had wound her in white velvet; how pale Putter-messer, her reading lenses glimmering into an old green book, directed him with sharpened voice to crowd his mind with impurity—with everything earthly, soiled, spoiled, wormy; fi-nally how Puttermesser directed him to trail her as she weaved round Xanthippe on the floor, as if circling her own shadow.

Round and round Puttermesser went. In the instant of giving the golem life, the just, the comely, the cleanly, the Edenic, had, all unwittingly, consummated Puttermesser's aspiring reflec-tions—even the radiant *PLAN* itself! Now all must be consciously reversed. She must think of violent-eyed loiterers who lurk in elevators with springblades at the ready, of spray cans gashing red marks of civilization-hate, of civic monuments with their heads knocked off, of City filth, of mugging, robbery, arson, assault, even murder. Murder! If, for life, she had dreamed Para-dise, now she must feel the burning lance of hell. If, for life, she had walked seven times clockwise round a hillock of clay, now she must walk seven times counterclockwise round captive Xan-thippe. If, for life, she had pronounced the Name, now she must on no account speak or imagine it or lend it any draught or flame or breath; she must erase the Name utterly.

And what of Rappoport, Rappoport the golem's lure and snare, Rappoport who had played himself out in the capture of Xanthippe? He too must walk counterclockwise, behind Putter-messer, just as the Great Rabbi Judah Loew had walked counterclockwise with his disciples when the time came for the golem of Prague to be undone. The golem of Prague, city-savior, had also run amok!—terrorizing the very citizens it had been created to succor. And all the rites the Great Rabbi Judah Loew had pondered in the making of the golem, he ultimately dissolved in the unmaking of it. All the permutations and combinations of the alphabet he had recited with profound and holy concentration in the golem's creation, he afterward declaimed backward, for the sake of the golem's discomposition. Instead of meditating on the building up, he meditated on the breaking down. Whatever he had early spiraled, he late unraveled: he smashed the magnetic links that formed the chain of being between the atoms.

Puttermesser, circling round the torpid Xanthippe in her shroud of white velvet, could not help glancing down into the golem's face. It was a child's face still. Ah, Leah, Leah! Xanthippe's lids flickered. Xanthippe's lips stirred. She looked with her terrible eyes—how they pulsed—up at Puttermesser.

"My mother."

A voice!

"O my mother," Xanthippe said, still looking upward at Puttermesser, "why are you walking around me like that?"

She spoke! Her voice ascended!—a child's voice, pitched like the pure cry of a bird.

Puttermesser did not halt. "Keep moving," she told Rappoport.

"O my mother," Xanthippe said in her bird-quick voice, "why are you walking around me like that?"

Beginning the fifth circle, Rappoport gasping behind her, Puttermesser said, "You created and you destroyed."

"No," the golem cried—the power of speech released!—"it was you who created me, it is you who will destroy me! Life! Love! Mercy! Love! Life!"

The fifth circle was completed; still the golem went on bleating in her little bird's cry. "Life! Life! More!"

"More," Puttermesser said bitterly, beginning the sixth circle. "More. You wanted more and more. It's more that brought us here. More!"

"You wanted Paradise!"

"Too much Paradise is greed. Eden disintegrates from too much Eden. Eden sinks from a surfeit of itself."

"O my mother! I made you Mayor!"

Completing the sixth circle, Puttermesser said, "You pulled the City down."

"O my mother! Do not cool my heat!"

Beginning the seventh circle, Puttermesser said, "This is the last. Now go home."

"O my mother! Do not send me to the elements!"

The seventh circle was completed; the golem's small voice piped on. Xanthippe lay stretched at Puttermesser's feet like Puttermesser's own shadow.

"Trouble," Puttermesser muttered. "Somehow this isn't working, Morris. Maybe because you're not a priest or a Levite."

Rappoport swallowed a tremulous breath. "If she gets to stand, if she decides to haul herself up—"

"Morris," Puttermesser said, "do you have a pocket knife?"

Rappoport took one out.

"O my mother, mother of my life!" the golem bleated. "Only think how for your sake I undid Turtelman, Marmel, Mavett!"

Huge sly Xanthippe, gargantuan wily Xanthippe, grown up out of the little seed of a dream of Leah!

Rappoport, obeying Puttermesser, blew aside the golem's bangs and with his small blade erased from Xanthippe's forehead what appeared to be no more than an old scar—the first on the right of three such scars—queerly in the shape of a sort of letter K.

Instantly the golem shut her lips and eyes.

The *aleph* was gone.

"Dead," Rappoport said.

"Returned," Puttermesser said. "Carry her up to the attic."

"The attic? *Here?* In Gracie Mansion? Ruth, think!"

"The Great Rabbi Judah Loew undid the golem of Prague in the attic of the Altneuschul. A venerable public structure, Morris, no less estimable than Gracie Mansion."

Rappoport laughed out loud. Then he let his tongue slide out, back and forth, from right to left, along the corners of his mouth.

"Bend down, Morris."

Rappoport bent down.

"Pick up her left hand. By the wrist, that's the way."

Between Rappoport's forefinger and thumb the golem's left hand broke into four clods.

"No, it won't do. This wasn't well planned, Morris, I admit it. If we try to get her up the attic stairs—well, you can see what's happening. Never mind, I'll call the Parks Commissioner. Maybe City Hall Park—"

Then began the babbling of Rappoport.

XII. UNDER THE FLOWER BEDS

arbage trucks are back on the streets. Their ferocious grinders gnash the City's spew. Traffic fumes, half a hundred cars immobile in a single intersection, demoralization in the ladies' lavatories of the Municipal Building, computers down, Albany at war with City Hall, a drop in fifth-grade reading scores—the City is choking. It cannot be governed. It cannot be controlled. There is a rumor up from Florida that ex-Mayor Malachy ("Matt") Mavett is scheming to recapture City Hall. As for current patronage, there is the egregious case of the newly appointed Commissioner of Receipts and Disbursements, said to be the Mayor's old lover; he resigns for health reasons even before taking office. His wife fetches him home to Toronto. Mayor Puttermesser undergoes periodontal surgery. When it is over, the roots of her teeth are exposed. Inside the secret hollow of her head, just below the eye sockets, on the lingual side, she is unendingly conscious of her own skeleton.

The *Soho News* is the only journal to note the Mayor's order, in the middle of a summer night, for an extra load of dirt to be shoveled under the red geraniums of City Hall Park. Parks Department diggers have planted a small wooden marker among the flower beds: DO NOT TOUCH OR PICK. With wanton contempt for civic decorum, passersby often flout the modest sign. Yet whoever touches or picks those stems of blood-colored blossoms soon sickens with flu virus, or sore throat, or stuffed nose accompanied by nausea—or, sometimes, a particularly vicious attack of bursitis.

And all the while Puttermesser calls in her heart: O lost New York! And she calls: O lost Xanthippe!

PUTTERMESSER
PAIRED

A t the unsatisfying age of fifty-plus, Ruth Puttermesser, lawyer, rationalist, ex-public official,
took a year off to live on her savings and think
through her fate. In the second week of her free-
dom—no slavery of paperwork, no office to go
to (a wide tract of her life already bled out in the
corridors of the Municipal Building, enough!)—it came to her
that what she ought to do was marry. This was not a new idea: it
had been her mother's refrain as far back as three decades ago or
more, ever since Puttermesser's first year in law school.

> Ruth, Ruth [her mother wrote from Miami, Flor-
> ida], there's nothing wrong with having a husband
> along with brains, it's not a contradiction. For God's
> sake pull your head out of the clouds! If you don't
> get married where will you be, what will happen?
> Alone is a stone as they say and believe me Ruthie
> Papa agrees with me on this issue not only double
> but triple, we didn't come down here to live in the
> heat with Papa's bursitis only in order to break his
> heart from you and your brains.

This innocently anti-feminist letter was now brown at the
edges, brittle; in the fresh tedium of her leisure Puttermesser
was sorting out the boxes stored under her bed. She was throwing things out. Her mother was dead. Her father was dead.
There would be no more reports of the Florida weather and no
grandchildren to inherit these interesting out-of-date postage
stamps and wrinkled complaints. Puttermesser was an elderly

orphan. For the first time it struck her that her mother was right: it was possible for brains to break the heart.

She bought a copy of the *New York Review of Books* and looked through the Personals. Brains, brains everywhere.

> Fit, handsome, ambitious writer/editor, non-smoker, witty, imaginative, irreverent, seeks lasting relationship with non-smoking female. Must be brilliant, unpretentious, passionate, creative. Prefer Ph.D. in Milton, Shakespeare, or Beowulf.

> University professor, anthropologist, 50, gentle, intellectual, youthful, author of three volumes on native Aleutian Islanders, cherishes the examined life, welcomes marriage or long-term attachment to loyal accomplished professional woman, well-analyzed (Jung only, no Freud or Reich please). Sense of humor and love of outdoors a must.

Among dozens of these condensed portraits Puttermesser could not recognize herself. She was hostile to the outdoors; the country air left her moody and squeamish—the peril of so many uneasy encounters with unidentifiable rodents, loud birds, monstrous insects, mud after fearsome Sag Harbor storms. She was no good at getting the point of jokes. Never mind that she didn't smoke; she was a committed liberal and regarded the persecution of smokers as a civil liberties issue. As for the examined life—enough! She was sick of examining her own and hardly needed to hear an Eskimo expert examine his. It was all fiction anyhow—those columns and columns of ads. "Vibrant, appealing, attractive, likable"—that meant divorced. Leftovers and mistakes. "Unconventional, earthy, nurturing, fascinated by Zen, Sufism, music of the spheres"—a crackpot still in sandals. "Successful achiever looking for strong woman"—watch out, probably a porn nut. Every self-indulgent type in the book turned up in these ads. Literature was no better. The great novels, rife with weirdos leading to misalliance—Isabel Archer

entangled with the sinister Gilbert Osmond, Gwendolyn Har-
leth's troubles with Grandcourt. Anna Karenina. Worst of all,
poor Dorothea Brooke and the deadly Mr. Casaubon. All these
bad characters—the men in the case absolutely, and many of the
women—were brainy. Think of Shaw, a logician, refusing to
allow Professor Higgins to wed Eliza, in open dread of fore-
ordained rotten consequences. And Jane Austen: with one hand
she marries Elizabeth to Darcy, clever with clever, and with the
other she goes and saddles Mr. Bennet with a silly wife. People
get stuck. Brains are no guarantee. Hope is slim.

The truth was this: Puttermesser had entered a new zone of
being. From the Women Attorneys Association she received a
questionnaire: *Aging and the Female Counselor*. Aging! Puttermesser! How could this be, when she had yet to satisfy Miss
Charlotte Kuntz, her piano teacher? At Puttermesser's last lesson
forty-five years ago, Miss Kuntz had warned her sharply that
such-and-such a sonatina needed work. It was just before
summer vacation. Puttermesser promised to toil over the
Tempo di Minuetto section all during July and August (the
Andante was easier), but she put it off and put it off. Instead
she wandered in a trance in and out of the children's room of the
public library; the rule was you could take out only two books at
a time. Frequently Puttermesser appeared at the library twice in
one day, to return two and to borrow two more. She read far
into the rosy shadows of the summer twilight. The lower half of
the sky was daubed with a streak of blood. "A beautiful day
tomorrow," Puttermesser's mild father said; "that's what a red
sunset means."

But Puttermesser's mother scolded: "In the dark! Again
reading in the dark! You'll burn out your eyes! And didn't you
swear to Miss Kuntz you'll practice every day during vacation?
You're not ashamed, she'll come back and you didn't learn it
yet? Nose in the book without a light!" In late August a letter arrived. Miss Kuntz was not coming back. She was moving upstate.

I am sorry to desert my post, Ruth, but it can't be helped. As you know, my father has grown rather infirm and I have been obliged to leave him by himself while traveling by subway to reach my pupils. It hasn't been easy. The change from the city will be a considerable relief. Here in Pleasantville we have purchased a modest though charming little house located just behind the Garden Street Elementary School, and I will be able to look after my father while giving lessons in the sunroom.

Let me urge you, Ruth, to keep working at your music. As I have often mentioned, you are intelligent but require more diligence. Always remember: Every Great Brain Delves Furiously!

By now Puttermesser had put off practicing for so long that her hair was showing signs of whitening. If alive, Miss Kuntz would be one hundred and four. Puttermesser had still not perfected the Tempo di Minuetto section, so how was it possible to consider a questionnaire on Aging?

Do you encounter discrimination on the part of judges? Employers? Clients? Court personnel?

Has your mental acuity or judgment noticeably slackened? If yes, how does this manifest itself?

Have your earlier positions (political, moral, societal) eroded? Are you, in your opinion, capable of new ideas? Flexibility? An open mind?

Have your earnings diminished? Increased? Are you treated with less respect? More? If more, how does your mature appearance contribute to this?

Has the feminist movement eased your professional situation? Are you harried less? More? No difference? How many times per week do you encounter sexist or ageist remarks?

Do you dye your hair? Use henna? Surrender to Mother Nature? If the latter, does this appear to augment or lessen your dignity among male colleagues? The public?

Miss Kuntz was no doubt under the ground in Pleasantville, New York, together with her father. In Puttermesser's cramped apartment in the East Seventies—a neighborhood of ophthalmologists and dermatologists—there was no room for a piano; the space near her bed could barely accommodate a modest desk. At night she could hear the high-school math teacher on the other side of the wall plunge her red pencils into an electric sharpener. Sometimes the math teacher did exercises on a plastic mat—unfolding, it whacked against the baseboard. A divorcée in her middle thirties who counted out loud with each leg stretch. She was working on her figure in the hope of attracting a lover. An announcement addressed to the math teacher had been thrust into Puttermesser's mailbox.

SINGLES EVENT!

ATTENTION, EDUCATED UNUSUAL SINGLES
TEACHERS' MIXER EVERY FRIDAY NIGHT 8:30 P.M.
MEET YOUR PEERS WITHOUT SNEERS OR TEARS
BRONX SCIENCE, HUNTER HIGH, STUYVESANT,
OTHER TOP SCHOOLS WELL REPRESENTED

$3 DONATION TO COVER PUNCH AND CHEESE

NOTE TO MALE TEACHERS: MORE MEN WANTED!
BRING YOUR (PROFESSIONAL) FRIENDS
CALL GINNY (718) 555-3000 FOR DETAILS

Puttermesser contemplated calling Ginny—she too was an educated unusual single. Instead she slid the sheet under the math teacher's door. The building, with its dedication to anonymity (each mysterious soul invisible in its own cubicle), was subject to jitters and multiple confusions. Mixups, mishaps, misdeliveries, misnamings. To the doorman she was Miss Perlmutter. If you asked the super to send the plumber you would get the exterminator. Without warning the pipes dried up for the day. You could try to run the faucet and nothing would come out. Or the lights would fail; the refrigerator fluttered its grand lung and ceased. All the refrigerators up and down the whole row of apartments on a single corridor expired together, in one extended shudder. You could feel it under your soles right through the carpeting. The building was a nervous organism; its familiar soughings ricocheted from cranny to cranny. Puttermesser could recognize by the pitch of its motor which floor the elevator was stopping on. She knew by the thump in the hall, and by the slap of sneakers heading back to the elevator, and by the rattle of all her locks, the moment when the new telephone book landed on her doormat.

Thump, slap, rattle. Something had landed there now; the sneakers were in flight. The chain-lock was still swinging and tinkling. Puttermesser laboriously fiddled with it, and then with the other two locks. Each required one turn followed by a quarter-turn. She worked as fast as she could. What if there were a fire? Robbery and rape or be burned alive: the New York predicament. All her neighbors had just as many locks; the math teacher had installed a steel pole that dropped into a hole in the floor.

The locks were undone. Puttermesser stuck her head out in time to see the flash of a yellow shirt at the end of the corridor. At her feet a chimney of huge flat cardboard boxes rose up. There was a smell of noisome cheese.

"Hey!" Puttermesser yelled. "Get back here! I didn't order this stuff."

"6-C, right?" the yellow shirt yelled back. "Pizza!"

"3-C. You want the sixth floor. I didn't order any pizza," Puttermesser yelled.

"You Morgenbluth?"

"You've got the wrong apartment."

"Listen," the yellow shirt called, "bike's in the street. Boss's bike. They take my bike I'm finished. Half-dozen veggie pizzas for Morgenbluth, O.K.?"

"I don't know any Morgenbluth!"

Like a piece of stage machinery, the elevator hummed the yellow shirt out of sight.

Fecal trail of stable—that cheese; some unfathomable sauce. Puttermesser kept her distance from ethnic foods. She had never tasted souvlaki; she had never tasted sushi. With the exception of chocolate fudge and Tootsie Rolls (her molars were ruined and crowned), gastronomy did not draw her. What she was concentrating on was marriage: the marriage of true minds. Reciprocal transcendence—she was not thinking of sinew, synapse, hormone-fired spasm. Those couples who saunter by with arms like serpents wrapped around each other, stopping in the middle of the sidewalk to plug mouth on mouth: biological robots, twitches powered by pitiless instinct. Puttermesser, despite everything, was not beyond idealism; she believed (admittedly the proposition wouldn't stand up under rigorous questioning) she had a soul. She dreamed—why not dream?—of a wedding of like souls.

Only the day before yesterday Puttermesser had taken out of the Society Library on East Seventy-ninth Street—an amiable walk from her apartment—a biography of George Eliot. A woman with a soul, born Mary Ann Evans, who had named herself George in sympathy with her sympathetic mate. George Eliot and George Lewes, penmen both, sat side by side every evening reading aloud to each other. They read science, philosophy, history, poetry. Once they traveled up to Oxford to see a brain dissected. Another time they invited Charles Dickens to lunch; he enthralled them with an eerie anecdote about Lincoln's death. They undertook feverishly cultural journeys to Spain and Italy and Germany, sightseeing with earnest thoroughness, visiting cathedrals and museums, going diligently night after night to the theater and opera. On steamers, for relaxation, they read Walter Scott. They were strenuous naturalists, pursuing riverbanks and hillsides for shells and fungi. Their house was called the Priory; nothing not high-minded or morally or artistically serious ever happened there. The people who came on Sunday afternoons—George Eliot presided over a salon—were almost all uniformly distinguished, the cream of English intellectual life: they were learned in Chaldaic, Aramaic, Amharic, Phoenician, or Sanskrit; or else they were orators, or else had invented the clinical thermometer; or were aristocrats, or Americans. The young Henry James made a pilgrimage to George Eliot's footstool, and so did Virginia Woolf's father. George Lewes was always present, small, thin, blond, quick, an impresario steering an awed room around the long-nosed sibyl in her chair. She depended on him; he protected her from slights, hurts, cruelty, shame, and from the critical doubts of John Blackwood, her publisher, who took her at first for a clergyman. It was a marriage of brain with brain, weightiness with weightiness. Dignity with dignity. And of course there was no marriage at all—not legally or officially. Lewes's wife, Agnes, was an adulteress who went on giving birth to another man's children; but it was an age of no divorce. George Lewes and George Eliot, husband and wife, a marriage of true minds admitting no impediment, were, perforce, a scandal.

All this Puttermesser knew inside out: it was her third or fourth, or perhaps fifth or sixth, George Eliot biography. She had, moreover, arrived at that season of life—its "autumn," in the language of one of these respectful old volumes—when rereading gratifies more than discovery, and there were certain habituated passages that she had assimilated word for word. "And yet brilliance conquered impropriety" gave her a shiver whenever she came on it; and also "Consider how a homely female intellectual, no longer young, falls into a happy fate." O happy fate! Somewhere on the East Side of New York, from, say, Fifty-third to Eighty-ninth, or possibly on West End Avenue between Sixty-sixth and Ninety-eighth, a latter-day George Lewes lurked: Puttermesser's own, sans scandal. It was now, after all, an age of divorce.

The shopping cart was squeezed between the refrigerator and the sink, folded up to fit into the little valley where the roaches frolicked. Wrestling it out, Puttermesser recalled her mother's phrase for a divorced man: used goods. Yet what else was there for her in the world but used goods? Puttermesser was used goods herself, in her mother's manner of speaking: she had once had a lover. But lovers are transients; they have a way of moving on—they are subject to panicked reconsiderations, sudden depressions, cold feet. Lovers are notorious for cowardice, for returning to their wives.

Puttermesser wedged the cart against the door jamb and bent to heave into it each big flat box. When all the pizzas were piled up inside the wire frame, she double-locked her top lock and triple-locked her bottom lock and trundled the cart down the corridor to the elevator. It was like pushing a wheelbarrow filled with slag. The elevator smelled partly of urine and partly of pine-scented disinfectant; with the cart in it there was barely enough room to stand. She poked the button marked "6," but instead of grinding her upward, the thing headed for the lobby, now and then scraping against the shaft.

Two very tall young women were waiting down there. One of them was carrying a bottle of wine without a wrapper.

"You getting out?"

"I was on my way up," Puttermesser said. "You brought me down."

"Well, we can't all fit," said the tall young woman with the wine.

"Just *try*," said the other tall young woman. "If you could just move your laundry—"

The tall young woman with the wine looked into the cart. "It isn't laundry. Smells like throw-up."

Puttermesser's spine pressed against the back wall of the elevator. The buttons were beyond her reach. A large black plastic triangle—an earring—swung into her face; the bottle of wine drove into her side.

"What floor?"

"Six," Puttermesser said.

"How about that. Is this stuff for Harvey's party? You going where we're going, Harvey's party?"

"No," Puttermesser said.

"Harvey Morgenbluth? On the sixth floor?"

"That's where I'm going," Puttermesser said.

The door to 6-C was propped open; all its chains were dangling free. A row of spidery plants in tiger-striped pots lined the foyer—a tropical motif. It was the sort of party, Puttermesser saw, where children run through shrieking, and no one complains. Ducks in police uniforms were shooting at evil-visaged porcupines in burglars' caps on a big color television in a corner of the living room, next to a white piano, but the children were paying no attention at all. A mob of them were chasing three little boys in overalls, two of whom seemed, as they sped by, to be identical twins. They raced through the living room and out into what Puttermesser knew had to be the kitchen (6-C's layout was the same as 3-C's) and back again. "No we don't, no we don't," all three were yowling. The two very tall young women from the elevator instantly made a place for themselves on the beige tweed carpet in front of the sofa, kneeling at the coffee table and pouring wine into paper cups, instantly hilarious; it was as if they had been dawdling there for hours. The sofa itself held a tangle of five or six human forms, each with its legs in one extraordinary position or another, and each devoted to a paper cup. Behind the children's screeches, a steady sea-noise burbled: the sound of a party that has been long underway, and has already secretly been defined, by the earliest arrivals, as a success or a failure.

This one was a failure: all ruined parties are alike. They pump themselves up, they are too boisterous, too frenetic, they pretend raucous pleasure. And this is true even of cousins and young aunts, of families. The Morgenbluth apartment looked to be all family—husbands, wives, untamed offspring. Sisters-in-law, like the pair from the elevator. A birthday for one of the little boys, probably—but there was too much wine, and no balloons; besides, the children were being ignored. Puttermesser wheeled the cart straight toward the white piano and began lifting the boxes out onto the top of it. Cracker crumbs were scattered over the keys; a cigarette, with its snout still burning, lay directly on middle C. The boxes climbed upward in precarious steps.

"Leaning tower of pizza," someone quipped, and from the tight little turn she caught in the tone of it, Puttermesser was certain that she was mistaken after all, that the noise all around was anything but domestic, that except for the children no one here belonged to anybody: no husbands, wives, cousins, aunts. It was the usual collection of the unattached. Roomful of the divorced on a Sunday afternoon in mild middle November. A "singles event": the math teacher, puffing on her mat three floors below, strained her torso in ignorance of the paradise of opportunity just overhead.

"It's about time we got some real food in here. You can't feed kids indefinitely on peanuts. Pretzels, maybe. Takes a grownup woman to remember nutrition. Any of these little sons of bitches yours?"

"I'd have to be their grandmother," Puttermesser said. It was the kind of remark she despised, and this stranger—a bearded man in his fifties, with a surgically squashed nose and oversized naive eyes, gray and on guard, more suitable to a kitten—had forced her to it.

He was pecking at the peanuts in his palm. "Well, you don't look it—they say it's all in the chin line. Twins are mine, but only on alternate weekends. With me it's always a double felony. Not to mention a couple of breakups. Marital. The way you spell that is m-a-r-t-i-a-l." He put out his hand, greasy from the peanuts. "Freddy Kaplow. How long've you known Harvey?"

The New York patter. Mechanical spew of the middle-aged flirt; he was practiced enough. And too stale for such young sons. Already finished with the second wife, the mother of the twins. No doubt a grown daughter from the first marriage. The daughter and the second wife were, as usual, nearly the same age.

"Tell Mr. Morgenbluth his pizza was delivered to the wrong apartment," Puttermesser said. "Tell him 3-C corrected the error."

"3-C corrected the error. No kidding, that's how come you got here? Cute, I like that. Boy-meets-girl cute."

Puttermesser took hold of her cart and began to wheel it away.

"There goes Mother Courage," Freddy Kaplow called after her. "Hey! No guts!"

The two young women from the elevator, still curled on the carpet, were being even more hilarious than before; on the sofa the row of tangled legs had become attentive. Three pairs of trousers (two corduroy, one blue denim), two of panty-hose. One of the men on the sofa—not the one in jeans—wore his hair in a ponytail, but was mainly bald in front.

Puttermesser tugged cautiously on the cart handle. "Excuse me, if you wouldn't mind, if I could just slide through here—"

"Hello there, pizza person, when do we eat?"

The balding man with the ponytail said, "I saw a bag lady the other day with one of those. She had it filled up to the top with piles of old shoes. All mixed up, no pairs."

"What'd she think she was going to do with them?"

"God only knows. Sell 'em."

"Eat 'em."

"Boil 'em in the bowels of Grand Central Station, *then* eat 'em."

"That's not funny," said a woman on the sofa. "I *work* with the homeless."

Puttermesser stopped. Pity for the ravaged municipality— reverberations from her days in officialdom—could still beat in her.

"In our program—it's a volunteer thing—what we try to do is

get them to keep diaries. We read poetry, we do E. E. Cummings. You have to make them see that we're all the same. They feel it when you're spiritually *with* them."

Another version of the New York patter. The wisecrack version and the earnest version, and all of it ego and self-regard. All of it conceit. Where was virtue, where was knowledge? Puttermesser was conscious of inward heavings and longings. She thought of mutuality, of meaning. So many indolent strutters, so much babble battering at the ceiling. That white piano with the crumbs. In no more than a quarter of an hour the windows behind the piano had begun to darken to blue dusk. Harvey Morgenbluth's beige tweed carpet, his paper cups, the hysteria of those hungry half-orphaned children running loose. Oh for a time machine! London in the grave twilight of a hundred years ago, Sunday evenings at the Priory. Cornices, massive draperies in heavy folds, ponderous tables and cupboards with carved gryphons' claws or lions' feet, old enameled landscapes hanging on tasseled cords from high roseate ceilings. A keyboard left open for the sublime and resolute hands. And in a great stuffed armchair in a shadowed corner, away from the lamp, the noble sibyl, receiving. Lives of courtliness, distinction; clarified lives, without tumble or blur. In George Eliot's parlor, a manner, or an idea, was purely itself. Ah, to leave careless New York behind, to be restored to glad golden Victoria, when the electric light was new and poetry unashamed!

In the foyer several of the tiger-striped pots had been overturned into puddles of wine; Puttermesser drew her cart through a patch of country mud. The spidery plants sprawled. A child's shoe lay flattened under one of the pots. A child's sock had become a glove for the doorknob.

And there, at the littered entrance of 6-C, stood a Victorian gentleman. He was not very tall; his cheeks and wrists looked thin. He was distractingly young, with a blond mustache, and he was actually wearing a hat—a formal hat, not exactly a fedora, but something more stately than a mere cap. He had on a capelike raincoat—partially unfurled at each shoulder, cola-brown, and grandly punctuated by big varnished metal buttons as shockingly bright as cymbals. Sherlock Holmes? Oscar Wilde? A dandy, in any case, self-consciously on display. One arm was held high, the other low, and in between rode a large flat rectangle wrapped in pale yellow paper and tied with a white string.

Puttermesser humbly backed her cart into mud to let the dandy pass. He slipped by her without taking any notice. She saw how she was invisible to him, of less moment than the tiger-striped pots displaced in his path. *She* had given way; the pots demanded his circumspection, and obliged him to go around them. It was worse than the Women Attorneys could imagine: the humiliating equation of a counselor of mature appearance with the walls and ceiling of 6-C's desolated vestibule. A doorknob is more engaging than a woman of fifty-plus. The man's face hurt Puttermesser; its youth hurt her. For an instant his head was perilously near hers—picking through the uprooted greenery, he tilted so close that she caught sight of the separate tender hairs of his mustache. His eyes were small and serious. Puttermesser thought with a pang how such a head, with such a dignified hat, and such snubbing colorless irises, and such an unfamiliar gravity of intent, would be out of place in Harvey Morgenbluth's living room, among the New York flirts. And that big flat package: a map? A map of the city, the world? An astronomical map. Andromeda. Ursa Major and Minor. Or a graph. A business graph. He was only a salesman, so never mind. Anyhow it was an illicit hurt: youth is for youth. An aesthetic error, a thin-skinned moral grotesquerie, to yearn after such a head, hat, cape; that nose, that mouth, those intimate hairs.

In her own apartment Puttermesser collapsed the cart and shoved it back into the alleyway between the refrigerator and the sink. There had been, she observed, a hatching: a crowd of baby roaches milled under the ray of her flashlight, then fled with purposeful intelligence. In God's littlest, the urge toward being and enduring; a soulless mite wills its continuity with the force and fury of our own mammoth human longing. O life, O philosophy!

All the same, Puttermesser sprayed.

In the morning she heard the brush of something in flight under her door:

> Dear 3-C:
>
> Just a note of thanx for yesterday's delivery—Freddy Kaplow (your pal and mine) gave me the dope on this. Sorry for the trouble and sorry I missed you! I'd love to return the favor, so if you ever need a passport photo in a hurry (no charge) or anything else in that line call on me. (I'm in the photography business, by the way.) I specialize in commercial reducing and enlarging but also in children's portraits. If you're interested in having a portrait done of the kids I can offer you a 25% studio discount in honor of your Good Deed!
>
> Yours hastily (on my way to work)
Harvey Morgenbluth
6-C
>
> P.S. Hate to mention it, but your insecticide smells all the way out here in the hall! This means the little visitors get to climb the riser pipe up to yours truly! Thanx a lot, neighbor!

A page out of the *National Geographic*: a pair of civilizations adverse in temperament can live juxtaposed in identical environments. Archaeologists report, for instance, that Israelite and Canaanites inhabited the same kinds of dwellings furnished with the same kinds of artifacts, and yet history testifies to intensely disparate cultures. 6-C's floor plan, Puttermesser reflected, was no different from 3-C's—she had seen that with her own eyes—but Harvey Morgenbluth had room for a piano and she did not. Harvey Morgenbluth gave parties and she did not. 6-C, the palace of exuberance. Harvey Morgenbluth had a business and Puttermesser currently had nothing.

Or, to reformulate it: despite exactly congruent apartment

layouts, Harvey Morgenbluth belonged to the present decade and Puttermesser belonged to selected phantom literary flashbacks.

The day was secretly bright behind a gray fisherman's net about to dissolve into a full autumn rain. The coursing sidewalks, still dry, had the spotted look of rapid dark rivers clogged with fish: all those young women in sneakers, clutching Channel Thirteen totes containing their office pumps and speeding toward desks, corridors, switchboards, computers, bosses, underlings. New York—Harvey Morgenbluth included—was going to work. And Puttermesser was idle. She was not idle: it was, instead, a meditative hiatus. She had stopped in her tracks to listen, to detect; to learn something; to study. She was holding still, waiting for life to begin to happen, why not? Venturing out for air, she was compelled to invent daily destinations—most often it was the supermarket over on Third, if only for an extra package of potato chips; she hated to run out. Or she fell in with the aerobic walkers among the more populated paths of Central Park, close to the protective rim of Fifth Avenue. Or she went mooning through the Morgan Library, the Cooper-Hewitt, the Guggenheim, the Frick; or kept up with the special exhibits at the Jewish Museum—the pitiable history of poor hollow Captain Dreyfus (hair-raising posters, Europe convulsed), shadowy old chronicles of the Prague Golem. New York, crazed by mental plenitude. The brain could not take in so much as a morsel of it, even at the rate of a museum a day. Paintings, jars, ornaments, armor, manuscripts, tapestries, pillars, flutes, violas, harps, the rare, the sublime, the celestial! Forms and illuminations, how was it possible to swallow it all down?

Hand in hand. The parallel gaze. No one knows lonely sorrow who has not arrived at fifty-plus without George Lewes.

From the express line in the supermarket (salty chips, cheese-flavored) Puttermesser headed for the Society Library, where she picked up the Yale *Selections from George Eliot's Letters* (pleasantly thick but portable, as against the nine-volume complete), then gravitated—why not?—to the Metropolitan Museum: the rain had started anyhow. Among the Roman portrait busts on the main floor Puttermesser ate a clandestine potato chip. A female sculpture in a niche—hallowed serenity wearing a head shawl—who certainly ought to have been the Virgin Mary turned out to be nothing more than a regular first-century woman, non-theological. She was what the Romans had instead of Kodak; yet Puttermesser resisted this pleasing notion. She was unwilling, just now, to marvel at the objects and hangings and statuary glimmering all around—the rare, the sublime, the celestial—in this exalted castle of masterworks. Her mind was on the *Letters*. George Eliot's own voice against Puttermesser's heart. She was tired of 3-C, of reading in bed or at the kitchen table. What she wanted was a public bench; why not?

From Rome she passed through Egypt (the little sphinx of Sesostris III, the granary official Nykure, with his tiny wife no higher than his knee and his tiny daughter, King Sahure in his headdress and beard, Queen Hatshepsut in *her* headdress and beard, and the great god Amun, and powerful horses, and perfect gazelles), and through polished Africa (Nigeria, Gabon, Mali), and through southern Europe, and through Flanders and Holland, and straight through the Impressionists. Immensity opened into immensity; there were benches in all those grand halls, and streams of worshipful pale tourists ascending and descending the high marble stair, but she did not come to the recognizable right bench until Socrates beckoned.

At least his forefinger was up in the air. The ceiling lights of that place—it was French Neoclassical Painting of the Eighteenth Century—seemed wan and overused. The room was unpopular and mostly empty—who cares about French Neoclassical? Puttermesser's bench faced Socrates on his death bed. Even from a distance away she could see him reaching for the bowl of hemlock with a bare muscular right arm. Socrates was stocky, healthy, in his prime. Part of a toga was slung over the other arm; and there was the forefinger sticking up. He was exhorting his disciples—a whole lamenting crowd of disciples, of all ages, in various griefstruck poses, like draped Greek statues. A curly-haired boy, an anguished graybeard, a bowed figure in a clerical cap, a man in a red cloak gripping Socrates' leg, a man weeping against a wall. Socrates himself was naked right down to below his navel. He had little red nipples and a ruddy face and a round blunt nose and a strawberry-blond beard. He looked a lot like Santa Claus, if you could imagine Santa Claus with armpit hair.

Puttermesser settled in. It was a good bench, exactly right. There were not too many passersby, and the guard at the other end of the long hall was as indifferent as a cardboard cutout. Now and then she stole a potato chip; the cellophane bag rattled and the guard did not stir.

> Assuredly [Puttermesser read in the *Letters*] if there be any one subject on which I feel no levity it is that of my marriage and the relation of the sexes—if there is any one action or relation of my life which is and has always been profoundly serious, it is my relation to Mr. Lewes.
>
> . . .
>
> I do not wish to take the ground of ignoring what is unconventional in my position. I have counted the cost of the step I have taken and am prepared to bear, without irritation or bitterness, renunciation by all my friends. I am not mistaken in the person to whom I have attached myself. He is worthy of the sacrifice I have incurred, and my only anxiety is that he should be rightly judged.
>
> . . .
>
> We work hard in the morning till our heads are hot, then walk out, dine at three and, if we don't go out, read diligently aloud in the evening. I think it is impossible for two human beings to be more happy in each other.

Impossible for two human beings to be more happy in each other!

A rush of movement along the far wall: a knot of starers had assembled just below "The Death of Socrates." They stared up, and then away, still staring; then up again. They were fixed on the lifted finger. Inexplicably it was directing them to look somewhere else. The knot grew into a little circling pack. Something was being surrounded over there, under Socrates' feet. The chips, the salt, the love adventures of the famous dead. Out of the blue Puttermesser fell into a wild thirst—George Eliot and George Lewes were traveling on the Continent, illicitly declaring themselves husband and wife. At home in England they were scorned and condemned, but in the enlightened Europe of the eighteen-fifties the best salons welcomed them without criticism, they were introduced to poets, artists, celebrated intellectuals; Franz Liszt played for them at breakfast, smiling in rapture with his head thrown back.

That fuss around Socrates. Puttermesser got up to see— anyhow she was in need of a water fountain. Some fellow had set up an easel. She inched her way into the starers and stared. The canvas on the easel was almost entirely covered: here were the mourning disciples, here was that prison staircase through a darkened archway, here were the visitors departing, here on the stone floor under Socrates' couch were the chain and manacle. That suffering youth hiding his eyes as he proffers the hemlock. All of it minutely identical to the painting on the wall: it was only that on the easel Socrates still had no face—the fellow in front of the easel was stippling out the strawberry-blond beard where it starts to curl over Socrates' clavicle. Puttermesser stared up at the painting and back down at the copy. One was the same as the other. You could not tell the difference. She stood at the rim of the crowd and through a kind of porthole watched the shadow of the lower lip gradually bloom into being; she had a better view of the easel than of the copyist. A bit of shoulder, a sleeve pushed up, a narrow hand manipulating the

CYNTHIA OZICK

brush—that was all. The hand was horrifically meticulous; patient; slow; horrifically precise. It worked like some unearthly twinning machine. A machine for uncanny displacement. The brush licked and drew back, licked and drew back. The ancient strokes reappeared purely. Puttermesser took in the legend on the brass plate—1787, Jacques-Louis David—and saw how after two centuries Socrates' nose was freshly forming, lick by lick, all over again. She licked her own lip; she had never been thirstier.

The drinking fountain was on another floor. She was gone ten minutes and came back to disappointment: the show was over. The room was nearly deserted. The fellow with the easel was dropping things into a satchel—he had already loaded his canvas onto some sort of dolly. He stopped to wipe a brush with a rag; then he rolled down his shirtsleeves and buttoned them. His shoes were beautifully polished.

Puttermesser's old neglected worldliness woke. She had not always been a loafer. Until only a little while ago she had moved among power-brokers, deputies, opportunists, spoliators, the puffed-up. Commissioners and chiefs. She had not always felt so meek. It is enervating to contemplate your fate too steadily, over too protracted a time: the uses of inquisitiveness begin to be forgotten. She thought of what she would ask the copyist—something about the mysteries of replication: what the point of it was. Plainly it wasn't a student exercise—not only because, though he was fairly young, he could hardly have been a student. He was well into the thirties, unless that modest orderly mustache was meant to deceive. And anyhow the will to repetition—Puttermesser knew she had glimpsed absolute will—was too big, too indecently ambitious, for a simple exercise. It looked to be a kind of passion. The drive to reproduce what was already there, what did it hint, what could hang from it?

She asked instead, "Did you get to finish the face?"

The young man held up an index finger in the direction of "The Death of Socrates." On the wall Socrates mimicked him. "It's finished, see for yourself."

"I mean in your version."

"What I do isn't a version. It's a different thing altogether."

An elbow-poke of enchantment—aha, metaphysics! "I saw you *do* it. It comes out exactly the same. It's the same thing exactly. It's amazingly the same," Puttermesser said.

"It only looks the same."

"But you're copying!"

"I don't copy. That's not what I do."

Now he was being too metaphysical; she was confused. She was confused by delight. He stood there folding things up—first the rag, then the easel. Above the mustache his nostrils gaped in a doubling victory of their own: George Eliot's observation of Liszt—when the music was triumphant the nostrils dilated. "If you don't want to call it copying," Puttermesser almost began— it was going to be an argument—but instantly quit. The syllables stopped in her mouth. Thin cheeks. Those bright hairs under such a tidy nose. Without his hat it was hard to be sure. Nevertheless she was sure. The Victorian gentleman in the vestibule of 6-C. The dandy who had snubbed her because a young man is incapable of noticing a woman of fifty-plus. He was noticing her now. She felt how she had coerced it. She had made him look right at her.

"Aren't you a friend of Harvey Morgenbluth's? We met at his door," Puttermesser said. "In the middle of that party."

"I don't go to Harvey's parties. I go on business."

"Well, I live right under him. Three floors down." Fraudulent. It would be right to admit that she had never set eyes on Harvey Morgenbluth. "Was that a painting you had with you? In that big package?"

Clearly he did not remember her at all.

"Harvey photographs my things," he said.

"He copies your copies."

"They're not copies. I've explained that."

"But the result is just the same," Puttermesser insisted.

"I can't help the result. It's the act I care about. I don't copy. I reënact. And I do it my own way. I start from scratch and *do* it. How do I know if Socrates' face got finished first or last? You think I care about that? You think I care about what some dead painter feels? Or what anyone with a brush in his hand thought about a couple of hundred years ago? I do it my way."

Puttermesser's terrible thirst all at once rushed back; she believed it might be the turning of her actual heart. Her organs were drinking her up and leaving her dry. She had abandoned all her acquaintance for the sake of the arrival of intellectual surprise. Mama, she called back to her mother through the dried-up marshes of so many lost decades, look, mama, the brain is the seat of the emotions, I always told you so!

In her mother's voice Puttermesser said, "It's used goods, isn't it? Shouldn't you begin with a new idea? With your own idea?"

"This *is* my idea. It's always my own idea. Nobody tells me what to do."

"But you don't make anything *up*—some new combination, something that never existed before," she urged.

"Whatever I do is original. Until I've done them my things don't exist."

"You can't say it's original to duplicate somebody else!"

"I don't duplicate." He was hitching his satchel onto his shoulder by its strap. "I reproduce. Can't you understand that? Babies get born all the time, don't they? And every baby's new and never existed before."

"No baby looks like any other," she protested.

"Unless they're twins." The canvas went onto the dolly. "And then they lead separate lives from the first breath."

"A painting isn't alive," she nearly shouted.

"Well, *I* am—that's the point. Whatever I do is happening for the first time. Anything I make was never made before." He gave her a suddenly speculative look; she was startled to catch a shade of jubilation in it. Did he talk like this every day of his life? She saw straight into the black zeroes of his pupils, bright islands washed round by faint ink. He poked one end of the folded easel toward her—it was all contraption, with wing-nuts everywhere. "What would you think," he said, "of helping me with some of this stuff?"

They walked with the contraption between them. The *Letters* were squeezed under Puttermesser's arm. Again immensity opened into immensity, hall into hall. They passed through majesties of civilizations, maneuvering around columns like a pair of workmen, drilling aisles through clusters of mooners and gapers. Precariously they wobbled down the great staircase. It was evident he could have managed all that equipment on his own; he was used to it. She was an attachment trailing along— an impediment—but it seemed to Puttermesser there was another purpose in this clumsy caravan. A kind of mental heat ran through the rod that linked them. He had decided to clip the two of them together for a little time. She understood that she had happened on an original. A mimic with a philosophy! A philosophy that denied mimicry! And he wasn't mistaken, he wasn't a lunatic. He was, just as he said, someone with a new idea. He had a claim on legitimacy. He was guilty with an explanation; or he wasn't guilty at all. The thing jerking and bobbing between them, with its sticks and screws, was an excitement—it made her keep her distance, but it led her. It was a sort of leash. She followed him, like an aging dog, sidelong.

Puddles on the pavement; she had missed the rain altogether. The street was silted with afternoon light. Puttermesser surrendered her end of the easel—she hated to give it up. Found! George Lewes, George Lewes in New York! He had a kind of thesis, a life's argument. He had nerve. "I'll come by," he said. "I'll drop in. The next time I have to be at Harvey's place. Here, take one of these. It tells all."

He set easel, satchel, dolly down on the sidewalk. Then he pulled out a little red case and drew from it a white card. There was a telephone number accompanied by two lines in red type:

> RUPERT RABEENO
>
> REËNACTMENTS OF THE MASTERS

Puttermesser, who had not laughed in a month, laughed: she was ready to be happy. "Do people know what this means when you hand it out?"

"It's self-explanatory."

She was still laughing; it made her as bold as an old politician. "Why would you drop in?"

"To explain the card." He bent to pick up easel, satchel, dolly. "Don't you want me to? Would you rather I didn't?"

"Come right now," she said. "I'm dying of thirst. I'll make some tea."

II. THE NIGHT READERS

uttermesser's favorite tea was Celestial Seasonings Swiss Mint—each tea bag had attached to it an instructive or uplifting quotation. Henry Ward Beecher: "Compassion will cure more sins than condemnation." Victor Hugo: "Laughter is the sun that drives winter from the human face." Ralph Waldo Emerson: "Make the most of yourself, for that is all there is of you."

The box too was imprinted with wisdom. Rupert Rabeeno read aloud, " 'I have always thought the actions of men the best interpreters of their thoughts.' John Locke," and twisted the box around. "This next one's Nietzsche. 'He who has a why to live can bear with almost any how.' "

Reading from the tea bag tags was only a joke, a diversion. What they were really reading from was *Middlemarch*. This was the beginning of a project: they were going to do all of George Eliot's novels—out loud, taking turns. The early chapters galloped, but after a while talk always seemed to intervene; they forgot what had happened at the start of a chapter, and had to repeat it. Sometimes they skipped the reading altogether. Rupert Rabeeno was not one of those people who allow their lives to be obscured by the vapor of the merely inferential. He was amazingly explicit: he made Puttermesser *see* things. In a month or so she had been led through all the particulars of his childhood. She knew the contents of his mother's dusty jewel tray—her high-school class ring, four pairs of screw-on celluloid earrings, one necklace of five-and-dime pearls, one broken watch in the shape of a violin—and exactly where his father used to keep the key to the store safe (in the toe of an out-of-style Buster Brown Mary Jane). His father had run a shoe store in a town outside of Atlanta. Rupert's two married sisters, much older, grandmothers several times over, were settled in Tampa and Dallas. He claimed, besides, two mothers. The first had died when he was only nine: it became his habit to dream over the sad remnants of her few poor trinkets. He thought he could catch a reminiscent sniff of her dress fuming out of the tray in her old chifforobe. His father had put it down in the cellar of the shoe store. His father's second wife—strong and rosy—worked in the shoe store just as Rupert's mother had, and to woo his affection rushed home to give him milk and chocolate graham crackers after school, just as his mother had. But he threw over his milk glass on purpose, and his stepmother watched him drag a spiteful finger through the spill, pulling the wet lines of it into a marvel of a cat with a lifted tail. After that he was sent for art lessons on Tuesday afternoons to a little local academy, where his classmates were mostly girls. Tap dancing was in progress just across the corridor, accompanied by a quaking piano; it was a humiliating place altogether. He didn't *sound* very Southern, Puttermesser noticed: he had left the South a long time ago, and had traveled everywhere. Some years back, he said, he had fallen into a "subject," his first, at the Louvre: it was the "Officier de Chasseurs à Cheval de la Garde Impériale Chargeant," by Théodore Géricault. And before that he had done some translating from the Catalan; and a stint, before that, in "The Changeling," on the London fringe, playing De Flores.

Puttermesser heard all this with a formidable sharpness—he was charging her with the will to take hold of him. It was as if he had given her a razor to cut him out with: the whole figuration of his history. He wanted her to know precisely what he added up to. He discharged everything he had done—he had done a lot—in a shower of color and anecdote; he was against elusiveness. Stories, worn through retelling, shot out from him: she felt the knots and burrs of reused thread. And portraits: his curly-haired sisters, their husbands (a couple of doctors, one a gastroenterologist, the other a pediatrician), their children, the strangers their children had married; but he was lost to all of them now. He had left his family behind. He spoke of the curiously perfected reflections of the bridges over the Seine, so that you couldn't tell which was the true world, the one in the air or the one in the river; and of the part-time job he had at eighteen, in a grimy record-pressing plant, listening over and over again for flaws in the grooves; and of how he had once been hired to teach English in a loft on West Fifteenth Street to fearful pathetic newcomers up from the Caribbean, under a half-mad "principal" who required every pupil to trace over the principal's model sentences in green ink; and of how the shoe store, always dark and unpopulated, like an empty movie theater with its double row of chairs back-to-back, had all at once surprisingly begun to flourish and bustle, fevered, it seemed, by his stepmother's quick run over the old brown carpeting—so that the two of them, his nearsighted father and his rubicund second mother, could dare to open a second store in the next town, called, like the first, THE PAIR FAIR.

It was almost too much. Puttermesser would not have minded a bit more mystery, the trail of something shielded, a secret stowed in a crevice. A spot, here and there, of opacity. He told her, with a compulsive comic vividness that shook her, of his clandestine night wedding, at twenty-three, to Cecilia Almendra, a little Argentine cabaret singer, who turned out to be a runaway. Señor and Señora Almendra found them and took the bride back to Buenos Aires—"before the consummation," he said. Señor Almendra (born Mandel, a refugee from the European cataclysm) raged; Señora Almendra sobbed. The girl had been registered at NYU and was supposed to be studying psychology; she never went to classes and wrote lying letters home. Her hours in the "carabet"—a filthy bar on Avenue A— lasted until five in the morning. A bedroom farce with an unrumpled bed.

In the decade or so since, Rupert had lived without romance—not that kind, anyhow. Paris, and then London, and then Pittsburgh. He was sick of being a seedy wanderer bartering the baubles of trick and knack. In granite Pittsburgh he worked for a provincial satrap, the monarch of an intrastate railroad, and for half a dozen years threw himself into designing billboards. His grand noisy posters, in riotous orange and purple and drumming red, jumped out at every station like oversized postage stamps connecting town with town. All the commuter lines that led to Pittsburgh were stitched together by Rupert's posters—he thought of them as brilliant beads strung on wire tracks. And he thought of himself as a polychromatic jack-in-the-box, ambushing the public. After the billboards, he switched to decorating cereal boxes. It pleased him that the selfsame jug, yellow and two-handled, overflowing with banana flakes, cropped up on tables from Tokyo to Tel Aviv; repetition wasn't far from continuity, and continuity not far from eternity. But in the end he didn't care for assignments and projects and campaigns. He disliked art directors and company bosses. Granite Pittsburgh crumbled for him; it was no better than a heap of sand draining through an hourglass. He missed being sovereign over himself.

Rupert Rabeeno was glutted with his own life—who isn't, and why not? He liked to tell it over and over, as if in the telling he could keep it from shrinking away into the smallness of the nearly forgotten. He let go of nothing he had ever known or seen or felt. Or not felt. Whatever had happened once he meant to make happen again. Reprise invigorated him. And Puttermesser was the same. It came to her in a rush of deliverance as wild as cognition, wilder than consternation—she was the same, the very same, no different! Whatever had happened once, she conspired, through a density of purposefulness, to redraw, redo, replay; to translate into the language of her own respiration. A resurrection of sorts. Wasn't her dream of having George Lewes again—a simulacrum of George Lewes—exactly the same as Rupert Rabeeno's wanting to make things happen again? Wasn't she, all on her own, a mistress of reënactment?

On a snowy afternoon in early January—Rupert Rabeeno was just back from delivering one of his great flat parcels upstairs at 6-C—Puttermesser decided to tell her idea about George Lewes. It was less an idea than an instinct; it was a burning; it made her shy. She suffered—he might mock her; she would be humiliated. And the awful discrepancy, the moat of age. The first George Lewes (would Rupert Rabeeno consent to be the second?) was born in 1817. George Eliot was born in 1819. A match altogether on the mark, generationally intelligent, so to speak; two years between them, she nearly thirty-five, he thirty-seven, as decently appropriate as could be. Puttermesser's shame stung. A hag. A crone. Estrogen dwindling in her cells. Rupert Rabeeno was too young—he was two decades too young—to be a candidate for a simulacrum of George Lewes. A gap like that is a foolishness in whatever century.

She watched him rummage in her clogged inch of pantry. He plucked up a can of tomato-and-vegetable soup and emptied it into a pot. Then he poured in some water from Puttermesser's blue teakettle and began to stir. She was used to this: he loved soup. He brought two or three cans every time he turned up.

She had calculated just how to get it said. An announcement. "October 23, 1854," she started off. And read: " 'I have been long enough with Mr. Lewes to judge of his character on adequate grounds, and there is therefore no absurdity in offering my opinion as evidence that he is worthy of high respect.' " The moist smell of onions heating in the soup curled around them. "Written," she explained, "right after George Eliot and George Lewes went off to Weimar together."

The soup splashed into two of Puttermesser's china bowls. "Why Weimar?"

"Goethe's city. Lewes was working on a book about Goethe. He was always working on *something*."

"Sit down and eat your veggies," Rupert Rabeeno commanded. "That woman's a prig. Too damn solemn."

Puttermesser said, "It's Lewes I'm thinking of." George Lewes, light-hearted, airy, a talker!

"He's on your mind a whole lot. So is she."

A clot of embarrassment coarsened her throat. "It's only a feeling," Puttermesser said. "A sort of . . . you know, a conceit. A literary conceit." She put her head down. It was unseemly. She was too old, by twenty years. "It's about ideal friendship."

He said, "I still don't see the point of Weimar. Going off somewhere. There's no point to it. We can stay right here."

So he understood her to the marrow. He was all quicksilver; he was ready. She saw how, once she had yielded up her little burning, he could better it, he could complicate it, he could shake the ash of theory from it and fire it into life. They drove through the rest of *Middlemarch* without interruption; or almost. Often she followed him out into the wintry town—after "The Death of Socrates" he had moved over to the Frick. In his own

133

place, on West Fifty-ninth, a studio with a Castro convertible, he boiled up a can of mushroom-and-barley. It seemed to Puttermesser that all the singles who had ever lived in this solitary room before him were roiling like phantoms in the steam. His suitcase was tidy and waiting—fresh shirts and turtlenecks, his shoe polish and his own toothpaste. His clothes were orderly, well brushed. She asked him where he kept his valet. He laughed; he was exhilarated. "No room for Jeeves! I hide him in my sleeves!" He showed her his favorite lamp—indispensable, he said, for snugness. He carried the lamp and the suitcase, she carried the shade. Laughing, they left shoe holes in the snow; at the curb the new snow was folding itself over last week's old black humps.

Rupert Rabeeno's lampshade was as wide as a bat's wing and cast phosphorescent reflections on the walls. At night under that greenish fishy light—3-C was now spookily undersea—they finished *The Mill on the Floss.* Rupert asked what next.

Puttermesser considered. "Not *Romola.* George Eliot said that book was what made her into an old woman."

"Let's do the life," Rupert said.

They tramped in the New York slush to the Society Library and took out all the George Eliot biographies there were, including the one Puttermesser had returned not long before. Rupert wanted to see how they matched up, whether someone writing about George Eliot in, say, the nineteen-eighties was going to turn up the same George Eliot as someone writing in the nineteen-forties, or in the eighteen-nineties. It was like reënacting a landscape a hundred years later, he said. The same grove of trees under the same sky, but different. What altered it was whoever was looking at it. Puttermesser almost followed the argument but was indifferent to it anyhow. Copyist's talk. She didn't care about any of that. She rejoiced, she was anointed. The germ of her secret seeing had breathed itself alive. Here they were, side by side, reading aloud, an indoor January pastoral; she had passed through the sacred gate, she had entered ideal friendship. Rupert's reading voice was dark, with now and then a sharp scratchy click in it, the call of some imaginary bird—it was a chirp she could not hear in ordinary conversation. It meant he was seized. Snared. Sometimes a tic convulsed his eyelid; he was agitated, he was engulfed. He surpassed her in her little burning, he urged her on.

In her cube of a kitchen she told him her convoluted work history, and admitted to sour Rappoport, with his wife at home in Toronto. Rupert, concentrating, beat at the soup—it was lumpy—and shook the eggs in their pan. After supper he cut her hair. The wisps fell from her nape and forehead, all over her shoulders and the floor. She watched in the mirror as he snipped, evening out the sides: it struck her that she was not yet a hag. Tiny hyphens of hair-cuttings fuzzed her neck; he blew them down inside her blouse and over her back. Her mouth in the mirror was content. Her tongue slipped out like a shining lizard. He never thought of her as too old. Nothing grotesque lay between them. She believed that now. They were friends, ideal friends. She saw how he had become more zealous than she.

When he went upstairs to Harvey Morgenbluth's she stayed behind. It was all business up there. She didn't care for Rupert's business; it opened into discord and combat. His business was postcards. He copied the masters. Harvey Morgenbluth photographed Rupert's doubles, in full color, and reduced them; then the photos were sent off to the printer and after that to a jobber for distribution. This was Rupert's living. "The Death of Socrates," for instance, with Socrates' face filled in, reappeared in packets of a hundred, sealed in transparent plastic. One hundred identically lifted Socratic fingers. One hundred identical youths bearing one hundred identical bowls of hemlock. There was a Rubens—"Venus and Adonis"—with a Cupid and a pair of dogs; there was van Gogh's "Irises" and Manet's "Woman with a Parrot." There was Turner's "Grand Canal, Venice," all ship and sky and water and misty distance. She thought him a genius—a genius ventriloquist; he could penetrate any style and any form, from a petal to an earlobe. He was at home in minuteness or in vista. The names of both painting and painter were printed on the back of each card—and also, in minuscule letters: RUPERT RABEENO, REËNACTMENTS OF THE MASTERS.

This was the subject of their small war. "If all it comes down to is postcards," Puttermesser said, "you might just as well send Harvey Morgenbluth into the Met with a camera."

"In the first place he wouldn't be allowed. Which," Rupert said, "is beside the point anyhow."

"No it's not. Every museum in the world sells postcards of its paintings."

"Exactly," Rupert said. "These are postcards of *my* paintings."

"It's a fraud."

This made him jolly. "Counselor!"

"I didn't say it's illegal. I'm not talking about copyright laws. There aren't any copyright laws for French Neoclassicals. That leaves you with your conscience."

"My conscience!" He reared back as if she had smacked him, and let out a scratchy laugh. It reminded her of the snap, as of an unearthly pod bursting, of his reading voice.

"People are going to look at *your* Grand Canal and think it's Turner's."

"I made it," he said, with so much clarity that Puttermesser felt she could stare right through the unpainted circles of his eyes into whatever murmured behind them.

This murmur swept her. She brought his whole head into her arms. "Rupert, Rupert," she said. A fabricator of doubles, but he had no duplicity. She nearly believed in his case: that these weren't doubles he fabricated. It wasn't a manner or mannerisms he took from his prototypes. It was—could it be true?—their power.

She recited: "'To see Kean act was like reading Shakespeare by flashes of lightning.'"

"What's that?"

"Coleridge said it about some famous actor."

And so their skirmish ended. She could not keep it up. If he didn't invent the work of his hands, he had, anyhow, invented himself. He wasn't a swindler, he wasn't an impostor. The postcards were his very own. She came on them in bookshops, and realized she had often seen them there before. A rack of his cards stood near the door when she went into a stationer's for a packet of envelopes. There on the top tier was Picasso's "Gertrude Stein"—that autonomous skull, tile forehead, mouse's chin. But Rupert had made it.

III. THE UNSPEAKABLE JOY

heir night reading under the sea-green lamp: the names of the long, long dead. Brabant, Bray, Chapman, Rufa, Cara, Sara, Barbara Bodichon, Edith Simcox, Johnny Cross. Specters. Of these, only Herbert Spencer survives recognizably on his own. George Eliot dared to beg him to marry her; she was infatuated. She had not yet met George Lewes. "I promise not to sin any more in the same way," she pleaded when Spencer turned her down; she could not imagine that he would end his days a bachelor. The philosopher of evolution could not evolve. "If you become attached to someone else, then I must die, but until then I could gather courage to work and make life valuable, if only I had you near me. I do not ask you to sacrifice anything—I would be very good and cheerful and never annoy you."

Rupert was reading this from the *Letters*. Puttermesser slammed down her eyelids. She had those pitiful phrases by heart. The abjectness, the yearning. Dry Herbert Spencer, a man shut off; no feeling could invade him. But one day he brought George Lewes with him to the *Westminster Review*, where George Eliot—she was still plain Miss Evans—was working as an editor. Lewes was playful, impudent, jokey; his face was pitted, he had a little neat nose with big nostrils. He was an apt mimic and told clever stories without a speck of meanness. George Eliot at first thought him ugly; she was ugly enough herself. People said he resembled a monkey; they said she resembled a horse. He had free tickets to the theater and invited her along. He reviewed plays, books, art, music. His mind was all worldly versatility. He wrote on French and German literature, he wrote plays, he made a study of insanity, he wrote on history and science and philosophy, on anemones and Comte and Charlotte Brontë. She translated Strauss, Feuerbach, Spinoza; she wrote on Matthew Arnold, Tennyson, Browning, Thoreau, Ruskin. She read Homer, Plato, Aristophanes, Theocritus; she read Drayton and a history of Sanskrit.

"What a pair, what a pair," Puttermesser said.

She had discovered something disconcerting: Rupert had confessed that until now George Eliot had been no more than a rumor for him. In high school in the town near Atlanta they had read *Silas Marner* in sophomore year. That was all of George Eliot he was acquainted with. The rest was new. He had never before looked into a biography of George Eliot. He had never heard of George Lewes or Johnny Cross or all those others.

"Why didn't you say so when we began? When we started reading?"

"I thought you could tell." He put his hand on her hand. How dependable he was; how eager to satisfy. "Anyhow I'm catching up. In fact I'm *caught* up. What do you know that I don't?"

She could not contradict him. It was as if he had swum into her brain and swallowed up its spiny fish, great and small, as they flickered by. Puttermesser was ravished: it was true, there was no difference between them. Under the sea-green lamp he was caught, he knew what she knew.

It was Lewes she wanted him to know.

They read until they were dried up. They read until their eyes skittered and swelled. The strangeness in it did not elude them: where George Eliot and George Lewes in their nighttime coziness had taken up Scott, Trollope, Balzac, Turgenev, Daudet, Sainte-Beuve, Madame d'Agoult (Lewes recorded all this in his diary), she and Rupert read only the two Georges. Puttermesser discussed what this might mean. It wasn't for "inspiration," she pointed out—she certainly wasn't mixing herself up with a famous dead Victorian. She was conscious of her Lilliputian measure: a worn-out city lawyer, stunted as to real experience, a woman lately secluded, eaten up with loneliness, melancholia ground into the striations of her face. The object was not inspiration but something sterner. The object was just what it had been for the two Georges—study. What Puttermesser and Rupert were studying was a pair of heroic boon companions. Boon companions! It was fellowship they were studying; it was nearness.

"George and George," Rupert said. "Practically a couple of twins."

"They were *lovers*," Puttermesser corrected.

In the mornings he snatched up his satchel and dolly and the clatter of his easel and headed for the Frick. Puttermesser marveled at the soaked threads of the canvas, glistening with bright heavy oil. In the evenings, after supper, they pushed on with the two Georges. A history of money and family. The money went to Agnes, Lewes's easy-going adulterous wife, and her brood of children by another man. Agnes in old age, very fat, with small fat fingers twiddling in her lap, supported until her death by George Eliot's earnings: they mooned over her photo in one of those bricklike volumes that littered the kitchen chairs. But to Lewes's sons George Eliot was "Mutter." One died young—she nursed and mourned him as if he were her own. Another was attached to her all her life. Lewes, meanwhile, was coaxing her to try her hand at writing stories, though privately he doubted whether she could master drama. Overnight she bloomed into greatness. And was a pariah all the same. Her brother Isaac, still in the Midlands of their childhood, would have nothing to do with her. She wrote him and he refused to answer. His sister was living with a man who had a wife. His sister could not be received in respectable drawing rooms. In the end the world came to her. Queen Victoria contrived to be presented to George Eliot.

Rupert read: " 'Our unspeakable joy in each other has no other alloy than the sense that it must one day end in parting.' " For twenty-five years George Eliot and George Lewes had their unspeakable joy—each other, and fame, and homage, and Europe, and a carriage of their own, and comforts, and the admiration of the best minds, and the hoverings and adorations of the young, among them Johnny Cross. Johnny Cross helped Lewes find a house in the country—he was good at all sorts of practical things. George Eliot called him nephew. "My dear Nephew," her letters to him began; and ended, "Your affectionate Aunt." He was a tall comely young man of twenty-nine, introduced to her by his mother on a holiday in Rome. After Rugby he went to New York to work in a branch of the family bank, and returned to London to do the same. George Eliot met Nephew Johnny Cross on George Lewes's fifty-second birthday.

IV. THE AWFUL DISCREPANCY

he death scenes and their aftermath fell to Puttermesser. They were familiar to her, and unimportant. It was the living Lewes she cared for, the salvational Lewes, the merry Lewes of transformation. George Lewes died at sixty-one, at the last of a dank November. He had always been sickly. During his final hours the doctors bustled in and out. In front of the Priory their coachmen cracked noisy jokes. George Eliot did not go to the funeral. Day after day she shut herself up in her bedroom with Lewes's books and microscope; she howled and howled. Only the servants heard.

Here Puttermesser stopped. It was over.

Rupert said, "We ought to do it."

"Do what?"

"Get married."

"*They* didn't marry," Puttermesser said, and closed the book.

"Hey, don't quit—there's more."

"No more Lewes."

"There's all the rest."

"You don't like her on her own. You called her a prig."

"That was before I knew her. Do the rest," he persisted.

So she went on with it. Two months after Lewes's death, George Eliot wrote to Johnny Cross, "Dearest Nephew, I do need your affection. Every sign of care for me from the beings I respect and love is a help to me. . . . In a week or two I think I shall want to see you. Sometimes even now I have a longing. . . . Your affectionate Aunt." And on a brilliant May day, at

St. George's Church on Hanover Square, sixteen months after she had howled over the parting from Lewes, George Eliot married Johnny Cross. The new wife was sixty. Johnny's mother had died within days of Lewes. He was an orphan of forty.

Rupert danced around Puttermesser's tiny bedroom, where they had set up the sea-green lamp on Puttermesser's teak desk. "Look at that, look at that!"

"She needed someone to lean on," Puttermesser said. "It was her temperament."

"The body was hardly cold!"

"You can't lean on a dead man."

"*Aha!*" Now he took her by the wrists. "Didn't I tell you that from the start? That first day in the Met? I told you—*I'm* the one who's alive!"

Puttermesser wondered at this. "Well, there's the honeymoon."

"I'll do the honeymoon!" Rupert said.

She watched him reconstruct Johnny Cross. Johnny Cross was anyhow a puzzlement. No one knew him really. He was expected to be "deep" and he wasn't. He was handsome and genial and athletic and rich. He was no intellectual, though he worked at it gamely, the same plucky way he chopped down a clump of trees or devotedly smacked at a tennis ball. He was a tremendous swimmer. He wasn't even remotely a writer, but he did turn out one astonishing book—astonishing chiefly because Johnny Cross had written it: *George Eliot's Life*. The title was as obvious and direct as he was. He plugged away at it after she died: it was a genuflection.

Rupert saw quickly that the heap of biographies they had been reciting from—including Johnny Cross's—were useless. Johnny Cross appeared in all of them, to be sure—which didn't signify he was *there*. You might find him but you couldn't get hold of him. Rupert did what he could to conjure up the true Johnny. In a way he remade him—Puttermesser thought it was a kind of plunder. Rupert was being preposterous and unfair, but she had to acknowledge he was ingenious. He went after unheard-of combinations and juxtapositions: a letter, then a paragraph from one of the biographies, then again a letter. He threaded in and out of whatever was at hand. And what emerged from all that prestidigitation was Johnny Cross in love—but not with George Eliot.

"Good God," Puttermesser said. "The one thing everybody knows for sure about Johnny Cross is that he loved George Eliot. He adored her! There never *was* anybody else for him. When she died he never married again. You can't just contradict what everybody absolutely *knows*."

But Rupert pressed on with his evidence. It was, he said, right there in Johnny's unnatural behavior in the first weeks after Lewes's funeral. George Eliot had pleaded with him to come and help her with the business matters George Lewes had always taken care of; Johnny was good at money. He arrived carrying Dante's *Inferno*. George Eliot was in her sitting room rereading the *Iliad*—in Greek, of course—to take her mind off her sorrow. Johnny said he was hoping to get started on Dante to take his mind off *his* sorrow; he was mourning his mother. The trouble was he had to read Dante in Carlyle's translation. The Italian he had picked up in Rome, with his mother, wasn't up to snuff. "Oh," George Eliot cried out to Nephew Johnny, "I must read that with you!"—she liked Dante better than accounting. They went at it word by word. She was massively patient. He was painfully attentive—this was his design.

Rupert held up *George Eliot's Life* under the sea-green lamp and chanted: " 'The divine poet took us into a new world. It was a renovation of life.' There, that's Johnny confessing."

"Right! You see?" Puttermesser said. "A renovation of life! He's telling us how he adored her—"

"You're not getting it," Rupert said. "The fellow was infatuated. With Lewes."

"Rupert, that's ridiculous."

"I don't mean what you think. I mean incarnation. He was

trying to jump right into Lewes's shoes—whatever Lewes was good at, Johnny was going to do. He was out for that. He was going to be Lewes for her. A reasonable facsimile. The idea was to impress on her that Lewes was still around. Accessible, in a manner of speaking. In another packet of flesh. The face was the face of Johnny, but the soul was the soul of Lewes. *That's* the point."

"Oh, I don't know," Puttermesser said, weakening. It was ridiculous and it was not.

"And the night readings. He kept a record just like Lewes. First Dante. Then she took him through Chaucer, Shakespeare, Wordsworth. The basics. He had to sweat it. All of it right there in her sitting room in the Priory, right smack under a big blown-up photo of Lewes. For all I know he had his bottom in the same chair Lewes used to put *his* bottom in. And doesn't he ask her to play the piano for him? The same music she played for Lewes? Then she turns sixty and Johnny kisses her hand."

"And then he marries her. George Lewes never did that! You keep ignoring that," Puttermesser said. "Marrying her isn't jumping into George Lewes's shoes!"

"You think she wouldn't have had a big church wedding with Lewes if she'd had a chance to? If the law had allowed it? Look, the minute such a thing gets to be possible—Johnny's definitely single—what does she do? She runs out to buy a trousseau."

Rupert fished up a book from the stack on Puttermesser's teak desk and wet his thumb. "They're sending letters right and left behind her back. Churning up the gossip. 'George Eliot had been seen at all the fashionable milliners and dressmakers in London. . . . Whatever money and taste could do to make her look not too unsuitable for a man of forty had been done.' And after a quarter of a century of snubbing her for living with Lewes, brother Isaac writes to congratulate her on her marriage to Johnny! And she's *grateful*. These are conventional folks, Ruthie, believe me. It's Johnny you've got to keep your eye on."

Puttermesser stared. "Why?"

"I'm telling you why. Watch him make himself into a second Lewes."

"*You're* doing that. You're making him into Johnny Cross, Reënactments." Puttermesser drew back. Her lungs felt fat from too much air. "You're making him into a copyist!"

Rupert gave a paradisal smile. "Isn't that what he had in mind?"

"He was in love! And she was lonely, she was missing connubial love. She'd been happy with Lewes, she wanted to be happy again—"

Puttermesser seized the *Letters* and shook out the pages with a ferocity. "Damn it, Rupert, *listen!*"

> A great momentous change is taking place in my life—a sort of miracle in which I could never have believed, and under which I still sit amazed. If it alters your conception of me so thoroughly that you must henceforth regard me as a new person, a stranger to you, I shall not take it hardly, for I myself a little while ago should have said this thing could not be.
>
> I am going to be married to Mr. Cross. . . . He has been a devoted friend for years, much loved and trusted by Mr. Lewes, and now that I am alone, he sees his only longed for happiness in dedicating his life to me. . . . Explanations of these crises, which seem sudden though they are slowly dimly prepared, are impossible. . . . We are going away tomorrow and shall be abroad two or three months.

"And then they went off together. That's how it is," Puttermesser finished. "A pair of married lovers. You can't just go and twist it into something else. You want to hear how she'd been feeling? *Here's* how she'd been feeling!" She was as pitiless as a conqueror. It was Rupert she wanted to conquer—Rupert's plan for Johnny Cross. She thumped a fist on the *Letters* and read out furiously, " 'Blessed are the dead who rest from their labors, and have not to dread a barren, useless survival.' That's why she married Johnny Cross!"

Rupert looked meditative; he looked serious. Puttermesser took him in all over again—he was narrow, and blond, and burnished, and small. He was brushed and orderly. The clear blank circles of his eyes needled out their steady black pupils. The pupils made deep fierce periods. They punctuated; they punctured.

"*We* ought to do that," Rupert said. "Not the going away part. The great momentous change—that part."

He *was* serious. It wasn't a snicker, it wasn't a crack tossed off. Puttermesser hated banter and flippancy; she had fled Harvey Morgenbluth's party because of banter and flippancy. Rupert was a Southerner—he wasn't infected by the New York patter. "Like a few other people in the world, he is much better than he seems—a man of heart and conscience wearing a mask of flippancy." That was how George Eliot had once described George Lewes—though not right away. Her first impression was of a miniature fop, gyrating his arms, too talkative, shallow. But Rupert was serious through and through.

"O.K.," Puttermesser said. "Let's do it."

She wasn't sure whether she had at just that moment agreed to marry Rupert Rabeeno.

"Let's not forget the honeymoon," he said.

"O.K." she said. "The honeymoon. You do it."

She watched him do the honeymoon. He did it fastidiously, with a sort of military instinct for the organization of it—slips of paper to mark the pages, volumes set in consecutive order ready to hand, quotations culled on cards. It was curious how well he had prepared himself. Out of the jumble they drew from every night—maps, letters, journals, biographies, memoirs, pamphlets, books and more books!—he was fashioning something clever, something out of the ordinary. A destiny. Rupert went about doing the honeymoon with the same heat of immanence he had blown into "The Death of Socrates." He read, yelled, sang, beamed. It was all for Johnny Cross, and Johnny Cross was only footnote and anticlimax. He wouldn't let her ride over his theory; she hadn't been able to deflect him. Puttermesser was jealous. Rupert had lavished nothing like this on George Lewes. Yet it really *was* happening again, a second round. Puttermesser was obliged to admit to herself the possibility that Rupert might be on the right track. The honeymoon of Johnny Cross and George Eliot was turning out to be purest mimicry of the honeymoon of George Lewes and George Eliot—the honeymoon that couldn't be called a honeymoon because there had never been a wedding.

Rupert did the wedding first. It was plausible to begin there, at the church at half-past ten in the morning. Lewes's son, two years younger than Johnny, gave George Eliot away. All of Johnny's relatives came—his sisters and their husbands and his cousins and his cousins' children. After the ceremony the bride and groom went back to the Priory with a pair of solicitors to sign their wills. Then they set out for Dover, to catch the next day's Channel steamer for Calais. In Dover they spent the night at the same hotel George Eliot and George Lewes had stayed at on their journey twenty-five years before. ("When Johnny was still a schoolboy!" Rupert crowed. "The same hotel!") When they reached Calais Johnny noticed how much younger and healthier George Eliot was looking—it was as if she were being renewed by every familiar mile along the old route. ("It *was* the old route," Rupert pointed out.) They were heading for Venice. Johnny took them down to Milan through Grenoble and Mount Cenis, exactly the itinerary Lewes had designed for what George Eliot had called their "deep wedded happiness." A week in Milan, as before, and then Venice.

Venice! "What stillness! What beauty!" George Eliot whispered. (Rupert, reading from George Eliot's journal, was whispering too.) "Looking out from the high window of our hotel on the Grand Canal, I felt that it was a pity to go to bed. Venice was more beautiful than romances had feigned. And that was the impression that remained and even deepened during our stay of eight days." But that was long ago, with Lewes. Their room was dizzily distant above the glistering water. In the afternoons the two Georges meandered through the basilica of San Marco, thinking it resplendent but barbaric. In the Scuola di San Rocco they were transfixed by the homely Mary of Tintoretto's "Annunciation." They bought lace and glass and jewelry, and floated around the lagoon in a gondola decked out with colored lanterns. Under the Rialto bridge the gondoliers rested their poles and warbled their lungs out, to bring up an echo out of the waves. ("*O sole mio,*" Rupert sang. "Now watch-a-John-nee," he sang.) Johnny Cross and George Eliot reached Venice a month after their wedding. It was fragrant early June. Sunlight and speckled cream palaces with ancient cracks running down their walls, and darkling shadows under the bridges—they intended to linger for an indefinite stretch of summer.

Instead they quit Venice in the second week.

"Panic," said Rupert. "The honeymoon's secret shock. Its mystery, its enigma."

"All right," Puttermesser said. "Get it over with. You don't have to milk it."

V. THE HONEYMOON

hey took a hotel directly on the Grand Canal and had all their meals brought to their room. Much of George Eliot's new wardrobe had come with them in trunks. She was cunningly and handsomely dressed, the elderly erupting collarbones covered by the lightest of wraps, the youthful waist disclosed. Lewes's death had left her ailing and frail; now she was marvelously restored. She was robust, she was tireless. She marched Johnny out to churches and galleries, and lectured him on architecture, painting, sculpture, history. He followed her ardently. He was proud of her, he was proud of himself. It was achieved. It was all exactly as it had been with Lewes. They stood before the same ugly Tintoretto Madonna and circled the gaudy bowels of San Marco. The June heat thickened; it began to feel tropical, though inside the old stone churches it was cool enough.

But there was something amiss with the air; the air was strange, and bad; there was something amiss with the drains. The view (though not so high up) from the windows of the Hôtel de l'Europe was just what it had been for that earlier pair, the two Georges—the Grand Canal knife-bright in the morning, blood-streaked at sundown, glowering at dusk. The canal below was itself no better than a drain. The air that rose from it was a sick cloud, a pustule of spew, a fume. The air was very bad. Their open windows gulped it in, especially at night when there was a flicker of wind. At night the stillness, the beauty: a pity to go to bed. Day after day they searched out gonging campaniles, out-of-the-way chapels, glazed portraits of holy babes and saints and bishops and doges, and when the heat ebbed slightly they rode round and round in gondolas, dazed by the blinding white cheeks of the palazzi. The beauty, the beauty!

In the evenings they settled in for supper at the snug oval table in their room. The napery was always blue, though the cloth, sweetened by some herbal soap, was changed daily, and a bowl of flowers, cut every afternoon, was set down on it to obscure the drifting smells of the canal. When the porter came to remove the trays—they ate simply, bread and fish and tea— Johnny and George Eliot were already sunk back into the *Inferno*. They had returned to Dante because it was clear that Johnny needed to brush up on his Italian now more than ever. Again she was lavishly attentive, especially to the difficulties of the syntax. She saw a kind of phrenological sturdiness in the coronal arch as his head lowered to the discipline of the page, a dolichocephalic head belonging to a long-boned six-footer. She was glad that he was as different in appearance from Lewes as could be—nothing about him was a reminder. Lewes had been little and vivacious—occasionally too quick—and brilliant and versatile. Johnny wasn't quick, but he was worldly enough; he was a banker who could tell when a man was bluffing. "Thou dost not know," she teased him once, "anything of verbs in Hiphil or Hophal or the history of metaphysics or the position of Kepler in science, but thou knowest best things of another sort, such as belong to the manly heart—secrets of lovingness and rectitude."

His character was solid, well-tried, he was steady and affectionate. It hurt her that she was so old, though *he* never thought of it. In Venice, despite all their happiness, she was consumed by it. Nothing could make her young again for Johnny: she knew it whenever she combed through the gray in her hair, or held the mirror to her eyes, with their bruised fleshiness run wild in the caverns beneath. Johnny was already well into balding, but the hair around his ears was dark and bunched with curls. His beard was frizzy. Behind it (his lovely mouth lost in the frizz) there perspired a striving boy with a nervous look. She noticed the look and understood. It was five weeks—almost six—since the wedding. They went to their beds every night as friends—he was her noble companion, her squire, her loyal pupil. How hard he tried! But he faltered over the Dante; she pointed with her finger, and he corrected himself. He was beginning to languish a little. The more she bloomed, the sounder she grew, the more he drooped. They had not yet lain as husband and wife.

It was exercise he was missing. He was, after all, a man of the outdoors, he played tennis and soccer and rowed and swam. Venice, all that water, and no rowing—it was only the sun-burned gondoliers and their indolent poles, it was only the dreamy floating, it was churches and galleries and pictures and history. Endless, endless history. Endless art. Endless beauty. He wanted some clean air, he wanted something strenuous.

("Pretty strenuous," Rupert intervened, "to keep on walking every minute in Lewes's shoes!")

He needed, he said, a swim. The Grand Canal was a cesspool; it was right at their doorstep, just under their windows, but you couldn't swim in the canal. The Lido wasn't far. They ought to get over to the Lido, the other side of it, where there was a good sandy beach. On the other side of the Lido they sat sedately on a bench, among ladies and their parasols, and watched the line of tidal waves. Johnny said he longed for a sea bath. The bath houses were nearby, and he had brought along his swimming costume. He would dash into the sea, have a decent splash, loosen up his limbs, and dash out again; it wouldn't occupy more than a quarter of an hour. She thought the weather wasn't suitable for such a venture: see, she said, raising the pedagogic finger that had so often guided him through the *Inferno*, you can feel the wind. I'm dying for a bathe, he said, it's the middle of June and hot as Hades. "Though the temperature is agreeable," she argued pleasantly, in that even, courteous contralto cherished by Lewes, and now cherished again by Johnny, "it has not the sort of heat that makes a plunge in cold water"—here she struggled to uncover a just simile—"as good as a drink to the thirsty."

They went back to their hotel. Johnny ordered an elaborate supper of lamb and tomatoes and pudding. The sommelier followed behind the porter with two small ruby bottles. She drank a glassful. Johnny drank several. He seemed roused, alert. She caught the thirst in his eye, and knew it was a shy celebration. The time had come. Over the last days she had observed his inwardness, his delicacy, his brooding. He had stood despondently before the very shapes and pictures that Lewes had looked on years before with so much brio and worshipful wit. Johnny was distracted. She was not surprised when, after the porter returned to clear the table, Johnny wiped his fingers with his blue napkin and declined to take up the Dante. She thought to tempt him with Comte—a diversion—but he turned away. She was discreet. The diffidence between them was natural. Until a month ago he had been a bachelor, doubtless no more celibate than any other handsome young fellow. But unlike herself—she had gone to bed with George Lewes for twenty-five years—he was new to the dignified rituals of conjugal intimacy. She made out some fresh tentativeness in him, a drawing away. It was restraint, it was mindfulness: he was whipping down animal nature until she was ready to give him a signal. She was a little frightened that he put the responsibility on her; but also excited. She, who was accustomed to leaning on a husband!

She retired into her dressing closet, a mirrored nook set apart, and chose a nightgown she had never worn before. She shut the door so that he would not see her too soon, and let down her hair. The nightgown feathered her bony shoulders with masses of concealing lace. In the looking glass it all at once struck her that, with her pleasant figure and loosened hair, she had the sweetness of a bride of twenty-two: she did not feel old at all.

When she came back to him she was disappointed that he was in his own bed. Nothing was different, it was like other nights. She had imagined he would be loitering at the window, say, listening for her, watching the black spirals the gondoliers' poles lanced into the water. She had imagined that he would wait until she hid herself—her little bride-self!—under her own coverlet, and then, hesitantly, tenderly, silently, he would set his limbs against her limbs at last. Instead he was a stiff hunch in the other bed. His trousers were folded on a chair. The small wind sent the window curtains grazing over his head.

On second thought she was charmed by this backwardness. She reminded herself that the initiative was hers, and how could it be otherwise? He was reticent, he was a boy. Perhaps she had been mistaken—possibly he had no experience at all. Below, sliding along the Grand Canal, a convoy of gondolas was flinging up laughter and voices and loud singing in an Italian remote from Dante's. Some locals on a lark, or a party of gondoliers and their wild girls. The air, bad as it was, swelled every sound into a roar. Then the line of gondolas passed and she was alone with him in the quiet. *"Bester Mann,"* she murmured, and added some syllables from Goethe—Goethe, whom Lewes had so much loved.

She sat on the bed beside him and caressed the circle of his ear. "Dearest, dearest John," she said. He kept his back to her and did not stir. She lifted the coverlet and lay down close against him. He had not put on his nightdress; he was still in that morning's shirt. He had discarded his cravat—it was a thick serpent on the floor. She touched her naked toes to the naked bulge of his calf; with one bold arm she embraced his wide chest. His upper body was hot. The leg was cold. She was right to have discouraged a swim—was he ill? "Johnny dear," she said. He did not answer. She was alarmed and faintly shamed: she removed her foot from his calf, and put her hand to the thigh of the other leg. It was cold, cold. Despite the trail of wind, the night was warm. It was growing warmer and warmer. The grooves flowing from her nose to the corners of her mouth, an old woman's creases, ran with sudden sweat; her armpits were sweated. She was not doing what he wished. She was too immodest, there was some mute direction he intended which she could not interpret. "Johnny," she pleaded, "dear boy, are you unwell? Look at me, Johnny dear, let me see your eyes."

He turned to her then, and showed her his eyes. They were unrecognizable—the rims of the lids as raw and bloody as meat, stretched apart like an animal's freshly slaughtered throat. Only the whites were there—the eyeballs had rolled off under the skin. An old secret shot through her like an intuition: a thing she had forgotten she knew. Johnny had a mad brother who was put away somewhere; Lewes had told her this long ago. Abruptly the eyeballs fell back into place. He was not normal. He was unwell. The bitter putrid wind, the drains, the polluted canal, the open window. He was breathing with urgency; every inhalation seemed hard won. She could not get enough air for herself. They were entombed in a furnace. Down below, the fleet of gondolas was returning, the raucous party from before, or another just as noisy—she heard blasts of laughter, and common street voices, and singing, and this time a tremulous guitar. She was standing now; her brain was shuttling so rapidly that it shook her—there was a doctor in Venice, Dr. Ricchetti, whom English people consulted. She ran to the bellpull on the farther wall, a little distance from the windows, to ring the hall porter.

A tremendous swipe—the scream of a huge bullwhip or instant cyclone—cut through naked space. A projectile of some kind—she had seen the smudge of it fly past her own back. A stone—a ball, a bone—tossed up by some loutish member of the crew below. Straight through the window. But the bed was empty. Johnny was not in it. The curtain was ripped away. The projectile had flown not into but out of the window. The projectile was Johnny. She bent over the window sill and shrieked. His elbows in their shirtsleeves dipped and rose, dipped and rose, like white fins. He was having his swim in the Grand Canal. The gondoliers mocked her cry: "Gianni, Gianni!" They leaped into the night water after him, but he would not be caught. For ten minutes they chased the white fins, and fished poor Johnny out by hooking his collar on one of their poles.

VI. THE MARRIAGE

Puttermesser had always hated that part. It was too ugly. She didn't like to think about it. Everything bright had ended with George Lewes's funeral. The rest was nothing. The rest didn't count. Johnny Cross, diagnosed as having been subject to "acute mental depression" on a single night of his life, came back to normal, never again had even a moment's worth of derangement, and died in 1924 at the age of eighty-four. But George Eliot weakened and failed. Six months after Johnny threw himself out of the window, she was dead.

Rupert remained cheerful. He didn't miss George Eliot; he had never admired her. Puttermesser too, under Rupert's influence, had begun to withdraw a little. Possibly George Eliot *was* a prig. She shouldn't have kept Johnny from bathing at the Lido; it was preposterous. She knew he was no good at foreign languages—he couldn't master Hebrew, and mixed up *hiphil* and *hophal*. Then why did she terrorize him with Dante? But Rupert was still harping on his idea—Johnny impersonating Lewes. After Venice, Rupert persisted, in the little time left to their marriage, George Eliot and Johnny Cross went back to the *very same house* Johnny had once helped Lewes buy. "The identical four walls!" he said. "Proof! What more do you want?"

Puttermesser was impatient. She was getting sick of Rupert's idea.

"George Lewes didn't jump into the Grand Canal, did he?" She pushed away the last volume of George Eliot's journal. "Johnny just couldn't face sex," she accused.

She looked around her bedroom. A flood of disorder. Heaps of those biographies and maps and memoirs and diaries. An engulfing crust on desk and dresser and floor. Miniature sky-scrapers on the window sills. It was enough. She wanted all those books out. Out, out! Back to the Society Library! The only tidy corner was over near her bed, where Rupert had stored several stacks of his postcards, straight as dominoes.

Puttermesser felt routed. It was as if they had come through a riot. Something tumultuous had happened; she was exhausted, as after intoxication or trance. Rupert had made it happen: this shivering precariousness, this tumult. He had cast out George Lewes, bright-souled George Lewes, and hauled Johnny Cross in. Rupert's impersonation of Johnny Cross impersonating Lewes! It was too alive. It jarred, it aroused. All through his telling it—his telling the honeymoon— she fidgeted, she kindled, she smarted. Rupert was a wizard. He made the honeymoon happen under her fingernails, at the root of her spine. She suffered. It was Lewes she wanted, only Lewes. Didn't the two of them—herself and Rupert—put their heads together under the lamp? Didn't they ignite every passage between them? Yet Rupert took Lewes from her and gave her Cross. Done! The honeymoon was done. Ugly, ugly. She hated it. She had always hated the honeymoon. Rupert pressed it under her fingernails, he pierced it like a pole to her spine.

Rupert said, "I finished up that Frick thing. Vegetarian tomato, all right?"

Puttermesser said she wasn't hungry for soup.

"Finished up yesterday. A nice Dutch landscape. I have to see Harvey about it when it dries—I'll ask him then. What's wrong with vegetarian tomato?"

"Ask Harvey what?"

"Well, it takes two witnesses. I'll get Harvey next time I'm up there. You figure out who else."

Puttermesser concentrated. "Two witnesses?"

"That's how many you need to get married."

So he meant it. She saw that he meant it. He had been serious about it before. He was serious about it now. Lewes! Lewes after all! Lewes had inspired him to it. Lewes had seduced him to it. Johnny Cross had gotten in the way, but the victory belonged to Lewes. Ideal friendship!

"I don't know anybody to ask," Puttermesser said.

"You know a lot of people."

"Not lately. Not this year."

"What about all those politicos in the Municipal Building?"

"I don't work there anymore and I'll never work there again. It was stupid to think I'd ever go back." She reflected on the webwork of her life. Her aunts and uncles were dead. The cousins, once a numerous and jolly gang, were scattered and aging. Half of them had been swallowed up by California—San Diego, Berkeley, Santa Monica, Lake Tahoe. By now most were senior citizens. And the receding gallery of all her old society: there they were, page after page in her little Woolworth address book, those ghosts of classrooms past and half-remembered offices, the detritus of her ascent to fifty-plus. Superannuated fellowship of gossip. Movie companions of yesteryear. They were all distant: either they were wrangling toward divorce, or they lived for their jobs, or they were tanning in the Caribbean, or they were absorbed in their children and their children's babies. Their children: the great genetic tide—the torrent—that separates those with offspring from those without. Three or four of Puttermesser's friends had already died in the lottery of early disease. In the roster of the living, there was not a soul she might want as witness to her wedding. Everyone was obsolete. She was clearing the way. A new life. Clean, pristine.

"But no, Rupert, you're the only one. It's only you. I don't have anybody else."

"I'm in lieu of the world," Rupert said.

She looked to see the mask of flippancy. But there was none.

"Oh no," she protested, and let his tidy head come into her arms. "You're not in lieu of anything."

Late on a Monday afternoon they took the subway all the way downtown to the Brooklyn Bridge station and went up to the second floor of the Municipal Building. The familiar corridors were wide, battered, gritty; it was as if the walls repelled light. To Puttermesser's surprise, the Marriage License Bureau was no longer there. It had crossed the road to Chambers Street and settled in a former bank the color of an elderly cat's scarred hide. On their way out, Puttermesser surveyed her old territory; inside what had been her own office only months ago, motes hung languidly on smuggled beads of illicit sun. Somewhere a toilet was running. It was relieving that no one recognized her. She was now among the generations of the politically vanished. Estrangement narrowed her throat; her eyes stung in the dimness. She marveled that she had once disgorged her law-yerly brain into this moribund organism, with its system of secretaries, clerks, assistants, its iron arteries shuffling with underlings.

On the trip back on the Number 6 line in the rush-hour crush, enveloped by the tunnel's grinding thunder, Puttermesser found herself smashed up against Rupert. The car swung like a cradle inside a concussion. Sunk into Rupert's warm shoulder, she felt herself without a past.

"A tomb," she told Rupert. "That place is a tomb."

"What?" he yelled out of the thunder.

"I'm thinking," Puttermesser shouted back, "that my savings are going down. I'll have to start again somewhere pretty soon. You too, Rupert."

"I don't *have* any savings."

The car screeched around a turn. "You can't do postcards for-ever," Puttermesser yelled. "Your talent's too big."

"It's just the right size to fit on a postcard. You should see the nice job Harvey's done on the Frick thing," he yelled back. "Harvey says O.K., did I tell you? About being a witness. And he knows two rabbis—one on the West Side who married him the first time, and one on the East Side who marred him the second time. On Second Avenue, in fact," Rupert hollered.

"You should give up the postcards. You should give up Harvey."

The train, arriving at a station, came to a violent stop. Putter-messer was catapulted away. A river of bodies rushed for the door. A forest of bodies sprang up between herself and Rupert.

"All right," Rupert mouthed from across the car, "I'll give up Harvey."

The wedding day was Wednesday—the rabbi on Second Avenue was free that night—and by then they had found the second witness.

Puttermesser said, "There used to be a thumping sound, remember? No, it was before you got here."

"Thumping sound?"

"Well, it's gone. It's been gone for weeks. She's quit doing it. I bet she wouldn't refuse us. She's the one," Puttermesser said. "She's right next *door*."

The math teacher explained that she had folded up her exer-cise mat for good. It was hard work, and didn't do the job. Anyhow it was too lonely. She was enrolled nowadays in one of those new health clubs for singles over on Madison. Her name was Raya Lieberman; she wouldn't at all mind, she said, helping out at a wedding, as long as it was after school. It was true she had Math Club on Wednesdays, but she was perfectly happy to skip it for once. "I've got as good an extracurric supervisory attendance record as anybody," she assured Puttermesser. "The best, considering what comes down the pike these days."

The rabbi's study was on East Ninetieth, in his apartment. On the telephone he had inquired whether a modest ceremony at 9:30 p.m. in his study at home would be satisfactory, given that it was such a small wedding party and given also—he had a homiletic inflection—that the congregational sanctuary couldn't in any case be secured in the evening on such short notice; and Rupert had agreed. It was beginning to snow again, so the four of them went by taxi—the bride and groom, and the two witnesses. Puttermesser sat in the back seat between the math teacher and Harvey Morgenbluth. Rupert, straight-spined in his stately hat and capelike raincoat, was up front with the driver. Puttermesser had on her best black patent-leather high heels. Rupert and the two witnesses were all wearing their galoshes.

"You ever done a thing like this before?" Harvey Morgenbluth asked Raya Lieberman, leaning across Puttermesser.

"I've been a bride, but not a witness. You?"

"Never done anything like this. How many times?"

"How many times what?"

"How many times you been married?" Harvey Morgenbluth urged across Puttermesser's lap.

"Once."

"With me it's twice. This is my second rabbi we're on the way to."

It surprised Puttermesser that Harvey Morgenbluth was a familiar apparition. She was habituated to his camel's walk and translucent flushed ears and phlegmatic oxlike forehead, well scored by parallel clef lines. It was not unusual for her to run into the math teacher on the way to the incinerator closet or the elevator, but now it dawned on Puttermesser that the flustered-seeming man whom she had often noticed weaving among the shabby old sofas in the lobby, hauling big square cartons, was Harvey Morgenbluth. Occasionally he pushed them on a dolly. No doubt some of those cartons contained Rupert's postcards. A sourness rose in her. Four inches by six; that was their size. That Frick landscape, a spacious van Ruysdael—a bridge, the gnarled roots of a tree, dark clouds, strange light (dawn or dusk or afternoon before rain), a hunter, a fisherman, a long road, deep vista, two riders, one mounted, the other standing by, red cloak thrown over a shoulder (Rupert loved cloaks, capes, togas), black horse crosswise in the road, blocking it, blacking it, dotting it, swallowing up sky and earth—all that mastery shrunk to four inches by six. Rupert on the side of diminishment, how could it be? At the Met, that first time, hadn't she seen in him voluminous will, the will to be proxy for the punctilious windings and reverberations of huge precursors? Was Rupert with all his amplitude always to be reduced via the technologies of Harvey Morgenbluth? He had promised on the subway to give up Harvey Morgenbluth. Rupert had never explained why a reënactment had to be a dwindling. If it was a dwindling, how could you call it a reënactment?

Puttermesser reminded herself that it was normal to be jittery on the way to one's wedding. Who knew what unhappy divinations Rupert was hurling at her in the front seat, from under his cloak?

Harvey Morgenbluth, still heavy across Puttermesser's knees, was trying to find out from the math teacher if she was available for dinner and a movie next Sunday. "We could go over to the Baronet on Third, or the Beekman on Second. Or look, I've got *Gone With the Wind* on tape, how about it?"

Puttermesser said briskly, "Don't you do those Sunday parties anymore?"

"Winding down, haven't had one in a bunch of weeks. The kids drove everybody crazy. And you couldn't get a type like Rupert—Rupert's a pretty open guy, but he wasn't interested."

Raya Lieberman said, "Nobody opens up nowadays. It's hard for people to be in touch. Everyone's a lonesome atom."

Harvey Morgenbluth whistled. "A lonesome atom, my God.

You *said* it." He turned to Puttermesser. His flushed ears were all attention. "By the way, how's the roach problem? You really want to beat 'em, try sodium fluoride around the pipes."

The rabbi's name was Stewart Sonnenfeld. He introduced Jill, his wife, and his teen-age son, Seth, who was at that moment writing a report on Chaucer's "Prologue" for his English class. The four poles of the wedding canopy were held up by Harvey Morgenbluth, Raya Lieberman, Jill Sonnenfeld, and Seth Sonnenfeld. Puttermesser had retrieved her mother's wedding ring from an old felt wallet she kept inside an empty plastic margarine container at the back of the vegetable bin in the refrigerator, to foil a burglar. The rabbi had cautioned Rupert to bring along his own wine-glass for the ceremony, so that morning Puttermesser had hurried into Woolworth's to buy one. Jill Sonnenfeld wrapped it in a paper napkin inside a paper bag, and Rupert stamped on it with his galosh. It exploded with a gratifying convulsion. In Puttermesser's apartment afterward Harvey Morgenbluth and Raya Lieberman each drank a styrofoam cup of champagne (Harvey's present) and ate a piece of wedding cake—Puttermesser made do with an Entenmann's chocolate layer from the supermarket on Third—and then the two witnesses went off together.

"Into the night," Puttermesser said. "They've gone off into the night, imagine that. Maybe it'll take."

Rupert was poking in the corner closet where he kept his equipment; he was dragging out his satchel. "Maybe into the night," Rupert said. "More likely upstairs to 6-C."

"*We* took," Puttermesser said.

Her heart—her fleshly heart—was curled around itself, like a spiraled loaf of hot new bread. Inside the cavity that rocked it, this good bread was swelling. Puttermesser waited for Rupert's head to come into her arms, against her heart's loaf. She waited for his voice, his dark reading voice, with its sharp click that could cut her with happiness, like a beak. The living, plain, pitiful flesh. Sometimes, for all the uproar of his history (he had handed over every winding of his life to her; he kept nothing back), he seemed new-made—as if she had ejected him from a secret spectral egg lodged in her frontal lobe, or under her tongue where the sour saliva gave birth to desire. He was her own shadow and fingerprint. She had painted him on her retina in her sleep. She felt him to be the smothered croak in her throat, a phlegm of chaos burst out of her lung. He had lived too long in her nerves, and her nerves were all wired to the transcendent. Desire, desire! She and Rupert—both of them—were too tentative.

He had pulled out his easel, and left it on the floor with the satchel. He crossed the living room to stand at the window. A hard wind hit the glass. There he was, mooning down at the snowy street below; she wondered if he was looking to see whether Harvey Morgenbluth and Raya Lieberman had really gone off into the night. The loaf in the middle of her chest ballooned; it grew and grew. Jealousy. Rupert's head struck her as still another loaf, all brightly honeyed against the snow-streaked panes. He had been born into the world two decades after her own birth. A long, long meadow, all grassy-green, stretched before him. Under his mustache the two points of his mouth were as elastic as a child's.

She saw that he was dusted over with gloom. He unbuckled one of his galoshes. He seemed indecisive about the other, but he shook it free. The race was behind them, the dream was dreamed. They had arrived at arrival. All wedding nights taste of letdown.

Puttermesser took off her black patent-leather high heels. They had walked in the snow only a little—out of the taxi, into the lobby—but her feet were still damp. She shivered from the feet up. She went into the bedroom to fetch her furry winter slippers. The dresser mirror arrested, fleetingly, the figure of a woman. How quickly that woman fled!

When she came back into the living room, Rupert was wearing his galoshes again. He was wearing his capelike raincoat and his stately hat. He had his folded-up easel under his arm and his satchel in his hand.

There was something in his face she recognized. An indifference had seeped into the gloom. It was as if she had turned invisible. It was as if he did not recognize her: *that* was what she recognized. A snub—almost a snub. His face hurt her. His youth hurt her.

"Rupert," she said. "What are you doing, Rupert?"

"I can't stay."

"You have to."

"I can't. I can't, Ruth. I can't stay."

"Rupert, take off your coat. Please, Rupert, please."

"No," he said. It was not indifference. It was a burning. He was inside a furnace; he was speaking out of a furnace.

Puttermesser called after him, "Rupert! What are you *doing*?"

"I can't stay."

In the little vestibule he set down his satchel and aimed the easel directly in front of him, clutching it like a burning beam; like a spear. He raised it high and plummeted after it back into the living room. He was running for the window. Puttermesser feared he would fling his lance straight through the glass. But he stopped. He put down the easel and with both hands lifted the window wide. A shock of wind knocked over the stack of styrofoam cups on the sill. The snow flew in, wet as a waterfall.

"Rupert, Rupert," Puttermesser pleaded. "Take off your coat. Shut the window. For God's sake, shut the window!"

He gave her his whole look then. She was falling into the tiny black holes at the center of his clean powerful eyes. She was falling and falling, but instead of vertigo or delirium or disorder there was only the candor of her own intelligence. She understood that he was altogether sane, altogether calculating, and as jubilant as a mathematician in the act of confirming an equation.

He picked up his things and walked out the door.

At the open window, hanging over the sill to catch sight of

him dwindling in the street, Puttermesser squinted into the snow. It was pointless to call down to him as George Eliot had called down into the Grand Canal, but anyhow she called and called; the snow blew into her mouth. She leaned into the wetness until her hair was all white with snow.

A copyist, a copyist!

PUTTERMESSER
AND THE
MUSCOVITE
COUSIN

I. HISTORY

verywhere it was a time of collapse: powers were falling, one after another. In Canada, at the edge of a forest, two ancient oaks (saplings when Caesar was crossing the Rubicon, said the Ottawa newscaster) came heaving down, struck from crown to root by a frenzy of lightning. For days the bitter smell of charred bark and ashen leaves drifted past nearby towns, arousing the nostrils of nervous dogs. In New York, a pair of famous editors, intimidating and weighty as emperors, in a flash of the guillotine were suddenly displaced; overnight their names tumbled into blackest obscurity. The young ruled, ruled absolutely; the outmoded old were forgotten, they were diminished and dismissed, and whoever spoke of their erstwhile renown spoke of vapor.

And on the earth's far-off other cheek, beyond the Pripet Marshes, beyond the Dnieper and the Volga, in the very eye of Moscow, where the cold cellar walls of Lubyanka Prison were wont to break out into pustules of bloody mold, like executioner's mushrooms, Communism was cracking, failing. The Soviet Union was on its way out, impaired, impaled, stumbling, exhausted, moribund—though who, in the ninth decade of the twentieth century, dared to suspect the death of the Kremlin?

Yet there were signs: fascism was pressing through the fissures. In Red Square, a mocking phalanx of blackshirts openly paraded. Thugs invaded the Writers' Union, yelling insults to Jews. Fossil Cossacks, old Czarist pogromchiks, renewed, restored!

Ruth Puttermesser, white-haired, in her sixties—retired, unmarried, cranky in the way of a woman alone—had no premonition about the demise of the Soviet Union; yet she believed in collapse. The skin on the inside of her elbows drooped into pleats; her jowl was loose and bunched, as if governed by a drawstring; the pockets under her eyes hung, and the ophthalmologist, attempting to dilate her pupils, had to lift the lids with deliberate fingers. All things fallen, elasticity gone. Age had turned Puttermesser on its terrible hinge.

She was as old now as her long-dead father: her father who, fleeing the brutish Russia of the Czars, had left behind parents, sisters, brothers—Puttermesser's rumored Moscow relations, aunts, cousins, a schoolboy uncle, all swallowed up in the Bolshevik silence, dwindled now into their archaic names and brittle cardboard-framed photographs. Puttermesser's Moscow grandmother, a blotched brown blur in a drawer: wrinkled Tatarish forehead, sunken toothless mouth; a broken crone, dim as legend. "Do not write anymore," Puttermesser's grandmother pleaded as the thirties wore on: "My eyes are gone. I am old and blind. I cannot read." This was the last letter from Moscow; it lay under the old Russian photos in an envelope blanketed by coarsely printed stamps. Each stamp displayed the identical profile of a man with a considerable mustache. Stalin. Puttermesser knew that the poet Osip Mandelstam had likened that mustache to a cockroach: whereupon Stalin ordered him murdered. Isaac Babel was murdered after months of torture and a phony trial. Mikhoels the Yiddish actor was murdered. All the Russian Yiddish poets were murdered on a single August night in 1952. Shot in the cellars of the Lubyanka.

And between Moscow and New York, a steady mute fright. The hidden warning in Puttermesser's grandmother's plaint was clear. *Stop! We are afraid of a letter from America! They will take us for spies, you endanger us! Keep away!* The old woman was famous among her children for eyesight so sharp and precise that she could see the alertly raised ears of a squirrel on a high branch in a faraway clump of trees. Puttermesser's father too had owned such a pair of eyes. Blue, pale as watery ink. Her poor orphaned papa, cut off forever from the ties of his youth: from his little brother Velvl, ten years old, his head in the photo shaved in the old Russian style, his school uniform high-collared and belted, with a row of metal buttons marching down his short chest. A family sundered for seventy years—the Great War, the Revolution, Stalin's furies, the Second World War, the Cold War: all had intervened. Puttermesser's papa, dying old of stroke, longed for his mother, for Velvl, for his sisters Fanya, Sonya, Reyzl, for his brothers Aaron and Mordecai. Alone in America with no kin. Never again to hear his father's thin fevered voice. Continents and seas lay between Moscow and New York, and a silence so dense and veiling that in the three decades since her papa's death Puttermesser had almost forgotten she had Russian relations. They were remote in every sense. She never thought of them.

II. A JOKE OUT OF MOSCOW

n the midst of that unstable period known as perestroika, when strange acts were beginning to flicker outward from a shadowy Soviet Union into the world at large, Puttermesser received a telephone call from Moscow. Half a century without a letter; not a syllable, not a breath; and now, out of the blue, out of the void, out (it felt) of *time*, the telephone rings (prosaically, unmiraculously) in an ordinary New York apartment in the East Seventies—Moscow! Forbidden, locked, sullen Moscow. Unearthly Moscow! A woman, panting,

high-pitched, overwrought, is speaking in German, and Putter-messer is able to follow most of it; hadn't she, after all, read Schiller's *Maria Stuart* in college? Also Goethe's *Hermann und Dorothea*? The panicky electric voice belongs to Zhenya, the daughter of the late Sonya—Sonya, the younger sister of Putter-messer's papa. Zhenya is Puttermesser's own first cousin! Tremulous, as if distance were composed of vibrating particles, Zhenya explains that she has no English, that she assumes Put-termesser has no Russian, that Zhenya herself, though now a pensioner, has been a teacher of German, but oh, the danger cannot be named, everything must be understood! *"Rette mein Kind!"* Zhenya wails, and Puttermesser hears, in the static of these Moscow sobs, her papa's blood crying up from the ground.

And so it was arranged: Puttermesser was to save Zhenya's child. She believed she understood from what. The old dark-nesses were creeping out all over a loosened Soviet Union: who could predict what mean-spirited ghosts of antique hatred were yet to be awakened? Certain newspaper accounts began to jump out at Puttermesser. In Kiev, young men passing under a window are flooded by the passionate sounds of a violin; they crash into the musician's flat and beat him unconscious. In Moscow, brainy students are shut out of the university by a relentless quota. Schoolchildren have their noses bloodied to the taunts of *Zhid! Zhid!*

And in New York—in the very hour of perestroika, of glas-nost!—Puttermesser picks up a joke that is at this moment circu-lating through Moscow: *Because there is a rumor of a delivery of meat, a long queue forms outside a butcher shop. After a four-hour wait, the manager emerges to address the crowd: "The meat hasn't arrived yet, but there won't be enough for everyone, so all the Jews must leave." Another four hours pass, and out comes the manager: "No delivery yet, but there won't be enough, so all the chronic grumblers against the regime must leave." Another four hours, and finally the manager announces: "Sorry, comrades, but there will be no meat*

*delivery after all. Everyone go home!" And a great moan rises up:
"Wouldn't you know it? The Jews are always getting favored!"*

How that poisonous joke with its bitter truths reverberated!
How Puttermesser felt for Zhenya's child! She set herself, over
several months, the task of letter-writing. She wrote to the State
Department, she wrote to her Congresswoman, she wrote to
her two Senators, she wrote to HIAS and NYANA. She visited
offices and consulted bureaucrats and filled out forms. She emptied a closet and bought extra pillows and sheets and pushed
aside chairs and hauled bookcases and made room for a new
sofabed. She listened in the subway for the consonants of Russian—once she grabbed the arm of a startled passenger and
asked for the story of his life; but the fellow turned out to be a
Pole. She went everywhere for advice, telephoned strangers,
was warned against the obduracy of officialdom and the barriers
to emigrés. Every day she schemed for the refugee's deliverance;
and at night, drained, insomniac, it sometimes seemed to Puttermesser that she could switch on, like a light discovering a hidden
stage, any scene from the past.

Under this aridly willed ray she saw her papa on a bed, lying
there dressed on top of the quilt, with his hands under his head,
the elbows jutting outward. He did not speak at all; his pale eyes
were open to nothing. He never blinked. It was three o'clock
and very bright; a big housefly was in the room, slamming itself
against the window, the wall, the high mirror above the dresser.
In the middle of the afternoon Puttermesser's papa had gone to
bed to mourn. His mother was dead—Puttermesser's Moscow
grandmother, whom she had never known, except as that dried-
out brown photo in the drawer. So many dead: Puttermesser's
papa; her papa's strangely Tatar mother; his shy and scholarly
father, also reduced to a cracked old Russian photo (a sick man's
face, solemn); all the lost aunts and uncles, the Muscovites, the
wartime sufferers; Velvl in his school uniform, with large round
pale eyes exactly like her papa's. Distant, oppressed, eclipsed.

The scattered graveyards. Puttermesser's papa and mama in Staten Island; and where were all those others, how to imagine the cemeteries of Moscow?

The refugee arrived at one o'clock in the morning in the middle of October, ten months after Zhenya's howl of *"Rette mein Kind!"* There was a night wind with a cold lick in its tail. In the empty street in front of her building Puttermesser stood waiting for the taxi from Kennedy. Wary, she kept fingering the wallet in the pocket of her cardigan.

The driver, without being asked, carried the refugee's bags— half a dozen of them—into the elevator.

"How much?" Puttermesser said.

"No problem. Fare's all taken care of."

"But she hasn't got any dollars—"

"She gimme *this*. Beats anything," the driver said, and pulled out a round plastic object. The face of it showed the head of Lenin against a background of the Kremlin, with two red stars in a silvery sky.

"It's only a watch? A cheap quartz watch."

"You kiddin'? It's outta Mars, where d'you get to *see* a thing like this?"

Puttermesser was impressed. The driver was right; the watch was a trophy. And the barter system had returned to Manhattan.

III. A SOVIET MARTIAN

er name was Lidia. She had flown on Aeroflot from Moscow to Bucharest to Prague. In Prague she switched to British Airways, which took her to Ireland for a two-hour refueling; after Ireland and before New York she landed in Washington—her ticket was a complication of airports. Her visa was a complication of fibs: she had convinced the American consul in Moscow that she would surely return—she was leaving behind a husband and two children. Sergei was the husband, the children were Yulia and Volodya. But she had no husband; it was all an invention. In reality Volodya was her boyfriend. The consul, she reported, was a nasty man. He looked at her as if she were a nasty worm. He thought everyone who applied for a visa was trying to put something over on him; he suspected that all of Moscow intended, hook or crook, to pour through the sacred gates of America and vanish behind them.

"You told him you had *children?*" Puttermesser marveled. "You didn't have to say a thing like that."

"I want he give visa."

"When the visa's up we'll get you in legally. I've been working on it. If we need to, we'll get an immigration lawyer," Puttermesser said; the fervor of salvation rose in her. "We'll ask for asylum."

Save my child! But it was no longer Zhenya's voice; it was the voice of Puttermesser's papa, longing for the remnant of the lost. The pathos of their fate, the Bolshevik upheavals, the German siege of Moscow, the hunger, the Doctors' Plot, the terror. *Rette mein Kind!*

"I get job," the refugee said. "I clean house for womans."

Puttermesser said doubtfully, "Would Zhenya want you to do something like that?"

"Mama, ha! What mama want!"

The refugee's laugh was a conflagration; Puttermesser was alarmed by such an eruption of mockery. There she stood, the Muscovite cousin, in the middle of Puttermesser's living room, a small space narrowed by the new sofabed and shrunken still more by these heaps of suitcases and bundles and boxes tied with hairy Russian rope. An ironic beauty of thirty-three, trailing clouds of alien air—or, if not air, some nameless extraterrestrial medium. A Martian. She looked all around, fierce and canny; she took things in. Puttermesser felt herself being tested and judged by those sliding satiric eyes the color of Coca-Cola, and by that frail china-thin nose ending in a pair of tiny tremulous nostrils. It was the longish nose of a Mesopotamian princess.

Her full name was Lidia Klavdia Girshengornova. She was an experienced biochemist—*eine Sportsdoktorin*, Zhenya had said, but after a while Puttermesser understood that this meant something like laboratory technician. She traveled all over the Soviet Union with her team—"my guys," she called them, big coarse country boys, half-literate and wild. A B-level track team trying to work itself up to international status and meanwhile playing the local competition. Lidia tested their urine daily for forbidden steroids—or else, Puttermesser speculated (she had read how the Soviets pumped up their athletes), it was Lidia's job to make sure that her guys were properly dosed. She was careful not to drink with them, but she wrestled and joked around, and she liked going to distant cities, Tbilisi, Kharkov, Vladivostok, Samarkand; especially she liked the trip to the Caucasus, where the hotels had a hint of Europe. She was amazingly up-to-date. Her lipstick was very red, and her hair was almost red, short over the ears, looped over one eyebrow. She wore black tights and a long turtleneck sweater that fell to the tops of her thighs. Puttermesser had often seen this costume on Lexington Avenue at lunchtime, near Bloomingdale's, and privately wondered at how *normal* her young cousin seemed: hadn't she been swaddled on a board at birth, like all infants in backward Russia? Only her shoes were unmistakably foreign. They smelled of Soviet factory.

IV.   THE GREAT EXPOSITION

n the morning Puttermesser set out her usual breakfast: toast and peanut butter. Lidia, suspicious, spread the yellow-brown stuff and made a horrible face. "What you call thees?" "You've never had peanut butter?" "*Nyet,*" said Lidia, so Puttermesser took her out to the supermarket. At a quarter to nine it was mostly deserted.

"Pick out whatever appeals to you," Puttermesser offered.

But Lidia, oblivious, in trance, was gaping down the long banks of freezers with their tall foggy doors, behind which lay mounds of spinach and broccoli and string beans and peppers and peas in richly bulging plastic bags. Her little nostrils fluttered as she moved past brilliant boxes of cereals and orderly shining rows of bottled olives and pickles and mustards, past gardens of berries and melons. And when Puttermesser put out her hand to pluck up a packet of cheese, Lidia whirred out a furtive whisper. "No! Not to take!"

"What's the matter? It's Jarlsberg, you might like it."

"They will *see!*"

"For God's sake, we're not under surveillance, we're here to *buy*, don't you understand?"

It developed that Lidia Klavdia Girshengornova had supposed they were visiting an exhibition hall. In Moscow, she explained, there were on occasion such dazzling fairs and expositions: a great public cavern set aside for gargantuan demonstrations of abundance, mainly foreign goods, strictly guarded. Hundreds came to gaze and marvel. To steal from a display, Lidia said, even the smallest item, could land you in prison.

The refugee had other misapprehensions. She thought the telephone was bugged; she was certain there was an official "listener" always on duty. She was innocent of polyester, and was astonished that the bed sheets were never ironed. She believed that every transaction had to be accompanied by a "gift." Her cases and boxes were cornucopias of shawls, scarves, colorful swaths of all sizes; varnished scarlet-and-black ladles and spoons hand-carved out of hardwood, decorated all over with flowers; ugly but clever little plaster ducks and cows; nested hollow dolls shaped like eggs, without arms or legs, each encapsulating a smaller doll, until the last stood alone, a tiny thumbelina. A circle of red spotted each miniature cheek, and each round head wore a painted babushka. Puttermesser was enchanted by these merry wooden faces redolent of old magical tales: dappled northern forests, silvery birdcalls and fragrant haycocks, a baba yaga's dark whim in an out-of-the-way cottage.

But Lidia gave her bundles an instantly entrepreneurial name: Russian folk art, she called it, with a salesman's snap in her voice.

Her voice was shrewd and deep, close to mannish. Puttermesser again felt herself being read by this voice; it took her measure with the speed of an abacus. Lidia, watching Puttermesser watching her unpack, held up one of the painted egglike dolls. "You like?" she asked. "You keep," and handed over the hollow doll with all its interior brood. A businesslike gesture. A payment of some kind.

Business was on Lidia's mind. "I tell before, I want clean for womans," she pressed.

"But you can do better than that. Something in a laboratory, something that could get to be permanent—"

"Just like mama!" Lidia laughed. She drew out a portfolio of photographs, many of them ragged and worn; Zhenya had sent them to show to Puttermesser. And here was Zhenya herself, sorrowing under summer sunlight, a puddle of shade under nose and lower lip. A dowdy plump aging woman in a patterned dress with a big collar. Flat face, eyes with the median Asian lid. Uncomplicated mouth, tightly shut; it made a narrow line. You could not imagine what this mouth thought or desired. Puttermesser's own cousin Zhenya, her papa's true niece! But the woman in the snapshot seemed generations removed. She looked old-fashioned. She looked . . . *Soviet*. The others, Puttermesser's papa's brothers and sisters, the abandoned, the longed-for, did not. Puttermesser was inflamed by the others—they were eternal, it was as if she was entering her papa's mind. Fanya, Sonya, Reyzl, Aaron, Mordecai! And Velvl's whitish pupils, his school uniform with the metal buttons, the very same picture Puttermesser had known all her life. Sonya's son, Lidia said, at twenty-one had been on a ship in the Great Patriotic War; a German torpedo sank it. And what had become of Velvl? Run over and killed by a Moscow tramcar in 1951. He left no children, and his widow married a Georgian. There were no happy stories among these photos. So many familiar pale round eyes. The sisters were redheads; Velvl was white-blond.

An ache fell over Puttermesser. It was grief for her papa's grief.

V. MORE HISTORY

very year in the spring, Lidia said, Zhenya made a pilgrimage to the grandmother's grave. When the Bolsheviks came, the grandmother's little dry-goods shop was taken away. It was no bigger than a cubicle, confiscated from the class enemy by the Soviet Peoples. There was winter hunger everywhere, so the grandmother took to peddling in torn shoes that had once belonged to her dead husband.

"What was she peddling?" Puttermesser asked.

Lidia shrugged. She knew only that it was illegal to sell anything privately; it was profiteering. The grandmother stood in the street at dusk and rattled the kopecks in her pocket, hoping to attract the day's last customer. A man in an official-looking black cap with a badge on it approached. He seized her wrist and manacled it to his own, and pulled her behind him over the hardened snow—but on the way she felt in her pocket with her free hand for a hole she had once sewn up, and broke through the threads, and dropped her few kopecks, one by one, through the open slit. They came to a terrifying building, all black stone on the outside, all cracked linoleum on the inside, where a man with a blue-and-gold collar—he seemed to be some sort of soldier—sat on a high bench and glared down at her. "Black marketeer! Capitalist! You sold goods, I saw you!" the man in the cap yelled. The soldier on the high bench demanded that she produce her profits. But her pockets were empty. "You make a fool of me?" the man in the cap yelled; he gave the grandmother a smack and let her go.

Lidia told this story indifferently. It was one of Zhenya's secrets, the kind she sometimes whispered behind the stove; it belonged to long ago. But Puttermesser stored it away with a pang: *this* was what had befallen her papa's mother! A starving wraith in her eighties, in broken shoes, peddling in the snow. (Her papa, separated by so many decades, by oceans and continents, had known nothing of it. Mourning, he had gone to bed in the middle of the day. The big housefly, looking to escape, slammed against the mirror. It slammed and slammed. There was no way out.)

VI. INTERVIEWS

idia had brought with her, for emergencies, a Russian-English dictionary. She never consulted it. It appeared she understood everything, and in her peculiar fragmented English she could convey almost anything. She had learned these jigsaw phrases in a night class, but had left after only five weeks—when she was not on the road with her team there were so many better things to do on bitter winter evenings in Moscow. You could go to someone's room and warm yourself with drink. A party, with strangers, for which you paid an entry fee. Or, rather, you could drink if you came with your own bottle of vodka. She had met her boyfriend in such a room, a largish room in a communal flat with high old ceilings stippled with grimy plaster roses; before the Revolution it had been part of a grand house owned by aristocrats. Her boyfriend, Lidia said, was really *after* her; he was always pestering her to get married.

"Are you sure he isn't just looking for a chance to get out of the country?" Puttermesser asked.

Lidia beamed; surprisingly, her teeth were magnificent.

"He want go Australia," she said, and slid into laughter.

Sometimes the telephone would ring at four in the morning, and then Lidia leaped up from her sofabed to catch it before it could wake Puttermesser. But Puttermesser always woke, and it was always Volodya.

"Can't he *count*?" Puttermesser said testily. "Doesn't he know what time zone he's in?"

"He afraid I stay in America," Lidia said. "He afraid I not come back."

"Well, isn't that exactly the point?"

"Just like mama!"

Mama, Puttermesser was learning, was preposterous. It was not admirable to be just like mama.

"Please, now we speak business," Lidia urged. "I want clean for womans."

The interviews began. Puttermesser put up a notice in the elevator:

> Companionable Russian emigrée, intelligent,
> charming, lively, willing to clean house,
> babysit, general light chores. Reasonable.
> Inquire 3-C from 8 p.m.

Then she blotted out "Russian emigrée"—it was too literary, and smacked of Paris or Berlin in 1920 (she thought of Nabokov)—and wrote instead: "Soviet newcomer." The neighbors streamed in; Puttermesser was acquainted with few of them. A couple arrived carrying a small girl in pajamas and asked for a pot to warm milk in while they looked the Russian over. The child broke into a steady shriek and Lidia dismissed them with a scolding; she didn't want to deal with *that*, she said. The bachelor journalist from 7-G, who occasionally nodded at Puttermesser in the lobby, confessed that he already had perfectly satisfactory help; what he was interested in was a chance to hear a grass-roots view of Gorbachev.

"Gorbachev!" Lidia scoffed. "Everybody hate Gorbachev, only stupid peoples in America like Gorbachev," and threw open the substantial valise that occupied her nightly. It was crammed with cosmetics of every kind—eyebrow pencils, rouge, mascara in all colors, a dozen lipsticks, hairnets, brushes, ointments and lacquers in tubes and tubs. Puttermesser could identify few of these emulsions and was helpless before all of them. (But ah, look, so they *did* have such contrivances in the puritanical socialist state!)

The journalist, offended, retorted that Gorbachev was certainly an improvement on, say, Brezhnev; but Lidia went on creaming her pointed little chin.

Puttermesser turned all around, like a cat in a cage. There was no place to sit down in her own living room. A pair of young men from the top floor were reclining on Lidia's sofabed. One of them inquired whether she knew how to use a vacuum cleaner. Lidia laughed her scornful laugh—did they think she was a primitive?—and asked how much they would pay per hour.

It was difficult to tell who was interviewing whom. Lidia had a head for numbers. She was quick, she could mentally convert dollars into rubles in an instant. She was after money, that was the long and the short of it. Day after day, Puttermesser tried to lure her cousin out—to a museum, or to the top of the Empire State Building. That would be a sight! But Lidia lifted an apathetic shoulder: she liked *things*, not pictures. And she had seen the New York skyline in the movies. She was waiting for evening, when the interviews would resume. The doorbell shrilled until midnight. What she wanted was to clean house and get dollars.

She settled finally on the family in 5-D. It was a three-bedroom apartment; there were three children. The husband did something in computers, and four times a week the wife took a bus downtown to Beth Israel Hospital, to work as a volunteer in pediatrics. They were a socially-conscious, anti-violence couple; though easy and unrestrained with their children, they banned toy guns, monitored and rationed television, and encouraged reading and chess. Two of the children had piano lessons, the third was learning the violin. "Call me Barbara," the wife told Lidia, and embraced her, and said what a privilege it was for her family to be in a position to provide a job for a refugee. She promised that they were going to be friends, and that Lidia would soon feel at home in 5-D—but if she had any anxieties or complaints she should immediately speak up: there was nothing that could not be negotiated or adjudicated. Lidia was impatient with all this effortful goodness and virtuous heat. She had chosen the Blauschilds only because they had offered her more dollars than anyone else.

"Varvara, ha!" Lidia yelped after her first day. "Foolish womans, teacher come for music, children hate!" And another time: "Dirty house! Children room dirty!" She had never in her life seen such disorder: shoes and shirts and toys left in heaps on the floor, every surface sticky, the sink always mountainous with unwashed pans and dishes, papers scattered everywhere. She disapproved of Varvara altogether—why would anyone run out to work for nothing? And leave behind such a vast flat, so many rooms, and all for one family, they lived like commissars! Only dirty! The chaos, the slovenliness!

"You don't have to *do* this," Puttermesser said. "You didn't come to American to clean houses, after all. Look, we need to go see the people at the agency. To get you past the visa stage. It's about time we took care of it."

Lidia's brown eyeballs slid cautiously sideways in their long shells. She lifted her shoulder and dropped it again.

VII. ANOTHER INTERVIEW

P uttermesser was privately glad of the four hours Lidia spent upstairs in 5-D every afternoon; it was a relief not to be obliged to visit so incessantly. Sometimes Lidia would talk of God and His angels, sometimes of the splendid old churches the Revolution had destroyed; and now and then she pulled out a certain dream book, which, if read prayerfully and with concentration, could foretell the future. Lidia was a believer in the world of the sublime. She was moved by icons, by Holy Mother Russia. She told how she often wept at Eastertime, and how Jesus had once appeared to her in a dream, looking exactly like a holy painting on an ancient icon. At such moments poor elderly Puttermesser, with all her flying white hair, saw her Muscovite cousin as some errant Chekhovian character misplaced in a New York living room: *"How lovely it is here!" said Olga, crossing herself at the sight of the church.*

"But there's another side to all that, isn't there?" Puttermesser said. "What about the Beylis case?"

Lidia had never heard of the Beylis case.

Puttermesser, a reader of history, explained: "The blood libel. Pure medieval insanity. A Jew named Mendel Beylis was accused in a Russian court of killing a Christian child in order to drain his blood. Imagine, a thing like that, and in modern times, 1913! The clergy never intervened. So much for Holy Mother Russia."

Lidia sent out her riddling smile, half secretive, half derisive. "Not happen now."

"And the attack on the Writers' Union? That was just this year!"

Puttermesser knew what Lidia was thinking: just like mama.

On a rainy night toward the middle of November they took the subway to the Bronx. Puttermesser had set the appointment with the agency for seven o'clock, so as not to interfere with her cousin's hours at the Blauschilds'. Lidia seemed nervous and reluctant. "We pay?" she asked. "Not at all. It's a service organization. They hire some staff, but they're mostly volunteers." "Like Varvara, work for nothing, foolish!"

In the cramped little office Linda sat morosely in a cul-de-sac of filing cabinets, noiselessly snapping her scarlet fingernails. The woman behind the desk had a doctor's manner: her aim was to make a diagnosis followed by a recommendation. She was, she said, a refugee from the Soviet Union herself. She had arrived five years ago, and had a son in high school: he was currently on the math team at Stuyvesant. Her husband, formerly an engineer, was employed as a salesman in a men's clothing store. The adjustment had been difficult at first, but now they were well settled. They had gone so far as to join a synagogue—in Kiev such a thing was inconceivable.

Lidia looked away; all this was for Puttermesser. It had a seasoned professional ring. Except for a mild brush of accent, there was nothing foreign about the interviewer. The woman was even stylish, in the way of the boroughs beyond Manhattan— she wore a scarf at her throat, meticulously knotted and draped, held by a silver pin in the shape of a lamb. She drew out several sheets of Cyrillic text and in a rapid cascade of Russian began to question Lidia. Despite a practiced series of nods she was not unkind. Puttermesser observed that her cousin was staring obsessively at the pin on the scarf; she was inattentive, lethargic. In Lidia's darkly unwilling mutter Puttermesser heard the desultory streak of cynicism she had lately come to recognize. She could spot it even in the unaccustomed syllables of Russian.

And then the Muscovite cousin rose up. Her eyes shot out

lightnings. Her fine teeth glinted. A roar of Russian galloped out of the cave of her mouth. The little office was all at once a Colosseum, with the smell of blood in the air.

"Good God! What was *that* all about?" Puttermesser demanded; she had restrained herself until they were nearly home. In the subway Lidia had made herself inaccessible. She pinched up her eyebrows. Her mouth narrowed into a tight line, like Zhenya's mouth in the snapshot. "Commissar!" she said.

They climbed the stairs in a stench of urine at the Seventy-seventh Street station, and nearly stumbled over a homeless man asleep on the concrete. The slanting rain wet his motionless face and neck. An empty bottle in a paper bag rolled past a muddy leg. Lidia hesitated; she was instantly cheerful. "Like in Soviet!" she cried, and Puttermesser understood that her cousin loved mockery best of all.

Lidia threw herself on her sofabed and crumpled up the papers the interviewer had given her and tossed them on the carpet.

"That woman only wanted to help," Puttermesser said.

"Rules. Much rules."

"Well, they must be worth it. *She* sounds happy enough over here."

"Such womans!" Lidia said. "My guys on team more smart."

The living room was now Lidia's domain entirely. Puttermesser almost never went in there. It was strangely scrambled and unfamiliar, a briar patch behind a barrier of hedgerows—Lidia's boxes and bundles and valises and plastic bags with their contents spilling out. The sofabed was always open and unmade, a tumble of blankets and pillows. Empty soda cans straggled across the top of the television. Orange sticks and an emery board lay on the edge of a bookshelf. Half-filled cups of coffee, days old, languished along the baseboards. Was this the Blauschild influence? Was chaos spawning chaos, 5-D leaching downward into Puttermesser's spare and scholarly 3-C?

But Puttermesser had another theory; the fault was her own.

She had been too solicitous of her young cousin, too deferential, too dutifully and unsuitably ceremonious. *Oh, that's all right, you don't need to think about that. Just leave it, I'll take care of it. Don't worry about it, you really shouldn't, it's fine the way it is.* These were the stanzas of Puttermesser's litany. It was incantation, it was "manners": she had treated Lidia as an honored guest, she had fallen at her feet—because she represented the healing of a great unholy rupture; because it was right that a rush of tenderheartedness, of blood-feeling, should pour into the wilderness of separation. To be blessed with a new cousin overnight!

The first week Lidia had grimly taken the broom—wasn't this what was expected? as a sort of rent?—and swept up after their meal. "Oh please don't trouble," Puttermesser said each time. Thereafter Lidia didn't. She left the lids of her cream jars on the bathtub ledge. She left her dirty dishes on the kitchen table. She left her wet towels on the living-room credenza. It soon came to Puttermesser that her cousin, though spurning atheism, was otherwise a perfected Soviet avatar: she did nothing that was not demanded. Released, she went straight to the television and its manifold enchantments: cars, detergents, toothpaste, cheeseburgers, cruises. An exhibit more various and abundant than any to be seen in the great halls of Moscow, and all unnaturally vivid (no green so green, no red so red, etc.) against an alluring background of meadows, hills, rills, fountains, castles, ferris wheels. The soda cans on top of the set multiplied. There was no reciprocity for Puttermesser's mandarin politesse.

"What did that woman at the agency *say,*" Puttermesser pursued, "that made you explode like that?"

"She say make Lenin go in trash."

"Lenin? You weren't discussing Soviet history, for God's sake, were you?"

"Medals. I bring much medals."

Lidia spilled them out then: a whole rattling green plastic bag of little tin effigies of a small boy. The bag had a word printed on it: фотография.

"Lenin when child, you see? Komsomol prize for children. Junk! Nobody want! I buy hundred for kopeck." The mocking laugh. "Woman say not allowed do business, big law for tax. Commissar!"

VIII. ENTREPRENEURS

very morning Lidia ate black bread and sour cream—she had chosen these herself from the neighborhood exhibition—followed by strong tea with plenty of sugar. Then she disappeared. She was always back in time to go up to 5-D to clean for Varvara. She confessed that she had grown to hate Varvara's children. They were selfish, wild, indulged; they knew too much, and still they were common—this is what people used to say about Khrushchev.

Puttermesser made no inquiries about Lidia's absences. The scene at the agency had shown what questions could lead to. But she noticed that Lidia never went out without carrying one or two of her many bundles.

At eleven o'clock, when Lidia was gone, Varvara came down to see Puttermesser.

She glanced into the living room: "Mess! Looks like *my* digs! And you don't even have kids."

"Is there a problem?" Puttermesser said. "You don't have to be embarrassed, I mean if things aren't working out with my cousin—"

"Oh, Lidia's a jewel! I wouldn't *dream* of losing her. She's enriched our *lives*," Varvara said. "She just *fascinates* the kids. She tells them Russian fairy stories—they're pretty grisly, the wolf always gets to eat somebody, but the kids love it. And Bill and I don't mind. It's not really mayhem like the stuff they feed them on TV. It's just imagination, it's harmless."

And Puttermesser, in the bloody theater of her own imagination, saw her cousin dissecting the limbs of Varvara's children via the surrogacy of wolverine fangs.

Varvara peered past the kitchen. "Is Lidia home?"

"She's out for a while."

"Taking in the Big Apple? That's nice. Hey," Varvara said, "I just want to get the two of you to come to a very special party. A private fund-raiser for SHEKHINA. You know SHEKHINA?"

"It's that magazine. The one that advertises itself as having nothing in common with MOTHERWIT," Puttermesser said.

"I told Sky about your cousin, and he said she'd be a terrific draw. Sky's a good friend of mine. We worked on the Neighborhood Visionary Project together years ago, when we all lived out in California. And before that we were both on the board of the All-University Free Expression Process, but that was before I met Bill. And before Sky had that nasty second divorce— basically she kicked him out. Bill *hates* Free Expression, he thinks it starts you on the road to violence. Bill's a *real* pacifist."

Puttermesser recalled the Free Expression Process, a fad of two decades ago: it had flourished in the age of streaking, when a naked student—a rosy blur of frontal flesh—would fly down the aisle of a lecture hall and dash across the stage. The Process specialized in "demonstrations" in which a forbidden word was chanted without pause for exactly two hours (fuck and asshole were the natural favorites); this was known as "neutering," and the goal of the Process People, as the press termed them, was to neuter all the naughty words.

Varvara said, "I guess *you* were never a Process Person. Wrong generation, after your time, right?"

But Puttermesser didn't believe in generations; such a notion was not in her philosophy. She supposed that what distinguished human beings, whatever their age, was temperament, proclivity, character. Until someone reminded her of it, she often forgot she was old. "I remember their slogan," she said. " 'Everything Comes Up Crystal.' "

"Right! Wasn't that beautiful? And the other one, the one on the T-shirts? 'Dirt Busters.' Cute! Once we did a double-Process on turd. Four hours of it. Turd, turd, turd, turd. Well, all that's long ago—B.K., before kids! We take baths with the kids, though. The whole family, two by two, cross-gender."

Varvara looked to be in her forties. Her face was both large and small. Her cheeks and forehead were very wide, her chin was broad and long, but bunched in the middle of all that unused space were the crowded-together eyes, round little nose, round little mouth. A family of features snug in a big tub. You could not tell from such a visage—it was, in fact, a "visage," a bit Dickensian, a touch archaic—that it belonged to an idealist.

Schuyler Hartstein, by contrast—Varvara's old friend—had exactly the sort of head one would expect of a social visionary. Puttermesser had happened on it now and again on television panel shows, a long-skulled baldish rectangle dangling a blond ponytail from its rear and (actually) a curly-ribboned monocle from its front. On such panels—they were not infrequent— Schuyler Hartstein always took the idealist position. He was called Sky not as an abbreviation but as a metaphoric allusion: the cloudlessly vivid cerulean of his poet's orbs. (Not at all the color of Puttermesser's papa's eyes, a wan blue diluted by the sad gray wash of memory and remorse.) In Schuyler Hartstein there were no hesitations, reservations, qualifications, impediments. He had a sunny blond face and all the social thinker's certainties. Around his neck hung a gold chain, at the end of which swung the two Hebrew letters that spelled "life." He was well-known for piety, and on Sabbath mornings could be seen in a white velvet skullcap, jammed down by means of a bobby pin over the upper hump of his ponytail.

Though a loyal socialist, Sky Hartstein was a ferocious entrepreneur. The periodical he had founded was by now almost two years old. Its name, familiar to Blake, Milton, the Swedenborgians and the theosophists, originated in Jewish mysticism: it referred to the radiance of the Divine Presence, and, kabbalistically, to its female aspect. It worked for the cutting-edge feminists; the Catholics liked it (it reminded them of Mary), the Buddhists had no quarrel with it, and the Hare Krishnas were enthralled. *Shekhina!* You could even find it in the dictionary. Still, the magazine was more celebrated for the manner of its launching than for its contents, a mixture of global utopianism and strenuous self-gratulation (they seemed to be the same thing). Sky Hartstein published his own poetry in his own pages. The famous advertising campaign at the start of SHEKHINA had been devised by Hartstein himself: its headline was POLITICS AGAINST MOTHERWIT—MOTHERWIT being a sober old periodical devoted to rationalist traditions, cautious liberalism, and an impatience with ponytails. But the war between SHEKHINA and MOTHERWIT was one-sided: MOTHERWIT remained aloof. It was only a story that MOTHERWIT had consistently rejected Sky Hartstein's poetry; MOTHERWIT published no verse at all. The vengefulness of Sky and his SHEKHINA was rooted in something worldlier, and more urgent, than the neglect of contemporary poetry. Sky Hartstein believed that, politically speaking, there were no enemies anywhere, except in one's own bosom. ENMITY IS ILLUSION, emblazoned on a dove's wing, appeared on the masthead. ONLY PLOWSHARES! cried out from the subscription blank.

Puttermesser knew all this because she had subscribed to SHEKHINA for its first year and then quit. She was addicted to magazines. She read TLS, NYRB, THE NEW YORKER, ATLANTIC, MOTHERWIT, HARPER'S, COMMENTARY, SALMAGUNDI, SOUTHWEST REVIEW, PARTISAN REVIEW, and THE NEW CRITERION. She did not read THE NATION; there was no reason to—it was more than a century since Henry James had written for it. She dropped SHEKHINA partly because she was indifferent to Sky Hartstein's verse—tiny uplifting telegrams consisting of very short lines—

but mainly because the radiance of the Divine Presence, insistently beamed out month after month, had begun to dim. Also, she couldn't help noticing that not all the swords had been beaten into plowshares. Sky Hartstein had the habit of taking wish for fact, and even the wish struck Puttermesser as improbable. He advertised in his own Personals columns for a wife, and meanwhile SHEKHINA's editorial positions were mist, fog, vapor, all passed off as "spirit," and sometimes as "rage." You knew beforehand that when you opened the magazine you would find the nasty anger of the pure-hearted.

The only surprise for Puttermesser was that Lidia's employer had turned out to be one of Sky Hartstein's old comrades.

"Wait'll you meet him!" Varvara crowed. "He's got this *mind*."

"But why does he want to meet Lidia?"

"Oh come *on*," Varvara said. "Isn't it obvious?"

When Lidia returned some hours later, she was not alone: she was pulling along behind her a tall young man.

"Pyotr," Lidia pronounced.

"Hiya," the young man said. He held out his hand. "I'm Pete. Peter Robinson, ma'am. I manage the Albemarle Sports Shop, d'you know us? Over on Third? Third and Ninety-fourth?"

"Pyotr," Lidia repeated. "Have *clean* eyes."

It was true: Lidia had hit on it exactly. Those were innocent eyes, guileless and unsoiled by wit. Pete Robinson—Pyotr— explained that he was from North Dakota, and was better acquainted with woods and farms than with the New York pavement. He had been in the city—had been transferred from the Seattle branch—less than three months, and the people! The variety! Back home, and even in a place like Seattle, you wouldn't ever get to run into someone like Lidia!

The three of them settled around the kitchen table. Pyotr wore a sweater with a V-neck and under it a plaid wool shirt. He had a big pale slab of a brow with a lick of shiny hair bouncing down over it like a busy tongue. He seemed as clarified and classified—as simplified—as a figure on a billboard. And Robinson! Puttermesser thought of the resourceful Crusoe; she thought of that radio series of her childhood: JACK ARMSTRONG, THE ALL-AMERICAN BOY! As quick as you could say Jack Robinson, her cousin had landed his prototype.

Lidia was joyful. "Pyotr help," she said.

And once again she turned the green plastic bag upside down—the one with фотография printed on it. This time not a single medal depicting the child Lenin fell out. Instead, a stream of green bills: all-American money.

"What's going on?" Puttermesser said. "Where'd you get all this?"

"Ma'am?" said Pyotr. "This gal's been working in my store all day. I've got to get back there myself pretty soon. She lured me out with that smile."

Puttermesser gave her cousin a skeptical look. "What is it, another job?"

"Ma'am," said Pyotr, "we're getting ready for Christmas, never too soon for that, so we're clearing out tennis rackets and ski poles from the middle of the floor. Nice big space, it's where we're putting the *tree*, y'know. Well, we get the tree up, and in comes this little lady with this funny way of talking, and next thing you know she sets herself up and she's in business. Right in the biggest traffic area we've got."

"Traffic area?" Puttermesser wondered.

Pyotr nodded. "You bet. It's our busiest season. If you don't mind my saying so, what you've got right here in this little gal is free enterprise, the real thing. They don't have it where she's from, y'know?"

Sitting at a card table he had found for her, under a Christmas tree decorated with colored light bulbs in the shape of miniature sneakers and footballs, the Muscovite cousin had sold—in a single morning—her whole stock of Lenin medals. For three dollars each. What lay strewn on Puttermesser's kitchen table were three hundred American dollars. And her cousin still had, in inventory, plenty of scarves and spoons and limbless hollow dolls.

Not to mention an all-American boyfriend.

IX. THE IDEALISTS

he SHEKHINA fund-raiser was held in one of those mazy Upper West Side apartments where it is impossible to find the bathroom. You wander from corridor to corridor, tentatively entering bedrooms still redolent of their night odors, where the bedspreads have lain folded and unused on chairs for months. Sometimes on these journeys there will be a bewildered young child standing fearfully in your path, or else an unexpected small animal, but mostly you will encounter nothing but the stale mixed smells of an aging building. Such apartments are like demoralized old women shrouded in wrinkles, who, mourning their lost complexions, assert the dignity and importance of their prime. The bathroom sink, if you should happen to locate it in the dark (the light switch will be permanently hidden), is embroidered with the brown grime of its ancient cracks, like the lines of an astrological map; the base of the toilet, when you flush it, will trickle out a niggardly rusty stream. And then you will know how privileged you are: you have been touched by History. Artur Rubinstein once actually lived here; Einstein attended a meeting in what is now the back pantry; Maria Callas sang, privately, on a summer night, with her palm pressed down hard on that very window sill; Uta Hagen paid a visit to the famous tenant, whoever it was, before the present tenant.

"Kakoi teatr!" Lidia cried; she was leading Pyotr by the hand. He followed docilely, shyly. Puttermesser saw how he was dazzled by the doubly exotic: enigmatic New York, where a Muscovite beauty could suddenly take you over and swoop you into an event more curious than any you might run into in the great Northwest! A spacious carpeted room; rows of folding chairs; sofas pushed against the walls, and long maroon draperies drawn over two sets of windows, like twin curtained prosceniums. A fresh copy of SHEKHINA had been placed on each chair.

"Oh look," Varvara said, opening hers, "here's an article by Kirkwood Plethora!"

Puttermesser asked, "Isn't your husband coming tonight?"

"Bill won't have anything to do with Sky, it goes back years. They just won't reconcile, but I'm not into any of that."

"Doesn't he mind? I mean if you're still loyal to someone he doesn't—"

"We're separate *people*, for God's sake!"

Pyotr leaned forward timidly. "Who's this Kirkwood Plethora?"

"The *film*maker," Varvara explained. "She's right over there, in front of the fellow who wrote that big play. The play about the flying bus filled with gays and lesbians? Plethora's the one who went to the Sudan to do a movie about the oppression of the animists . . . ssh! It's starting."

Applause. The evening's host, a woman in the middle fifties, dressed in jeans, a creased shirt, and several rings and bracelets, materialized out of the lost rear recesses of the apartment. Puttermesser picked up the magazine she had been sitting on and began to riffle through it, until she came on one of the poems Sky Hartstein liked to sprinkle through each issue:

> The unneeded
> are needed
> for our satisfaction.
> We are bloated
> with such satisfactions.

Enough!
Let us turn
and satisfy ourselves
with the sublime.

The title was "The Marginalized." Puttermesser, attentively rereading, was unsure what or who the unneeded and the marginalized *were*: were they the despised of our world whom we abuse by our injustices, or were they our own greedy feelings, of which we should be ashamed? (SHEKHINA, she noticed, tended toward the frequent use of "we" and "our," pinning on its readers, willy-nilly, any sin currently in bad repute.) Or was this poem only another of Sky's wistful advertisements for a new wife?

Pyotr was caressing Lidia's raw little hand, each finger with its blood-red hood. Lidia wore her reddest lipstick and her most detached smile; she was fondling the buttons of her new leather coat. The polished leather shone like black glass, and Puttermesser was all at once put in mind of the boy Dickens in the blacking factory. Child labor! One of the causes of messianic Marxism. Lidia had bought the leather coat in a shop on First Avenue run by immigrant Koreans—Varvara had told her where to find it—and had paid for it with the profits from her Lenin medals. The label said Made in China: sewn, for all anyone knew, by eight-year-old slaveys chained to their machines. In her gleaming leather coat and black tights, Lidia seemed unimaginably remote from Zhenya: Zhenya with that sun-crossed squint, that loose proletarian dress, flat fearful mouth, imploring scream.

Puttermesser looked all around—who was in this room? Varvara had already spotted the most celebrated: Bert Waldroon, the playwright and activist, and Kirkwood Plethora, grown surprisingly elderly by now, her trademark single earring masking a hearing aid. There was, besides, a young seminarian, the leader of Men for Women, an all-male feminist organization dedicated to the removal from Scripture of every "he" pronoun referring to God; the idea was to substitute phrases such as Profound Essence, Divine Fundament, Illimitable Spirit, Goad of the World, Omni-Gendered Sole Purpose, Soul Engenderer, and so on. There were some of Sky Hartstein's fellow-poets, including the one who accompanied himself on the zither, and another who wrote bilingually, in order to promote Esperanto. There was a tepid novelist whose books sold fairly well despite her estrangement from grammar and spelling; it was said that it took two copy editors to get her through her native tongue. And there were, of course, the politically consecrated—atheists mainly, apparently unoffended by what they called Sky Hartstein's "religious orientation." The rest were the unsung and the undistinguished, though not the unmarked: they were immensely recognizable by virtue of the adoration that enflamed them. They were, like the atheists, hot believers in Sky Hartstein's credo. In the pages of SHEKHINA it went by the name of Spiritual Polity.

The introducer in jeans was just finishing her money pitch—"Remember, Sky's the limit!"—when, in thickening applause, Sky Hartstein ascended out of his chair. (You couldn't say he got up out of it.) It was, he began, "for me personally," an amazing week. On Monday he had been invited to the White House to meet with the Vice President, who wanted to learn more about the Spiritual Polity concept. On Tuesday TIME and NEWSWEEK ran photos of the Vice President and Sky in fraternal embrace, and the VILLAGE VOICE published Sky's remarks in full. SHEKHINA was making its way! On Wednesday His Holiness, the Dalai Lama, granted Sky an audience, and what do you suppose they talked about? Those little toy cars you operate by remote control, how they are subject to movement by an invisible force . . . only imagine the golden smile of His Holiness, a lover of mechanical and electronic contrivances, an engineer-manqué perhaps, but also, foremost and formidably, a metaphorical metaphysician. The little cars stand for the power, from afar, of divine influence drawing on human will. . . . Sky Hartstein's speech rushed on in flooding sheets, a torrent of sweetness and light (though, Puttermesser secretly thought, the sweetness was Nutra and the light was lite). He swept the Beatles into the Psalms and the prophets into organically grown vegetables. He quoted from Blake and recited the sleep-giving properties of melatonin. He excoriated greed and selfishness, oh especially these! Greed and selfishness polluted both Republicans and Democrats, those equal sewers of armaments and national arrogance. Let all borders dissolve, let the nations vanish away, let all peoples be bound up in lovingkindness! Let us remember our hopes and extol our visionaries! Let glasnost spread its healing tent over the earth, and restore us to origins, to openness of heart, to classlessness, to the end of want—let the poor rise up from their wretchedness according to the verdant primal promise of that genius who once labored long in the British Museum! Karl and Groucho, Lenin and Lennon: Sky ventured this little joke, he didn't care how stale, and anyhow it wasn't a joke at all—the robust and pliant tissue of Spirit joins like to like, and unlike to unlike; ah we happy many!

Everyone knows, he went on, about the excesses of Stalin, the gulag, the terror, the KGB, informers, shadows, spies, interrogators, torturers; and yet in an early time, before the darkness of perversion descended, before the betrayal of the noble scheme of universal aspiration, there was the little holy seed of human redemption. The Great Experiment had failed in its first venue, yes, but if the seed were to be replanted, there ought to be a witness to give testimony to its fertility, to its potential, to its futurity. And the witness was here, in this room, at this moment.

Puttermesser thought: how simple-minded this righteousness is; but what does he want with Lidia?

"Imagine one born into the Experiment," Sky Hartstein said, "after its best days are done. When the veil of perfidy has fallen over it. After it has attenuated. When it is plain that what is required for the Experiment's resuscitation is a more favorable environment and another go. Still," he said, "to one born into the Experiment, no matter how late, there must cling some small amount of the Pristine. The Revolution leaves its residue. Intimations of the Beginning. A trail, a wisp, an aroma of what was *meant*. Tell us," he said, widening his arms in Lidia's direction, "what you have inherited from the Beginning."

Lidia snatched her chapped knuckles out of Pyotr's faithful grasp and jumped out of her chair. "You think was in old days clean?" she cried. "Never clean, no! Stupid mans! Stupid womans!"

Bert Waldroon, the playwright, began to hiss. The host in jeans, worrying about the disruption of her party—a table at the back of the room was stacked with oatmeal cookies and a wholesome pyramid of apples—broke in plaintively: "But wasn't Communism once a truly beautiful hope? At the start? In principle? And remember that for serious progressives the goals of socialism are still viable—"

Lidia uncoiled the tight windings of her laugh. "Foolish American peoples!" she yelled. "In Soviet stupid peoples more smart! My guys on team more smart!"

Varvara whispered furiously, "Sit down! You're ruining the meeting!"

"Communism," Lidia yelled. "What Communism? Naive! Fairy tale always! No Communism, never! Naive!"

There she stood, her pointed little chin in the air, her elbows firm—a Saint Joan of disillusionment, a commissar of mockery: a perfected Soviet flower. She trusted no one, she trusted nothing. She was no more rooted than a dandelion's head when it has turned into feathers and is ready to fly. For the first time Puttermesser liked her cousin nearly as much as she deplored her.

X. A TEA PARTY

n the middle of the night the telephone rang. Puttermesser found herself catapulted out of a fiercely undulating dream: waves and waves of barbed wire were unrolling before her. Her apartment was ringed round with barbed wire: it crisscrossed the windows, it closed off the kitchen, it followed the baseboards and led right into Lidia's living room and surrounded her sofabed. Thirstily heading for a drink of water, Puttermesser leaped over the wire and caught her shin on one of the twisted barbs. Blood was spilling down her ankle, flowing between her naked toes. . . .

It was Volodya, calling not from Moscow but from Sakhalin. Sakhalin, the Czar's penal colony, where Chekhov had gone to investigate prison conditions. A distant island in the inconceivable Sea of Okhotsk, below the Arctic, its southern tip irritably fingering Japan. Talk about Mars! Puttermesser turned in her bed, drove off the bad dream, and listened to the murmur of Russian. Lidia in Russian was a different Lidia: she flew among the rococo gasps and trills of those brilliant syllables as lightly as on a trapeze. Her laugh, embedded in Russian, was a different laugh: it was free to do its stunts.

"Do svidanya," Lidia breathed out—it was a sly caress—and hung up. "Volodya want do business in Sakhalin," she explained.

"Don't people get arrested for trying that? Isn't it dangerous? Zhenya's grandmother—" Then Puttermesser remembered that Zhenya's grandmother was her own grandmother too: an old woman in a black babushka dropping kopecks through a hole in her pocket to foil the pitiless. In Puttermesser's mind her papa's mother went skittering across the steel crust of snow again and again, forever, a snatch of movie reel played over and over.

The thirst in her dream had pursued her into the kitchen. She filled the kettle for tea and put out two cups. The windows, cleared of their silver thorns, were black. It was half-past three.

"You don't mean *private* business," she said. "Isn't that what they call economic crime—"

Lidia released her amiable shrug. "Perestroika," she said.

"Really? People aren't afraid of breaking the law anymore?"

"Apparatchik rules," Lidia spat out. "*Volodya* not afraid!"

"But I thought you said he was thinking about leaving the country. Going to Australia."

"First get much rubles. First Sakhalin."

"I don't suppose you can buy a leather coat in Sakhalin. Not with such deep pockets anyhow," Puttermesser said, pouring the water over the leaves and letting it darken to mahogany. She didn't mind that her cousin had converted her away from tea bags.

"I buy coat in America, give Volodya."

"You're out of a job now," Puttermesser said mildly.

They sipped their tea. Lidia produced the half-dozen oatmeal cookies she had been slipping into the pocket of her new leather coat—emptying or filling pockets seemed to be in the family line—at the very moment Varvara was firing her.

"Foolish Varvara," Lidia said. Nibbling her cookie, she looked almost childlike; her nostrils vibrated.

"Well, what did you expect? The woman invites you to the center of her life and you insult everyone in sight. The way you answered Sky Hartstein. You heard it, those people actually get asked to the White House. SHEKHINA's getting famouser and famouser."

"PRAVDA also famous," Lidia said. "Nobody read. Read to make joke."

And in that instant, as "PRAVDA" dropped among the oatmeal crumbs in Lidia's red mouth, Puttermesser understood her dream. All that barbed wire! It was a platitude of a dream. She had transformed her apartment into the gulag—it was that simple, so stupidly transparent that it would make Freud yawn. Sky's speech had brought it on; or else Volodya had: the eeriness of a call from a former penal colony just as she was bleeding on barbed wire.

"That book you've got?" Puttermesser said. "That dream book?" It was asinine to ask for it, but she did: she felt a shudder, a mystical quake, traveling from Sakhalin to herself—something strangely predictive.

She had never seen Lidia more alert. Her thin neck swerved like the neck of a small quick animal—a pony, or a hyena—as she dashed through the hedge of her bundles to fetch the dream book, and it came to Puttermesser that she had finally struck home with her cousin. Until now what had she been for Lidia if not a harassment and a bore? How old and irrelevant she must seem to a lively young woman, a flirt, a foreigner, a beauty!

Lidia returned with the book in her hands as if she were displaying a crown on a cushion. Here was a believer, an adorer; the cynic, the pessimist, had vanished. Her shrewd eyes had shrunk to the size of two narrow brown seeds. "What in dream? I look, I find."

Puttermesser waved all around. "Barbed wire. All over the place. Across the windows, everywhere. I got cut on it and blood poured out. I mean *poured*."

Lidia considered; she put her head down to study what appeared to be a sort of index—dream topics?

"Does it list barbed wire?"

"*Nyet.*"

"Prison?"

"Prison not in dream. Dream here, in house." Lidia bent over the pages, turning them so slowly that the ceiling light flashed off each one. "Ah," she said. "*Krov.*"

"What's that?"

An elongated vowel lingered. A ghostly word. "Blooood," Lidia said. "Where blooood come?"

"No, no," Puttermesser said crisply. "It isn't blued. It doesn't rhyme with food, it rhymes with mud. Out of my leg. My foot. My toes."

"*Khorosho,*" Lidia said. "Better from foot. Blooood from head mean you dies." She stopped to study some more; she was uncommonly serious. "Peoples dream blooood from foot, they make holy future. You holy womans. You"—she struggled to translate—"saint."

Puttermesser stared: her ironic cousin was altogether drained of irony. The mystical shudder that led to bitter Sakhalin fell away. Her cousin was . . . what was her cousin? —Anything shoddy, anything that broke at a touch, parts that failed, faulty mechanics, the switch on the living-room wall that suddenly gave out, the leak in the kettle, a crack in the plaster, the bus that was late in coming—all these were occasions for Lidia's satiric call: *like in Soviet!* Proof of a corrupt and shabby universe. Puttermesser knew what her cousin was: an apparatchik of blemish and smirch, wart and scab, disdain and distrust. *Like in Soviet!* She was either too suspicious or too credulous. She was a skeptic who put her faith in charlatanism.

"I think," Puttermesser said darkly, "you would be a lot better off throwing out such a silly book and getting hold of an English grammar instead."

The little brown seeds of Lidia's eyes swelled. She slapped the dream book shut. "What for I need English? I go Sakhalin with Volodya! Make big business in Sakhalin!"

"What are you talking about?"

"Volodya say come, get much rubles. Marry maybe."

A gray blur, as if a piece of sky were getting hosed down with diluted whitewash, had begun to brighten the windows. It was still too early for dawn, but the blackest hours of night were receding, and in that morning light that was not quite light, spun together with the sharp cartoonlike brilliance of the ceiling fixture, Lidia was sending out a phosphorescence of her own.

"You came for asylum! You came to escape! I spent months paving the way before you got here," Puttermesser said. "I tackled every goddamn bureaucracy, public and private. For God's sake, Lidia, what do you think this is? A *vacation?*"

"I come work," Lidia contradicted.

"You're here as a refugee."

"Refugee? What mean refugee?" Her face was a lit stage; every filament of her hair burned red and redder yet.

"Don't tell me that out of a million words *this* is the one you don't get! Listen, where's that dictionary—dig it out! Unless it's sold? Via Peter Robinson's miscellaneous merchandise outlet—"

"Ah, Pyotr," Lidia said sweetly. "Tall mans, same like Volodya—"

"Go get the goddamn dictionary!"

So for the second time that night Lidia broke through the hedge and heap of her belongings—the spoons, the dolls, the shawls, everything she had brought to peddle in America—and came back with a book: Russian-English, English-Russian.

Puttermesser looked up "refugee" and right next to it found эмигрант.

"Read that," she commanded.

"Emi-*grahnt*," Lidia read.

"That's what you are. That's what I've been working on. That's what I understood from Zhenya."

"Zhenya? Zhenya say this? I am emi-*grahnt* like you is holy womans," Lidia blazed, and stretched out her long, long laugh, as elongated as the vowel in blooood, as crucial as inspiration. "What mama say! What mama want!"

XI. THE FAREWELL

n the end Pyotr wept. Lidia had been gone only a day; she had managed her ticket—New York to Moscow, a direct flight—all on her own.

"This Korean place on First Avenue?" Pyotr said. "She asked me to go over there with her. To try on this *coat*. That was only day before yesterday."

"She did mention that you and her boyfriend are about the same height," Puttermesser said.

"I mean I knew it was a present, but I didn't know who *for*. She said it was for her brother in Moscow. She said she was having it shipped."

"Lidia doesn't have a brother."

"All the time she was planning to leave."

"But not before clearing a profit," Puttermesser said.

"Those dolls went like hot cakes. She must've made around nine hundred dollars off them, never mind what she got for the rest of the stuff."

"Russian folk art. The spoons, the shawls."

"Those Lenin medals? That was just to see how things'd go."

"To test the market," Puttermesser offered.

"She walked out of my place with maybe two thousand smackers. Even this weirdo book went—like half English, half Russian? Would you believe it, in a *sports* store? She picked up ten bucks for it."

"She didn't sell that dictionary!" Puttermesser cried.

"It was your idea, wasn't it? She said you were making her do grammar instead." Pyotr drank and sobbed. "I *liked* that funny Russki talk."

They were sitting in Puttermesser's living room. It was, in its way, another tea party—but there was booze in the tea cups. Pyotr had brought along a bottle of vodka to celebrate with Lidia; it was a month ago to the day that she had revealed herself in the Albemarle Sports Shop.

But Lidia was far above the round earth, heading for the death of the Soviet Union.

Crumpled plastic bags littered the carpet. The sofabed was just as Lidia had vacated it, an anarchic jumble of cushions and twisted sheets. Ripped pairs of pantyhose sprawled gauzily over a parade of Coke cans. Lidia's various scents—lotions, nail polish, hair spray—wafted like the wake of an apparition.

"She didn't even tell me she was going," Pyotr wailed.

Puttermesser looked into Pyotr's clean wet North Dakota eyes. Jack Armstrong, the All-American Boy: gulled.

"The Great Experiment," she said, and emptied what was left of the booze into poor Pyotr's innocent cup.

XII. LETTERS

December 12

Dear Ms. Puttermesser:

I hope you'll forgive this somewhat embarrassed intrusion. Barbara Blauschild, your upstairs neighbor and an old pal of mine, kindly gave me your name. I understand you attended our fund-raiser about two weeks ago, in the company of that interesting young lady who raised a ruckus—Barbara tells me you're her relative. Barbara also tells me she released the young lady from her employ on my behalf. (She had hired her for compassionate reasons.) I very much appreciate the depth of Barbara's friendship, but she's always been precipitate. (We keep up our friendship despite the fact that her husband hasn't spoken to me in years. The truth of the matter is that Barbara and I used to be an item 100 years ago, back in California, and Bill's never gotten over it.)

I admit (again) that I'm a little embarrassed to be asking this. It's just that when the young lady with the Russian accent stood up in our meeting with all that fire in her face—not that she exactly knew what she was talking about—it struck me that I would like to get to know her. What's tricky here is that Barbara, having let her go, now declines to approach her. So I thought you might be willing to help. (I am a sucker for red hair.)

> Sincerely,
> Schuyler Hartstein, M.A.
> Editor and Publisher, SHEKHINA

December 15

Dear Mr. Hartstein:

Thanks for your note. My cousin has returned to the Soviet Union. She did, however, leave behind a number of cosmetic materials on the top of the toilet tank. None of these were unusual or worthy of remark. Yet only recently I found, concealed under her bed, a half-used bottle of hair coloring.

> Sincerely,
> Ruth Puttermesser, Esq.

From Tel Aviv, in German (in Puttermesser's unavoidably maladroit translation):

> Hotel Royale
> 23 Juni

Liebe Ruth!

As you can see, because of the pressure of circumstances I have emigrated to *das Land, wo die Zitronen blüh'n* (Goethe). I have been here only two days. Lidia is now living in Sakhalin. In the summer it is not a hardship to be there. She is six months pregnant, and she and Volodya (he is her boyfriend since last year) will marry very soon. He is very busy setting up a business with other ambitious young men. You probably do not know, because until now it has been kept as secret as possible, that a number of paleolithic mammoth tusks have been dug up by farmers in Sakhalin. Volodya's plan is to buy the tusks from the locals and resell them in the West. He and his colleagues are in at the start, so the investment will not be great. I am told that these tusks are very beautiful and actually resemble fossilized wood. Lidia is somewhat doubtful about their authenticity, but you know my Lidia—such a skeptic! Nevertheless she is putting all the money she earned in America into the business. Even if the tusks are not authentic, she believes they can easily be passed off as such to potential collectors, since value is as value seems.

I am glad she is safe in Sakhalin, safer than she would be in America. Lidia told me that she was forced to attend an extremely dangerous political meeting in New York, where all the participants had knives and guns. Some of the guns went off. I am sorry you did not spare her this fright. Even before that, she told me, she was made to travel to a distant place at night, where a woman official of some unsavory and possibly secret organization tried to dragoon her into signing certain papers—a scheme of indenture, apparently. I am very dismayed to hear of such things in your country, especially knives and guns at a public meeting in a palatial hall where the people are, as Lidia explained, well-dressed. Some of the women, though not all, as stylish as Raisa Gorbachev!

The night I left Moscow there was a riot in our street. This is because the USSR is falling apart. Some say the death knell has already been sounded. [In the original: *das Tautengeläut ist schon geklungen.*] The rioters shouted unpleasant slogans and wore unpleasant uniforms and broke many windows, but they did not (at least not obviously) carry knives or guns. I thank God that Lidia, who did not wish to accompany me here, is for the time being in quiet Sakhalin. Who knows where fate will finally place her? She confided to me that the baby is regrettably not Volodya's, and she was pleased to have me quit the USSR—she feared I would disclose the truth to Volodya. She assures me that you, dearest Ruth, know who the father is, and that he is a nice boy. I, however, have always been afraid that Lidia would get into trouble with one of the athletes on her team. But the team has been disbanded, since there are no more official Soviet teams.

I will write again when I begin to understand this new place. In the meantime, please write *auf deutsch* to the above address (it is a hotel being utilized as an absorption center for new immigrants) and tell me all you know about the baby's father. Lidia says he has a typically Russian name and actually sells icons for a living (but they are of course only reproductions). Where in America could she have unearthed such a person?

Your new-found cousin
Zhenya

PUTTERMESSER
IN PARADISE

Knit and unravel,
commands the Gavel.
Do and undo,
till nothing's true.

—A Song of Paradise,
translated from the Akkadian

ery deep is the well of the past. Should we not call it bottomless?"

It was Thomas Mann: the opening sentences of *Joseph and His Brothers*. Ruth Puttermesser, sitting under the green lamp in her lonely bedroom one moment before her death, sitting with the weight of that mighty tale of a magus pressing into her ribs, was thinking of Paradise: very deep is the well of Paradise; should we not call it bottomless?

It happens that in the several seconds before we die the well of the ribs opens, and a crystal pebble is thrown in; then there is a distant tiny splash, no more than the chirp of a droplet. This seeming pebble is the earthly equal of what astrophysicists call a Black Hole—a dead sun that has collapsed into itself, shrinking from density to deeper density, until it is smaller than the period at the end of this sentence. Until it is less than infinitesimal.

Puttermesser heard (she did not feel) the pebble's electric *ping!* as it pierced the veil of the sluice that lay at the bottom of the well—or, rather, as it flew through the impalpable membrane that marked the beginning of bottomlessness. And at the bottom of this bottomlessness—in Eden oxymorons are as esteemed as orchids—there was PARDES. PARDES is a Hebrew word, as befits so messianic a thought: it means an orchard, it means a garden, it means Paradise—derived, no doubt, in this intertwining of the vines of civilization, from the Greek PARADEISOS.

Yet as Puttermesser sat alone in her bedroom under the green lamp, with the magisterial Mann pressed against the framework of her skeleton, it was still one whole instant before her death, and she was as far from entering Eden then as she had been at the moment of her birth. The radiator exhaled its familiar little winter sigh, and over bed, books, and desk the green lamp threw out a cavelike velvet halo. Under Puttermesser's hand and eye Mann was speaking:

> There are deeply chamfered trains of thought out of which one does not escape, once in them; associations cut and dried from old time, which fit in each other like rings in a chain, so that he who has said A cannot help saying B or at least thinking it; and like links in a chain they are, too, in that in them the earthly and the heavenly are so interlocked one into the other that one passes willy-nilly, and whether speaking or silent, from one to the other.

Puttermesser's mind flew into and behind these phrases like a spirit that can pass through walls. Exegetical onomastic Puttermesser!—what was she musing on in the nanosecond of life still allotted to her? She was thinking of Paradise, yes, but (because the earthly and the heavenly are so interlocked one into the other) she was also thinking how names have their destiny, how they drive whoever holds or beholds them. For instance: the poet Wordsworth giving exact value for each syllable. Or Mann himself—Man, Mankind, seeking the origins of human character in Israelitish prehistory. Or how one Eliot reins in the other Eliot: "the jew squats on the windowsill"—that's Tom—rebuked by Deronda's visionary Zion—that's George. And James the aristocratic Jacobite, pretender to the throne. Joyce's Molly rejoicing. Bellow fanning fires; Updike fingering apertures; Oates wildly sowing; Roth wroth. And so on. Puttermesser: no more cutting than a butterknife.

The earthly and the heavenly are so interlocked that one passes

willy-nilly, and whether speaking or silent, from one to the other.
Without transition? Without interim or hiatus or breath? Without fear?

Puttermesser is about to be murdered and raped—in that order. She was murdered before she was raped. The intruder—the murderer, the rapist, in that order—slid, slipped, crept into her bedroom through the slightly raised window behind Puttermesser's reading chair. The window was raised because, though it was February, the apartment, like so many apartments in New York, was stifling. The radiator was a fiery accordion, belching out its own equatorial weather.

There was a kind of kick or knock; the intruder was standing on top of the radiator. The rubber on the soles of his sneakers gave out a burning smell.

She saw him then; she saw the knife, a long blade on a spring, as far in its intent from the work of a butterknife as Tom is from George. "Frank," he said; and how strange it was that he spoke his own name! Or perhaps, whatever the deed to come, it is not within the scope of human aspiration to remain anonymous. "It's me, Frankie," he said. And then, in familiar movietone, "Do what I tellya or ya dead."

So, in those last seconds, she secretly undertook to call him Candide—for his frankness, for his candor. His face she did not see; it was fully hooded in what she supposed was a ski mask. She supposed it was a ski mask not from ever having glimpsed one of these—when had exegetical onomastic urban Puttermesser, now close to the biblical threescore and ten (but she was not to reach it), ever scaled a magic mountain capped with snow? It was all newspaper knowledge: who hasn't read of muggers in ski masks?

Candide inquired: "Whatchoo got in here's worth somethin?" Under the ski mask a pair of eyeglasses glinted; his head was horrible, supernatural, a great woolly maroon knob with two ferocious headlights. In the bedroom closet he found Puttermesser's old typewriter. He didn't want it. He gave it a kick. He opened a dresser drawer and scrabbled around in it and pulled out Puttermesser's papa's silver watch; it went right into his pocket. It was an old-fashioned wind-up watch.

Candide inquired: "Rings? Earrings? Where you put em?"

But she had none of these things. Exegetical onomastic urban puritanical Puttermesser! A necklace or two might have saved her life.

Her eyes fled to the one possibly desirable object within reach: on the teak table in the corner of her bedroom stood a computer. Puttermesser had acquired this device as a hand-me-down; she was now technologically ascended. Harvey Morgenbluth, upstairs in 6-C, had bought himself a newer model. The old one was already obsolete; superseded—though good enough for a novice like Puttermesser. These machines were spawned in "generations," Harvey Morgenbluth explained, and succeeded one another with the rapidity of fruit flies. Puttermesser was reluctant to give up her workhorse typewriter for a fruit fly; she felt much as her turn-of-the-century predecessors had felt when they were obliged, willy-nilly, to move from gas lighting to electricity, or from Dobbin's warm flanks to a motorcar. Still, humanity was turning on its temporal hinge, and Puttermesser was obliged, willy-nilly, to turn with it.

"You can take that," she said to the horrible woolly knob, with its lit-up peepholes. "Just take it and go."

"You got rings? Earrings? No?" He lifted the computer off the table, wrenching it free of the keyboard; the wires trailed. Then he set it down on the floor and gave it a kick. "Where you keep em? Rings, bracelets, hah?" She watched him shut the bedroom door and barricade it with Harvey Morgenbluth's obsolete old model. There was no escape. The computer's silent glass mouth was indifferent, though she had brought it to life often enough, a genie spewing alphabets. Lately Puttermesser had begun to type out improbables; or the genie had.

Secreted inside the computer's dead mouth, improbable, impalpable, were these curious fragments:

> My father is nearly a Yankee: *his* father gave up ped-
> dling to captain a dry goods store in Providence,
> Rhode Island. In summer he sold captain's hats, and
> wore one in all his photographs. From Castle Gar-
> den to blue New England mists, my father's father,
> hat-and-neckware peddler to Yankees! Providence,
> Rhode Island, beats richly in my veins.

> My younger sister was once highly motivated as a
> scholar, but instead she married an Indian, a Parsee
> chemist, and went to live in Calcutta. She has four
> children and seven saris of various fabrics.

Not a single syllable of any of this was true. She had no sister, whether younger or older. There was nothing of New England in her veins. Her history was bare of near-Yankees. She had never known her grandfather, dead now for more than seventy years; that grandfather, sickly, had never left the wretched little village of his birth in cold corrupt old Russia. It was her papa who had run from the Czar's depredations and passed through Castle Garden's great hall: an immigrant speck in an im-migrant tide.

The genie in the computer was revising Puttermesser's ancestry, it was dreaming Puttermesser's dreams—even her newest dream of Paradise:

> Here is how it will be [the genie had written in
> Puttermesser's voice]. I will sit in Eden under
> a middle-sized tree, in the solid blaze of an in-
> finite heart-of-July, green, green, green everywhere,
> green above and green below, myself gleaming and
> made glorious by sweat, every itch annihilated,
> fecundity dismissed. Day after celestial day, perfec-
> tion of desire upon perfection of contemplation,
> into the exaltations of an uninterrupted forever. In
> Eden all insatiabilities are nourished: I will learn

about the linkages of genes, about quarks, about primate sign language, theories of the origins of the races, religions of ancient civilizations, what Stonehenge meant. I will study Roman law, the more arcane varieties of higher mathematics, the nuclear composition of the stars, what happened to the Monophysites, Chinese history, Russian, and Icelandic.

Ah, false, false! Paradise, when Puttermesser was transported there, bore no resemblance to this hungry imagining. Paradise, when Puttermesser was transported there, was . . . but no. No and no. First it is necessary to get through the murder and the rape.

Clearly the computer had no interest for Candide. He was looking for something portable. Puttermesser undid the band of her wristwatch and tossed the watch across the room to where he was standing. He caught it with one hand, examined it, dropped it to the floor, and stepped on it. The plastic face crackled under his sneaker. "Garbage," he said. "Worth ten bucks. Don't dis me, lady."

And then she did not know what to do. "Try the kitchen," she said. "The spoons and things." She thought: let him just open the bedroom door, and she would fly through it and get away.

"Sterling?" inquired Candide.

"Oh yes," Puttermesser assured him. There was nothing in her kitchen drawers but stainless steel.

"O.K.," he said. "I'll go look. But don't you move, lady."

He shoved aside the computer and opened the door. The green lamp reflected greenly in the ski mask's portholes. "Hey wait," he said, and felt for something in his pocket.

It was a narrow rope. In no time at all—his fingers were admirably quick—he had tied her wrists to the radiator. With a twist of the rope she was flung to the floor. There she lay, contorted, staring through the rungs of the chair.

He went out and came back.

"You lyin to me, lady. It's all garbage in there."

"There's cash in my purse."

"Where you keepin it, hah?"

She was weeping now—a painful mute weeping, as if her vocal cords had been suddenly cut.

He found her purse—it was right there on the dresser—and turned her wallet upside down. Through the rungs of the chair she saw the falling fan of cards and green bills. But there was a raging light in the holes of the mask.

Candide said: "I don't like no credit cards and I don't like no chicken shit."

How quick and fastidious his fingers were! He wiggled the knife and made it shimmer and shiver; then he put the handle to his lips, like a flute, and kissed it. He pushed the chair out of the way to clear a space, and stood astride her, a sneaker close to each ear. She could smell the rubber soles of his sneakers, but the rubber smell was oddly mixed with vomit and she understood that it was her own vomit; she was vomiting, and she felt defiled by her own vomit, and also by a terror so frigid that it left her unaware of the spasms that must be convulsing her esophagus. It seemed to her important—she sensed this acutely—not to offend him by crying out, but her breath ran thin, it was anyhow not possible: he had placed the weight of *Joseph and His Brothers* on her breasts, and was heaving downward with one powerful flattened palm. He began efficiently, with the throat— the vocal cords were sliced through instantly—and then crisscrossed the blade rapidly over the ears, lopping off (it was unintended) half a lobe on the right ear. Her breath ran thinner now, but she could taste the rusty wetness that was her blood. Then he repositioned her torso, ripped the knife through her underpants. . . .

But enough. By then Puttermesser was in Paradise. Like the excruciations of labor (but how could Puttermesser know this? she had never given birth), dying, even agonized dying, generates its own amnesia. And since the rape was committed after the last living sigh had left her body, there was nothing to erase from Puttermesser's posthumous cognition. For her, the rape never happened at all.

It is sometimes supposed that in Paradise one is permitted to bend over the bar of Heaven, so to speak, for a final contemplation of one's abandoned flesh. This is a famous untruth steeped in a profound illogic. Had Puttermesser been able to view herself tethered, bloodied, torn, mutilated, stripped, striped, violated—had she taken in so malignant a scene, so degenerate an act: the lower quarters of her carcass still hot, the tissues still elastic, yet resistant to easy penetration because the wall of death has already blinded every cell, death its own stricken fortress; had Puttermesser seen that engorged member crash through the entryway to the lately untrodden tunnel between her elderly thighs, had she seen the ski mask smeared with vomit, and the wily fingers that held the knife lavish vomit on that ramming organ—she might have been swept and rent by a pity so enduring that Paradise could not tolerate or sustain it.

That is why a last look is not allowed. That is why there is no pity in Paradise. And that is why Paradise is cold-hearted.

A second misconception: Paradise has no gate or door or vestibule. Simply, one arrives—or, rather, since this is Puttermesser's history, Puttermesser was all at once *there*. Or *here*: though this too misrepresents. In Paradise there is no before or after, no over there or right here, no up or down, no then or now, no happy or sad. The last phrase may puzzle. No sadness in Paradise is to be expected; but no happiness? Isn't happiness the *point* of Paradise?

Return for a moment (but in Paradise there are no moments: no hours, minutes, or seconds) to that earliest word in the world's earliest tale: PARDES. The orchard, the garden. But PARDES is also an acronym for a way of understanding—even for understanding the meaning of PARDES itself. Dismiss the vowels and consider: PRDS. All the letters tied in a bouquet constitute

PARDES. (Or Paradise. Or PARADEISOS.) But taken one by one, each letter contains its own meaning. Now follow closely:

P. This stands for *p'shat*.
R. This stands for *remez*.
D. This stands for *drosh*.
S. This stands for *sod*.

Now follow closely again; these are words for adepts. (And be patient. We will come back to Puttermesser. Only see how mistaken she was in dreaming that Paradise is a place to study in! In Paradise everything has already been learned; all intellectual curiosity is slaked.) Then let us begin:

P'shat is the obvious sense: the readiest meaning.
Remez is the allusive sense; that which is hinted at or inferred.
Drosh is the induced sense; an interpretation; that which requires investigation and must be drawn out. A theory, in short.
Sod, ah, *sod*: this is the secret meaning.

In Paradise, it must be said at once, only Scriptural languages are spoken. You will recognize Hebrew (of course), Sanskrit, and Arabic. The tongues of other hallowed texts may be less familiar; yet all these sacred tongues are interchangeable—i.e., their speakers are not aware of any differences, whether in their own speech or in the speech of other Paradisal denizens. Puttermesser, for instance, imagined she was uttering the syllables of her native New York; in actuality, she was speaking the archaic Hebrew, bold and blunt, of Genesis. —But to continue:

Paradise in its obvious sense: it is where you find yourself when you die. (Simple!)
In the allusive sense: there are hints in Paradise of how your life deserves to be judged. Also hints of indifference to all that.
Paradise interpreted: this Puttermesser is sure to accomplish.
The secret meaning of Paradise: it resides solely in the pupil of the Eye of God.

Even before her ascent to this place, these formulations were not new to Puttermesser. What chiefly struck her was that

PRDS in all its branches had nothing to do with any idea of the future: yet wasn't Eden particularly known as the World-to-Come? So here was still another misapprehension: Puttermesser, like all mortals, had erroneously assumed that Paradise *was* the future. It was, she thought, immortality.

But as she wandered through its various neighborhoods, she came on living persons, in full health; she was certain they had not died. There were theaters and concert halls and movie houses and video shops; there were poetry readings. She stopped to listen to one of these: a middle-aged Russian, disheveled, red-haired, out of breath, a trifle irascible. His Old Church Slavonic, recited at a rapid clip, had the explicit inflections of the streets that sidle away from the Nevsky Prospekt. And then (this was perhaps *remez*) Puttermesser understood that all this was what in an earthly vocabulary would be called hallucination. Surely the living were not in Paradise. She looked around for W. H. Auden, who had befriended the Russian poet, and who was unarguably dead. But she saw and heard only the still-alive and lively Russian. There were flowers at his feet; she recognized tulips, red, yellow, and white, and gladioli, and violets, and a patch of tiny impatiens. The trees were indistinguishable from earthly trees. Everything had an inner fluorescence.

It was plain, then (she had arrived at *drosh*), that Paradise was the place—though it was not exactly a *place*—where she could walk freely inside her imagination, and call up anything she desired. But anything she might call up would inevitably be from the past—what else had she brought with her, if not the record of her own life? Yet if, as she now somehow knew, there was, in fact, no past or future in Paradise—and only a puzzling present, with a flesh-and-blood not-yet-resurrected poet declaiming from a lectern in a flowery realm famously reserved only for the deceased—then what was it she was actually calling up?

The lost, the missing, the wished-for. The unfinished and the unachieved. Not the record of her life as she had lived it, but as she had failed to live it. If she was curious about a poet (and yes, she was curious about the Russian, who, like her own papa, had escaped a ferocious tyranny; and also she was a little bewildered by him, even a little suspicious, because hadn't he once slyly declared for polytheism, or at least against monotheism?)—well, there he suddenly was. She could hear him out; she supposed she could, if she liked, ask him anything at all, and he would have to answer her; he was, after all, a simulacrum, a palpable vision, and wholly subject to her newly celestial will. Whereas— while she lived—he had been a remote figure, inaccessible, dis- tantly lofty and strange. She had felt his exclusions, his hauteur, his rebuff.

But now the whirlwind of her mind could command his pres- ence. His presence or anyone's! She had only to *think*, and the thought would appear incarnate before her. Ah, delightful! Splendid! It was, in truth, Paradise.

No rebuff could go unrepaired.

At nineteen she had been enormously in love, and was rejected.

The man's name was Emil Hauchvogel. He was twenty-two. He had a beautiful head, molded like a Roman sculpture, and he was a student of philosophy. His voice was blurred, very faintly, by a thread of foreignness pulled along the edge of the vowels; as a child of eleven or twelve he had fled from Hitler's Germany with his parents. In Frankfurt his father had been a well-off wholesaler, and though the family had arrived as impoverished refugees, Emil's father worked his way up and managed to establish himself securely enough in the same business. Emil reflected this paternal striving and success: he had the confident air of a young lord, but not in the sense of easy inheritance. He was trained for ambition.

Emil's college was small, bucolic, venerable, revered. Putter- messer's college, a patient subway ride from the Grand Con- course in the Bronx, was urban, mobbed, brash. She too longed for philosophy, but it was too hard for her. Her brain was not subtle enough: desire wasn't capacity. There were questions she could barely grasp the import of, and theories that floated by like so many indefinable cloud-shapes. What did Thrasymachus intend? Was it possible to trust the Nicomachean Ethics? Is pleasure an activity or merely a feeling?

One morning in early January she read a notice on the bulletin board just outside the cafeteria:

NEW ENGLAND WINTER WEEKEND RETREAT
SUBJECT: CAN THERE BE MORALITY WITHOUT GOD?

Puttermesser knew what she thought. An ethical imperative without a divine order to implant and enforce it was unlikely, was no imperative at all. The unheated bus rattled and groaned uphill for miles on a narrow highway between wintry fields. The claws of naked branches were black against the snow. In her old galoshes Puttermesser's feet grew numb. The dozen other students ate their sandwiches or catnapped; now and then they sang; the pompoms on their hats bounced. Wound in scarves, clapping their woolen mittens in time with the singing, the live breath steaming like teakettles from their rounded mouths, patches of red brightening their cheeks, they seemed as remote from metaphysics as their lunch bags and knapsacks. Yet weren't they all heading for Emil Hauchvogel's college to talk of God?

Emil met the bus in the parking lot behind the dormitories. The dorms were mostly empty, he explained: everyone had gone home for New Year's, and the little group of philosophers would have the whole campus nearly to themselves. It wouldn't all be High Thought—in one of the halls there were skis and sleds ready for use. It was instantly clear that Emil was the organizer. Puttermesser got off the bus with cramped legs and a full bladder. Wherever she turned, the ground was white. The low college buildings peeped out of the snow like miniature

Swiss chalets. Puttermesser's citified heart rose in her well-bundled ribs.

First there was toast and vegetarian soup, and then came the sledding. It was already dusk. Puttermesser went on her belly down the long hill, forgetting to steer: she ended half-buried in a snow mound. "That's not the way," Emil said. He was in charge of everything and everyone. At the top of the hill he eased himself down flat on the sled, and Puttermesser climbed on. The length of her lay against his back and rump and thighs. His legs stuck out well beyond the curve of the runners. The two of them rushed downward like some mythical double creature, or else it was only the wind that rushed; her body resting on Emil's, Puttermesser felt warm, cradled, lazy, even sleepy. The slope seemed infinitely longer than before, the descent dozingly slow. "See?" Emil said when they reached the bottom of the hill. "It's all in the *hands*. You have to control the direction, you can't just go hurling yourself any old way."

And after that he paid her no attention at all. From a little distance she saw him helping with the straps of a pair of skis. The skier breathed out teakettle steam and had ruddy cheeks under a pompomed wool hat; nevertheless she had not been on the bus. She belonged to Emil's own tribe; she belonged to this superior landscape. Streamers of white-blond bangs swayed under the wool hat. With a fierce and ready shriek she plunged through the blue-black dark, a flying crescent on a falling path.

In the morning all the philosophers, still scarfed and mittened, met in a latticed gazebo. Heaters had been set up in the middle of a ring of benches; icicle spears hung down from the eaves. The shorter icicles were bunched like bundles of clear fat chandeliers. The sunlight on the snow cut blind streaks across Puttermesser's sight. It was too brilliant, and far too cold, despite the wafting heaters, to sit still. The philosophers from Emil's college—the ones who were at home here, the natives—grouped themselves all together on one side of the gazebo, apart from the philosophers who had come on the bus. "The city mice and the country mice," Emil objected, and made everyone stand up and change places. As for the cold, he said, the clarity of the air would clarify thought. "Purity of heart is to will one thing," he said. "That's Kierkegaard," muttered yesterday's skier.

Then Emil lectured. His thesis was religion and art. At the beginning of all civilizations, art and religion were ineluctably fused: a god was a statue or a painting. The gods spoke through their physical representations. Ra, for instance, the supreme Egyptian deity, expressed himself through a golden disk atop a falcon's head; "my skin is of pure gold," sang the sun-priests of Ra.

"You see?" Emil said, pacing around the heaters. The sun illumined the pale disks of his eyes; he had turned himself into Ra. How beautiful he was! In the dazzling morning light the skin of his face was of pure gold. "Once the God of the Jews forbade art in religion, then art was released—released forever—to follow its own spoor. Once art was exempted from idol-making, from religious duty, it could see what it wished, it could record what it liked, it could play and cavort and distort—whatever it pleased! And all without obligation to sanctity. Pious obeisance was dismissed—unwanted! Excluded! Art was free to be free! The Second Commandment had kicked it out of religion! You see?" Emil said again, looking all around; he had a princely pleasure in his own wit.

But was it wit in praise or dispraise? Puttermesser, bewilderment contracting her throat (unless she was starting to catch cold?), could not be sure. Was he mocking the Second Commandment, or lauding it? Was he an atheist or a believer?

"So if art can thrive best in the absence of religion," Emil concluded, "if in fact there *must not* be any religious connection in order to have a truly autonomous art, then the same applies to morality, doesn't it? Art didn't really become art until it shucked off God. And morality won't really be morality until it too gets rid of God."

A jumble of city voices protested. "That doesn't follow!" "You haven't proved it about art anyhow!" "Sophistry!"

But all the country philosophers applauded.

Puttermesser was silent. She knew what she thought: she thought Emil was shocking. He was certainly a novelty, but he was more arrogant than novel. He was spontaneously eloquent, but he was too self-aware: he was an egotist. She thought all these things, and felt her own shame, because she had nothing to say, she could invent nothing so startling; she was empty. But how beautiful he was, how vehement, how extraordinary were his mind-passions! He was against God with all the fervor of a mystic; he was a purist; he found even the idea of God to be perfectly useless. And he was a visionary in search of converts against God.

Puttermesser understood she was being shaken with a violent infatuation.

By now all the philosophers had spoken, one by one, each in turn. The gazebo was serious and orderly. Icicles, warmed by the sun, were leaking idle drops from their tips. The dripping sounds fell in a syncopated pattern. Puttermesser sat, a pariah in her muteness; a simpleton.

Emil was standing right in front of her. "You didn't come all this way just to be obstinate? In which case you could at least disclose which view your obstinacy intends to serve," he said.

Puttermesser could not answer.

"You're obstructing the movement of the meeting. *Say something.*"

She offered miserably, "It's God who makes us good."

"That's how children think," Emil said.

The city and the country philosophers sent out their morning smiles. What contempt they had for her!

Emil bent and said quietly into her ear, "You're not being very effective here, are you?"

And this whispered judgment—*you're not being very effective here*—infiltrated Puttermesser's brain with a deadly permanence.

It stung; it endured; she remembered it always. He had cut her down, he had belittled her.

A second meeting in the gazebo was called for the afternoon. Emil had supplied everyone with a printed schedule. The philosophers ignored it; instead they went out to the hill to slide and flirt. The two camps were willing enough, by now, to mix freely, and in the sharp light of the horizonless snow Puttermesser could no longer tell who was city and who was country: all those reddened frozen faces, and the smell of damp wool, and teasing spite spiraling into laughter. God and morality were left unresolved. The laughter rolled up and down the hill. Puttermesser lashed her scarf over her nose and mouth, butted her head into the wind, and trekked out to the gazebo.

Only Emil was there.

"Nobody came," he said.

But *she* had come; was she nobody?

"The magnet of youth appears to be stronger than magnitudes of thought," Emil said. "They'd rather kiss in the snow."

"So would I," Puttermesser said. How reckless she was, to speak in such a way!

"As long as you could be sure that God lurks behind every kiss?"

Puttermesser said soberly, "I think we're indebted to a sublime force at all times, whether or not we acknowledge it."

"You need to read Bertrand Russell. You need to be disabused of myth. You ought to look into Kant. Kant said that if God exists, and if we act out of love or awe of God, or out of confidence in a divine reward, then our conduct isn't morality, it's prudent self-interest. Listen," he finished, "one of these days when I'm in the city I'll give you a call."

"Why?" Puttermesser asked; she was in full earnest.

"To teach you how to seek virtue in a Godless universe," Emil said.

They met at the information booth in Grand Central Station.

Puttermesser arrived half an hour late, and condemned herself. She had been afraid to set out. She was afraid of Emil Hauchvogel; she was afraid of her own inferiority. At twenty-two he had absorbed all of Schopenhauer and Nietzsche; he read George Meredith and Ronald Firbank; he could recite whole speeches from *Timon of Athens* and *A Midsummer Night's Dream*, and knew a dozen arias by heart. He could say the names of French and Italian film directors, and tell you which were their most nuanced scenes, and what kind of lens the cameraman used to control the lighting. He was capable of certain striking ruminations on Turing and Gödel. And of course he was at home in German.

It was a warm April evening. Puttermesser had never expected to see Emil Hauchvogel again, and here he was; they were heading for a concert at Carnegie Hall. She recognized that her fear of him had flattered him; it was the pleasure of her awe he must be after. He was not above enjoying such a thing; he knew he deserved it. His brown hair sprang abundantly and ardently upward, as if it had a different rule, or route, for spring. Puttermesser wore her only dress-up things: a bright green angora sweater and a tan corduroy skirt in the new style, nearly all the way down to her ankles, like an illustration in a Victorian novel. She saw he was not pleased with her clothes; she guessed that he had a low opinion of angora and corduroy in the concert hall. She was an experiment that was already failing.

After the concert she declined his offer of a cigarette (she never smoked); she hung back when he proposed a nearby bar, and drew him instead into Howard Johnson's. He watched her drink her ice-cream soda to the lees and tapped his cigarette ash into his empty coffee cup. "You should learn something about music," he announced, but he did not say he would teach her. He did not speak of a Godless universe or of an ethics viable in the absence of divine power; she had prepared herself, and had searched out Bertrand Russell and *The Critique of Pure Reason* in the college library. But now it was something else: it was Ives and Milhaud, Copland and Thomson, Schoenberg and Bloch. It left her all at sea.

They rode the subway to the Bronx. He returned her to her door with his cigarette locked between his lips. And then, with a thieving and frightened motion she would suffer over for the rest of her life—it was bold, almost savage—she put her hand to his mouth and snatched away the cigarette and dropped it on the corridor floor. Her little finger grazed his upper lip; she had touched his flesh. His look was darker than surprise. Instantly she was thrown down into humiliation. She had lost him; she had lost him. She held out her hand for goodnight, but he was already fixed on the elevator across the hall.

It was the beginning of her education. She went back to the library and found a textbook called *The Enjoyment of Music* and sat down with it grimly, like a zealot. She studied the elements of the orchestra—strings, woodwinds, brasses, percussion instruments; she read up on style, from Gregorian chant all the way through to the post-Romantics; she learned about key and scale, about transposition, modulation, chromaticism, harmony, dissonance, counterpoint; she allowed herself to be swept away by the idea of fugue, oratorio, chamber music, opera, a cappella, symphony, concerto, chorale. She accumulated names: Scarlatti, Berlioz, Schumann, Schubert, Chopin, Liszt, Mendelssohn; she fell into the lives of Mozart and Mussorgsky.

She neglected her courses and toiled for a week. And all the while she never heard a note. She could not recall any part of the concert in Carnegie Hall: she had been preoccupied with listening to Emil's listening, how he took a breath, how he tilted his face, how he surrendered to the sounds, whatever they were. He understood the sounds; she could not. Behind his shut eyes they rushed riverlike, ravishing; she saw him flooded with their peculiar code and tattoo and swell. But she was ignorant and deprived. There was no music in her head. Her head was a chamberless nautilus, incapable of echo.

She memorized a whole stanza of Bach's Cantata Number 80, *Ein' feste Burg ist unser Gott,* and copied out into her notebook: *chorale fugue, D major, 4/4, 3 trumpets, timpani, 2 oboes, first and second violins, violas, and continuo (cello, basses, organ).* It was all mind-stuff. It never occurred to her to get hold of a recording, and anyhow she was impatient. She was studying in order to write to Emil. She thought he could not turn away from a letter about music; she would tell him she was catching up; the next concert wouldn't be Greek to her; and besides, she intended to write him in the language of Bach and of Emil's own childhood in Frankfurt-am-Main.

So Puttermesser wrote Emil Hauchvogel a letter in her college German. She was certain there must be mistakes in it. She hoped he would overlook them and be charmed; or, if he declined to be charmed, he would at least see how seriously she was attending to his instruction: *You should learn something about music.*

She wrote, "Truly there would be reason to go mad if it were not for music." It was Tchaikovsky translated into German. And next to it she wrote: *"Das ist doch Du!"*

There was no reply. She supposed he was ignoring her; she had offended him with that lunatic gesture of the cigarette. It was torn from his mouth, his lip had felt her little finger—when she had meant only to free him to say his goodnight as she shook his hand. But oh, the clumsiness of it, the frightened aggressive stupidity of her clumsiness! He imagined she was soliciting a kiss. A kiss! Never! They were formal and tentative friends—he was her teacher—in a formal and tentative friendship that decayed at the touch of her little finger.

After three weeks his answer came. He wrote fluently, in his ready familial German, and said nothing about her mistakes. At first she thought: aha, so there weren't any: how meticulous she had been, how she had labored to winnow them out! But that was only her vanity, her ambition, her desire; she quickly recognized that he was indifferent. He had meant the hiatus to speak for itself. He told her that it was a fine thing, this opening of her life to the glories of music; she would be enriched forever. As for *dem nächsten Konzert*, what bad luck, he was overburdened with term papers and course work and couldn't possibly leave his desk. *Mein Tisch*, he called it, as if it were an ordinary table and not a desk at all, and that made her think of the sticky soda-glass rings on the table at Howard Johnson's, and how he had doused his cigarette butt in his cup, how she had refused to go to a bar (what was the matter with her, she was nineteen!), how unpolished she must seem to him, how she had knocked his cigarette right out of his mouth, how stupid she was! (Though now she was capable of defining a fugue.)

Mein Tisch: she envisioned him at a vast seminar table, the youngest of the great philosophers, a polymath, a genius, an atheist.

When in after years she learned of Emil Hauchvogel's wedding, the pang that struck her chest vibrated like some wild interior gong. His wife, she heard, was a cellist; his little daughters were precociously, ferociously, musical.

In Paradise she married him.

She had long ago given up the idea of an ethics indebted to some hypothesis of divinity. She didn't care any more about God. She was obsessed with organ music, its heavy majestic ascent, its heavy molasses fall.

In Paradise Emil was invited to sit at Kant's *Tisch*. Sometimes Wittgenstein and Quine were there; once—what an occasion *that* was!—Plato turned up.

"What does he *look* like?" Puttermesser asked. She touched her little finger to Emil's mouth and let him kiss it.

"Short fellow. Big head, big nose, translucent ears, the usual poetic brow," Emil said. "Frequently meets with Maimonides. Tells me he's starting on Talmud, though he finds it a bit disorganized. Compared with his own stuff."

"What color eyes?" Puttermesser pressed.

"That's a funny thing to want to know."

"But what color *are* they?"

"White," Emil said. "All white."

"You don't mean he's blind?" The moment she said this she knew it was preposterous. In Paradise sight and insight are equally acute. Nowhere is it easier to thread a needle or grasp a point.

"It snows inside his eyes. You look in and it's always snowing there, like a pure-white field."

In Paradise Puttermesser gave birth at last. The child's skin was silken gold. They circumcised him and planted the tiny gold foreskin under an olive tree, and every olive on every branch began to take on the color of gold. And when all the olives had turned gold, the snow in Plato's eyes stopped, and his eyes were as gold as the olives on their branches.

In Paradise Puttermesser was happy—in her brain and in her heart, in her womb and in all her sexual parts.

But there is a flaw in Eden. The flaw is not what the stories tell us: there is no serpent. All the fruit trees are safe to eat from. There is no expulsion; there is no angel with a flaming sword. All those are children's tales. Timeless Eden is as sweet as Puttermesser and a million million others before her have imagined. In Paradise all yearnings become fact. All desires come to pass; in every instance the fulfillment exceeds the dream.

In Paradise Puttermesser is happy, oh happy!—in her sexual parts, in the golden beauty of her child, in the gold of Plato's eyes, and in the newest heat of her mind, which is everything it had not been at nineteen. In Paradise Emil whispers to her about her mind: how impressive, how effective, her thinking is. He kisses her little finger and calls her a Satrap of Thought. He calls Maimonides the Sovereign of Thought. He calls Kant the Emperor of Thought. He calls Beethoven the God of Thought. (In Paradise, even for Emil, God is admissible.)

Flaw? No, there is no flaw in Paradise. That is a vestige of Put-termesser's obsolete terrestrial notions. Paradise surely has no flaw; but it has its Secret. (PRDS, you will recall, ends in *sod*.) *Sod*: the secret meaning of Paradise! And alas for Puttermesser that she will now uncover it. It is integral to, coextensive with, the very grain of Eden, which is timelessness. Timelessness does not promise the permanence of any experience. Where there is no time, there is no endurance. Without the measure of clocks, what is lastingness?

If Puttermesser had married Emil Hauchvogel in ordinary life—if he had kissed her at her door, if a courtship had followed, and so on and so on—then it would be possible to calculate that the marriage "lasted" a certain number of years. But in the ever-lastingness of Paradise, what does it signify to say how long any-thing lasts?

In Paradise, where sight and insight, inner and outer, sweet and salt, logic and illogic, are shuffled in the manner of a kaleido-scope, nothing is permanent. Nothing will stay. All is ephemeral. There is no long and no short; there is only immeasurable isness. Isness alone is forever; or name it essence, or soul. But the images within the soul shift, drift, wander. Paradise is a dream bearing the inscription on Solomon's seal: *this too will pass.*

And that is the secret meaning of Paradise: Solomon's truth. It is the other reason for the notorious cold-heartedness of Para-dise; it is why everyone who is supernally happy in Paradise, happier than ever before, will soon become preternaturally unhappy, unhappier than ever before. A dream that flowers only to be undone will bring more misery than a dream that has never come true at all.

The secret meaning of Paradise is that it too is hell.

So it is with Puttermesser in Paradise. Emil and her little son evaporate; in sorrow she watches them pale like ink under water. Inconsolably, in her old familiar solitude, she walks through neighborhoods of illusion and phantasmagoria, witnessing loss and tragedy and heartbreak—each following a great and joyous victory.

She sees Henry James, the Master, growing rich on the triumph of a play, the very play that once failed humiliatingly on the London boards; but she already knows (as the Master himself will soon know) that paradisal success will end in jeers and feebleness.

She sees elation dissipate and ignominy conquer.

She sees the divinely palpable Dickens celebrated in every corner of Eden. Then she sees him led back, a grown man, to the blacking factory where the boy had suffered.

She sees a hooked fish returned to dread: her father's life, tossed back to the Czar.

She sees the alphabet fleeing from having been invented.

She sees infants searching for the wombs that had expelled them.

She sees Science longing for Alchemy.

She sees a bearded young man clutching a book of the history of humankind, weeping because he has been made into a godhead; she sees him mourning the deadly fruit of his apotheosis.

Remorse coats the celestial streets with a remorseless ash, as white as the snow that has returned to the sockets of Plato's lost eyes. For every display of splendor there is the debilitation of decay. She sees the towers of civilizations gleam and fade. She sees infatuations wither. She sees small heaps of char: the embers of tremendous loves, loves as famous as Dido and Aeneas, or Rachel and Akiba. She sees the lofty tells of ambition dwindling into resignation and defeat.

Puttermesser, whose name means nothing more troublesome than butter-cutter, walks through the white ash of Paradise, herself a shadow though casting none, and longs for the plain green earth.

She has seen into the *sod* of PARDES, so this is what she sings:

At the point of a knife
I lost my life.
>   *Butter, butter, butter,*
>   *butter knife.*

If I were alive I wouldn't fault
anything under the heavenly vault.
>   *Better, better, better,*
>   *better life.*

Better never to have loved than loved at all.
Better never to have risen than had a fall.
>   *Oh bitter, bitter, bitter*
>   *butter*
>   *knife.*

A Note About the Author

CYNTHIA OZICK is a novelist, essayist, playwright, and short story writer whose work has won numerous awards, including the American Academy of Arts and Letters Straus Living Award, four O. Henry First Prizes, the Rea Award for the Short Story, and a Guggenheim Fellowship. She lives in Westchester County, New York.

A Note on the Type

This book was set in Monotype Dante, a typeface designed by Giovanni Mardersteig (1892–1977). Conceived as a private type for the Officina Bodoni in Verona, Italy, Dante was originally cut only for hand composition by Charles Malin, the famous Parisian punch cutter, between 1946 and 1952. Its first use was in an edition of Boccaccio's *Trattatello in laude di Dante* that appeared in 1954. The Monotype Corporation's version of Dante followed in 1957. Although modeled on the Aldine type used for Pietro Cardinal Bembo's treatise *De Ætna* in 1495, Dante is a thoroughly modern interpretation of the venerable face.

Composed by Creative Graphics, Inc.,
Allentown, Pennsylvania
Printed and bound by Quebecor Printing,
Fairfield, Pennsylvania
Designed by Anthea Lingeman